The CYBORG and the SORCERERS

Lawrence Watt-Evans

A Del Rey Book

BALLANTINE BOOKS • NEW YORK

A Del Rey Book
Published by Ballantine Books

Copyright © 1982 by Lawrence Watt-Evans

Library of Congress Catalog Card Number: 81–22865

ISBN 0–345–30441–1

Printed in Canada

First Edition: June 1982

Cover art by David B. Mattingly

DREADFUL ENCOUNTER

He was across the room and snatching up the submachine gun at the same instant that he fired the snark at the door and put some distance between the girl and himself.

The door vanished behind a cloud of brown powder; the range was close to the maximum, so the snark's energy beam did not penetrate completely, just left a large oval scar of rough raw wood. Drifting dust darkened the already dim room. Slant then released the submachine gun's safety, and waited for the dust to clear.

The darkness abruptly dispelled by a vivid yellow glow from the door; it swung open, revealing a black-robed figure holding aloft a staff.

The light came from the head of the staff, and Slant felt an electric tingle in his skin. Behind the wizard—there could be no doubt that this was a wizard—were three other men, clad like the council chamber guard, holding drawn swords . . .

He sighed regretfully. Time to become Cyborg Warrior again!

Also by Lawrence Watt-Evans
Published by Ballantine Books:

LURE OF THE BASILISK

SEVEN ALTARS OF DUSARRA

Dedicated to my father,
Gordon Goodwin Evans

Chapter One

HE LAY BACK ON THE ACCELERATION COUCH AND WON-
dered idly whether he had been officially decommissioned, and whether anybody left alive had the
authority to decommission him. He had no idea, and there
was no way he could find out. He had been under total
communications silence when the D-series destroyed Old
Earth's military—and probably its civilization as well—and
since then, of course, there had been no signal at all from
his home base on Mars. There could be little doubt that his
superiors were all long dead; if the war hadn't killed them,
the passage of time would have. The fourteen years of subjective time he had spent in space worked out to about three
hundred years of outside time, and he doubted very much
that anyone on Old Earth had been making breakthroughs
in geriatrics after the war was lost.

In fact, it was entirely possible that there was no one at
all left alive on Mars or Old Earth. Even if he chose not to
believe the enemy propaganda broadcasts he had picked up
all those years ago claiming total victory, he had overheard
enough ordinary ship-to-ship chatter to know that his side
had lost the war quite decisively. That didn't mean that the
other side had won, but it did mean that the world he had
grown up in was gone forever.

None of this proved he hadn't been decommissioned;
there might be enough odd survivors scattered about to

1

have formed a successor government, and it was possible that some general somewhere, in a fit of tying up loose ends, had put an official stop to the IRU program.

Of course, it didn't matter what anybody said or did, or what was legally or technically true. As long as he and his damned computer hadn't received their release code they were still an IRU, and as long as they hadn't received their recall code they would continue their current open-ended reconnaissance. It didn't matter in the slightest whether he had been decommissioned or not, because if he tried to do anything about it the computer would burn out his brain.

If he had been left to his own devices he would have surrendered long ago, immediately after he learned that his side had lost and Old Earth's rebellious colonies had conquered the mother world. He had tried to convince the computer that that was the sensible thing to do, that there was no point in fighting on. He had tried to explain that there was no one left alive who knew their release code or recall code.

The computer hadn't cared at all. Its programming was very explicit in forbidding anything resembling surrender, and it reminded him unnecessarily that it was programmed to kill him if he disobeyed that programming. The Command's method of ensuring the loyalty of its IRU cyborgs and making certain that none of them fell alive into enemy hands was very simple; any attempt at surrender, or any sign of cooperation if captured, and the thermite bomb at the base of his skull would go off. They had assured him that such a death would be quite slow and painful, and he had believed every word. At the time he even thought it a good and clever idea; since the D-series, he had cursed it at great length.

It didn't matter at all whether he had been decommissioned or not, but it was something to think about, and after fourteen years alone with his ship that was a precious commodity.

He hadn't been in space all that time, of course; there had been half a dozen planetfalls. Unfortunately, in accordance with his orders, they had all been on enemy worlds, with the computer rigorously enforcing the strictures against fraternization with the enemy. He had remained alone, regardless of how many people he encountered.

It didn't bother him too much. He had been selected, after all, to be able to endure all the hardships that might befall an Independent Reconnaissance Unit cyborg, and loneliness was one of those hardships—perhaps the worst of them. Contrary to the popular myth, to the superman image the government press spread that attracted so many candidates, there was no need for an IRU pilot to be a perfect physical specimen with the build of the proverbial Greek god; in fact, such a physique would be a definite disadvantage in the undercover work an IRU might have to perform, as it would be far too likely to attract notice. It wasn't the body that was important, because regardless of what a candidate started with he would be rebuilt, his skeleton reinforced with steel, his muscles stripped and reconstructed, his nervous system rewired to inhuman speed and accuracy, all without changing his appearance.

It was his mind that had to be special. Drugs and hypnotic conditioning could do only so much; modern neurosurgery and hormone regulation helped, but still, only certain rare individuals had the sort of mind that could adapt to the demands put upon it as an IRU. There was the loneliness, first and foremost, and the incredible boredom of piloting a one-man ship between the stars.

It was known right from the start that an interstellar war would have to drag on for decades, while the ships from each side crossed the vast empty spaces between stars. The speed of light, as Einstein had long ago explained, was an absolute limit on starship velocity. Human technology still remained below that limit, so that journeys to even the nearest stars took years—and Old Earth had spread her colonies beyond the nearest stars. The contraction of time experienced at near-light velocities helped considerably, so that a human being could make a voyage of several light-years in a few subjective months, but still, those months added up. Ordinary craft carried a dozen people at the very least, who frequently came to hate each other—but who were not alone. IRU ships were strictly solo. The pilot of an IRU had to be able to survive those months and years alone without quite going mad.

The drugs and hypnosis helped. After fourteen years, though, they didn't help much.

Besides handling the loneliness, an IRU cyborg had to be capable of doing his job; he had to be a starship pilot, an interstellar navigator, an assassin, a spy, a saboteur, a soldier. The IRU fleet was the elite of Old Earth's military, and was expected to do everything too complex or too subtle to be handled by brute force—not that the Command had been stinting of brute force; an IRU ship carried as much armament as could be crammed into it.

He had gone over all this more often than he could count; whenever an entertaining train of thought petered out, he found himself reviewing once again why he needed to be entertained in the first place. He was an isolated survivor of a defeated military force, one of Old Earth's elite; he was IRU 205, code-named Slant.

It occurred to him, as it sometimes did, that he hadn't always thought of himself in those terms; there had been a time, long ago, when he had been a civilian. His name had been . . . oh, what was it? He had forgotten again. His hypnotic conditioning was supposed to blank out any memories of civilian life that might interfere with his efficient functioning, which generally meant everything relating to him as a specific individual. They had left all his impersonal knowledge of events and behavior on the grounds that it could be useful. They had erased his old identity—but the conditioning had been done fourteen years ago, fourteen years without reinforcement, far longer than it was meant to last, and he could sometimes remember his old name. He had been Samuel Turner, a nondescript North American sort of name, and he knew in an abstract way that he had grown up in North America, mostly in the northeastern area. He remembered streets, schools, parks, and a few years of college—but no names, no individual faces, no family life.

Trying to remember his name was an interesting diversion; enough of a block lingered to ensure that he never retained it for more than a few minutes. Once, several years earlier, he had developed an irrational fear that he might forget it permanently. This had been shortly after he had first managed to recall it at all, and he had had some idea that it might someday matter to know it. He had written it down somewhere, and had not looked at it since; it was comforting, in a minor way, to know that it was safely recorded. It kept the game of trying to remember it from becoming too frustrating; he could always reassure himself, when the name was reluctant to come forth, that he could dig out the note he had stuck in one of his books and read it. Knowing that made frustration bearable, and sooner or later the name would always come to him; he had never yet had to try and find the note, the exact location of which he had long since forgotten.

Having remembered his old name, he lost interest in it, and as his attention turned to other things he promptly forgot it again, as swiftly as ever.

He looked at the glass-fronted bookcase he had bolted to the forward bulkhead, which looked incredibly out of place in the sleek control cabin. It was jammed full of old bound books, mostly paperback novels and art histories, many of which held notes he had written to himself—one such note consisting simply of his name, whatever it was. He had spent his entire enlistment bonus on furnishing the ship, and most of the money had gone for the archaic cabinet and old-fashioned printed volumes. He derived a certain special enjoyment from handling the books that a computer library printout didn't provide; the action of turning the pages gave him a feeling of progress that the steady crawl of words on a screen or a calm recitation by the computer didn't, a feeling that he had accomplished something when he finished reading the book. He also found it easier to flip back pages by hand when he wanted to check back for something than to locate it in the computer.

And of course the art books had those lovely old flat, glossy photographs, far more appealing than any images the computer could conjure up. His computer had been designed for military use; it could pilot a ship, plan tactics, target and fire its weapons, analyze enemy ships or installations—but the fidelity in its video and holographics left something to be desired, except when he used the direct-control linkage, which he found uncomfortable and used as little as possible.

Therefore, despite the jokes his compatriots had made about his reading habits, he had stocked the bookcase and brought it along, and there it was. He had read every book in it at least twice, studied every photograph over and over. He had similarly exhausted the computer's library, both text and video—at least, he thought he had; it was hard to be certain. He had definitely gone through every title that sounded the least bit interesting. There was little else to do while the computer was piloting.

It occurred to him that he had spent all his time lately in the control cabin or the galley or the shower; perhaps he could find something to interest him in one of the other compartments. Perhaps it was time to rotate the decor in the control cabin.

He looked around the ovoid room. The thick chameleon fur carpeting that lined all the walls—and the floor and ceiling, which were indistinguishable from the walls—was a rich golden yellow, and had been for weeks. Three bright nylon tapestries were hooked into the carpet, one on either side and one directly opposite the bookcase; cylindrical lightbars were extruded from various points around the room, providing a pleasantly diffuse illumination. Fur carpet, bookcase, tapestries, lightbars—that was the entire room, except for the acceleration couch he lay on and the direct-control cable that was attached to it. He wondered if perhaps he could have spent his money better.

Of course, he had other furnishings in the aft storage compartments. There were several statuettes and small sculptures, and an assortment of hangings for the walls— everything from simple watercolors to tuned crystal-and-wire matrices that droned eerie music when blown on, either by Slant or by the ship's air circulation system.

It probably was time to rotate furnishings; the tapestries had had their turn. He could mount a few statuettes on lightbars; there were some electrostatic adhesive disks somewhere on board that would keep them secure on such makeshift pedestals.

It might, he thought, be a welcome change just to have different colors; he thought a command to the computer, and the golden chameleon fur turned glossy black. That was certainly more dramatic, with the extruded lightbars in bright contrast to the walls; the tapestries stood out vividly, red and blue and gold. The bookcase, haphazardly packed with multicolored bindings, stood out too clearly against the dark background; it looked sloppy. He turned the fur white.

That was better. The lightbars were scarcely visible, and although the bookcase still stood out, it seemed quietly dark now instead of bright and rowdy.

As usual, playing with the chameleon fur aroused his artistic interests. He had studied art history in college mostly because the courses happened to fit his schedule neatly—a detail of civilian life that he had, oddly, been allowed to remember—but he did have a genuine interest in color, form, and composition. That was why he had all the books and art objects; he had, he recalled, fancied himself something of a scholar in the artistic area, back when he was young and naive. He had thought that when the war was over he could retire honorably and spend his days studying mankind's attempts to create beauty.

Instead he was still out in space, crawling his way across the galaxy, playing out the role of spy and saboteur on behalf of an extinct nation, studying each world's capacity to destroy other words.

It could be worse; at least he was primarily interested in military targets. His mission was to determine of each world he came across whether it was capable of launching an attack on Old Earth, and where such capability existed, to destroy it if possible. He was to capture any new weapons he came across, so that they could be duplicated by his side back on Mars. It was not a particularly bad job, if one had to be an IRU. He had heard that some of his compatriots had been assigned terror missions, with instructions to destroy whatever they found and slaughter whoever they could; that was the sort of assignment he could not have handled. He wondered whether any of those IRUs were still, like himself, wandering about, unable to surrender. He hoped that there were none, that any such that might have existed were all long dead. He could justify his actions to some extent on the grounds that he was destroying war machinery, and therefore promoting peace, but there could be no justification for simply wreaking as much havoc as possible.

Of course, he knew his own justification was just a rationalization; he fought on because he had to, to survive, and probably a terrorist IRU would do the same.

That line of thought was depressing, leading back again to the prospect of having his brain burned out if he tried to surrender; he dropped it and looked about at the white walls. The tapestries stood out in dark contrast, and he decided white was too harsh. He was considering light blue, trying to envision it before he actually tried it, when a chime sounded, the computer's warning signal.

He started. It had been months since he had heard anything—really heard, through his ears—except the steady, quiet hum of the ship going about its business, and the little rustles and thumps he made in going about his own.

"What's up?" he asked the computer. He spoke aloud, unnecessarily, and his voice sounded strange in his ears.

"Ship is now entering a star system. Standard procedure calls for cyborg unit to assume control," it replied silently through the telepathic device in his skull.

Slant grunted and reached for the direct-control cable at the head of the couch. He had been disconnected for months, maybe years, letting the computer run the ship since they had left the last system, and his hair had grown down over the socket in the back of his neck; he pulled the hair aside and plugged the cable in. It took a moment's effort; he was out of practice and had to work entirely by feel, not having eyes in the back of his head. He suspected that the long disconnection had let his body's natural growth and healing processes twist the socket a bit out of line, as well. Eventually, though, the thousands of pin-contacts slid home, and he was in control of the ship, hooked directly into the main computer as well as in telepathic radio contact with it through the terminal in his brain.

It took two or three seconds before his piloting skills came back; for a moment the data came through as a jumbled mass of sensation. Then his conditioning took over, unscrambling the signals, and he felt the ship as his body, felt the gravity-well of the star-sun ahead, knew exactly the ship's relative velocity, knew what radiation, electromagnetic or otherwise, was reaching the ship. The interstellar hydrogen that served as some of the fuel for the fusion drive was much thicker here; that was usual in the neighborhood of a star.

He was decelerating steadily; the near-light velocities that were necessary for interstellar travel were downright dangerous within a system, where meteors, asteroids, or even small uncharted moons or planets might get in one's way. Although the computer had, of course, been slowing the ship for weeks, his speed still seemed uncomfortably great; an outer planet slipped by too quickly to examine properly, though he noted it was an ordinary gas giant of unimpressive size.

This system, the computer informed him, was listed as enemy-held and heavily populated. An attack force of conventional warships had been sent to this area, but there was no record of what had become of it, no indication whether or not it had reached this system.

He stepped up the deceleration and turned the scanners ahead, so that the next planet provided rather more information. According to the records, this one had a Marslike climate and had been lightly settled at last contact.

Slant found no evidence of life; there were no lights on the nightside, no radio emanations, no detectable electromagnetic radiation at all. There were a great many craters, not of particularly natural appearance, and considerable residual radioactivity.

It seemed that the war had reached this system. Regretfully, he settled back and waited for the next planet to come into range. Records indicated that this next one was the major population center, with some two billion people at last count. It was the second planet out, and assuming its orbit hadn't changed and had been accurately recorded in the first place, it would be found on the far side of the sun. By traveling in a hyperbolic path down close to the star, he could use its gravity to further decelerate the ship.

Accordingly, he took the ship in near the sun, and shortly thereafter approached the second planet at a velocity low enough that there was no perceptible difference between his subjective time and the time on the planet's surface.

The world swam slowly toward him, and he studied it closely.

There were no radio emanations, no large electrical fields, no microwaves, no sign of any technology or industry. Looping around the nightside, there were no lights above the level of a Class III town, but there were lights; there were hundreds of tiny, flickering lights, just barely detectable.

There was a good deal of background radioactivity. Slant guessed that the planet had been bombed back to barbarism but not utterly depopulated; those faint, unsteady lights could be campfires or small firelit towns.

He saw nothing of any interest here. He would be moving on, then, without landing. It had happened before; he had been through two systems where he found nothing worthy of his attention. He suggested as much to the computer. It disagreed, and drew his attention to the planet's gravitational field.

He had not given that any thought, since he knew of nothing man-made that had any significant effect on gravity; now he shifted his perceptions, and as the ship made another elongated orbit around the planet he studied the gravitational field.

It was slightly uneven, of course, with a few of the slowly shifting irregularities that indicated seismic activity. However, there was also a sprinkling of tiny localized disturbances; he saw them as a scattered array of little sparkles, like a swarm of lightning bugs seen from half a kilometer away.

That made no sense.

These were not movements; those he could have explained, since anything that moved large masses about altered the local gravity slightly. In these spots, though, the intensity of gravity seemed to flicker. There was no movement in any direction, but a variation in strength as if huge amounts of matter were disappearing and reappearing, flashing in and out of existence.

It made no sense at all.

"Computer," he asked silently, "could that be some sort of natural phenomenon?"

"No such phenomenon has been recorded or theorized."

"Any chance of instrument error?" After fourteen years, one couldn't expect every system to be in perfect working order; there had been various minor failures previously.

"Error is highly unlikely. No discrepancies or anomalies register in measurements of any other body."

"That's really weird." He spoke aloud, in a soft murmur.

"Analysis: It must be assumed that these anomalies represent human action. This system is listed as enemy-held, so it must be assumed that these anomalies represent enemy action. No such anomalies have been encountered previously, and library references indicate the theoretical possibility of a device called 'antigravity' with military applications, so it must be assumed that these anomalies represent enemy weapons research. Orders require that all detected enemy weapons research be investigated immediately."

"Weapons research? That's stupid. This planet hasn't got any technology; how could its people have developed antigravity? If they have antigravity, why aren't they using it for space travel?"

"Information insufficient. Analysis remains unchanged."

"Look, I don't want to investigate here; it's a primitive planet now, whatever it was before, and that can't be weapons research. It has to be some sort of natural phenomenon."

"That conclusion is contraindicated. Take appropriate action immediately or override option will be exercised."

"What? Oh, no, you don't!" He reached up to tear the plug from his neck but was not fast enough; there was a wrenching mental flash, and he lost control of both the ship and his own body. His limbs twitched spastically as the computer assumed control; then he lay still. He was able to use both the ship's sensory apparatus and his own, but all movement, even so much as blinking or breathing, was now under the computer's direct control; accordingly, his breathing was slow and mechanically steady, and he blinked exactly once every five seconds. He watched in helpless paralysis as the ship slid down from its observation orbit into a landing approach and swept across a vast expanse of dark ocean.

It was perfectly clear to him that gravity disturbances notwithstanding, this planet had been bombed from the nuclear age back to the level of bow and arrow. The computer, unfortunately, was not programmed to pay attention to such things. It assumed a high-level technology everywhere—or rather, it assumed nothing but acted according to orders based on false assumptions. Those damnable orders had kept him a wandering exile for years, and were now plunging him into a situation where he would probably have to roam over half a world killing innocent people who happened to get in his way before he could convince the computer that there was no secret enemy installation here developing antigravity weapons to use against the ruins of Old Earth. He had no idea what the disturbances actually were, and had no strong desire to find out; if there was anything on this backward burned-out world that could kill him, it was probably whatever was making those anomalies.

He had little choice, however. When the override released a few kilometers above the surface, to allow human discretion in choosing a landing site, he cooperated and made no attempt to head back into space. It would only have resulted in another use of the override, and if he was going to have to play spy again he might as well get it over with.

The planet was very Earthlike, with somewhat more than half its surface covered by ocean, the remainder a patchwork of green vegetation, golden beaches and deserts, and the gray and brown and black of bare rock in the mountains and badlands. There were icecaps, smaller than Old Earth's, at each pole; his orbit took him over an edge of one, though he was unsure whether it was north or south, having become disoriented while under the override. The computer's records told him that the planet had mild seasons, slightly less than terrestrial gravity, and four continents, of which only the largest was known to be thickly inhabited. He was coming down over this continent now;

it was enjoying the late summer of its four-hundred-day-plus year.

He skimmed past the coastal plain and into the foothills of a low, ancient, worn-down mountain range that the computer had picked as his landing area. The ship was still traveling at high velocity, at least for atmospheric travel, though it was decelerating fiercely; anyone below was probably seeing the biggest, brightest shooting star in years. If there were any radar or modar installations, though, they would see nothing; the ship was screened against every form of electronic detection its designers had known.

The hills below him were blanketed in thick forests, a deep, ominous sea of Earthlike trees—probably imported from Old Earth when the planet was first settled and terraformed. He turned the ship and more or less paralleled the mountains, continuing to decelerate.

A dim spot of orange light flashed by beneath, and he had the computer play back in slow motion and high magnification the record that was automatically kept of everything detected within "enemy" systems.

The light was a campfire, with a group of fur-clad men sleeping huddled about it. Spears and swords were in evidence; this was apparently not one of the worlds where a return to barbarism had brought peaceful coexistence.

Even at stop-frame and maximum magnification he could make out no details that seemed significant; he dropped the image and asked if the ship's records had any evidence indicating when the planet's civilization was destroyed. There was nothing very helpful; the only relevant item was that the war fleet targeted for this system had been scheduled to arrive about six months after the D-series had hit back home.

That was more than thirteen years ago by ship's time, and three hundred and four years ago by outside time. This ever-increasing differential between himself and the rest of the universe was something that Slant had long ago accepted, even though he did not really understand it. Relativity was beyond him, but he had had plenty of opportunity to observe its effects.

He was low over the mountains, and turned his attention

to getting the ship down in one piece. He suspected that the computer would interpret any increase in altitude as an attempt to avoid landing and use the override again, so that he had to dodge between the highest peaks instead of rising above them.

Of course, in allowing him to choose the landing site, the computer left him free to choose the worst possible place; he had done so on occasion in the past, as a petty attempt at revenge. The computer hadn't cared in the least; that was outside its programming. This time he didn't bother, but just set down in the first clearing that looked large enough in the area the computer had selected. None of the myriad systems failed. Fourteen years without maintenance made that something that Slant no longer took for granted, but the ship landed softly and smoothly and exactly where he wanted it. It immediately set about camouflaging itself; he left that to the computer and its subsidiary machines, unplugged himself, and went to the galley for a meal.

He had come down just on the night side of the dawn line, landing by infrared rather than visible light; by the time he had eaten the computer reported light in the east. He was resigned to the task of scouting out the "enemy weapons research," but he refused to be rushed, and took his own time in choosing supplies from the lockers.

He dressed himself in leather pants and a fur vest, which he hoped would not be too conspicuously alien to the local inhabitants; he could find no shirt that seemed suitable, and the computer reported warm weather, so he left it at that. It was very odd to wear clothes again; with every movement he was uncomfortably aware of the leather and fur brushing and rubbing against his skin. He considered a pair of boots for several minutes before pulling them on; his feet immediately felt cramped and sweaty, but he had no idea how much walking he would be doing, nor what sort of terrain he might encounter. Bare feet might not be suitable.

Remembering the swords and spears he had seen, he decided that he had best be armed; he dug out a Bowie knife, and after due consideration chose an old-fashioned submachine gun from the rack of firearms. The gun was perhaps the most terrifying weapon he had, or at least the most startling, with its chattering roar, blue smoke, and bright flash, and was useful at a considerable range and against large numbers—though in some situations it was undoubtedly less effective than a hand laser or a snark.

He found a belt, donned it, and stuck the knife in it; the gun he slung over his shoulder. He tied a leather pouch to the belt, stuffed a few foodbars and other miscellaneous supplies in it, and decided that he was adequately equipped.

There was a mirror in the shower; he stopped in and checked to see whether his long brown hair hid the socket in the back of his neck. It seemed to; he brushed it back with his fingers, trying to arrange it so it would not fall aside. He doubted very much that the locals would take kindly to a stranger with a gleaming chunk of metal and plastic embedded in his flesh.

When he had convinced himself that the socket would not show, he marched out the airlock onto the ship's wing.

The early-morning air was cool and pleasant; a slight breeze blew against his bare chest. The natural currents and rich scent of the surrounding pine forest were positively delightful after years of stagnant, recycled air smelling of metal and plastic and algae, and he breathed deeply as he looked about.

He had landed well on the inland side of the mountains, and the low, rounded peaks reared up in the east, great black shadows against the rosy pink of the dawn sky. On all sides of the ship there stood tall green grass, utterly Earthlike, and beyond the grass was a ring of pine trees, likewise completely terrestrial. Slant surmised that the planet had been lifeless before it was colonized; if not, the Terran flora—and probably fauna—must have driven out whatever was there previously. That was not an unusual pattern on colony worlds.

The morning sun lit the grass, and dew glittered on every side—but only at a distance. The heat that radiated from the ship had boiled off all moisture for a dozen feet in all directions, and Slant guessed that the ship's approach path was burned brown, if not black, from the heat of its passage. He could feel the warmth of the wing's metal through his boots, and it occurred to him that it might be a good idea to get off. He jumped carefully to the ground, landing with a great rustling in the tall grass. He regained his feet, and saw that the grass reached well above his knees.

A soft whirring drew his attention back to the ship; the service robots had finished camouflaging and were reentering their storage compartments, leaving the vessel smeared with mud and draped in plastic vines twined with real, freshly plucked grass. It still stood out dramatically in the center of the broad, level clearing, but was no longer immediately recognizable as a starship; the metal did not gleam, and the sharp edges and corners were softened.

Looking back under the wing, he saw that his guess had been correct; there was a trail of burned grass and scorched earth behind the vessel. He considered pointing it out to the computer and suggesting that it be camouflaged as well, but decided against it. The ship could take care of itself.

Scanning quickly around the edge of the clearing, he saw no sign of a road or trail. There was no evidence other than himself and his ship that any human being had ever been anywhere near this spot. He wondered why there was a clearing in the first place; was it completely natural?

It didn't matter, of course. It didn't seem to matter what direction he took, either, so he began marching directly away from the ship.

"A large concentration of anomalies representing enemy weapons research lies approximately one hundred kilometers to the planetary northeast. This landing area was chosen for that reason. Movement in that direction is indicated."

Slant made a slight noise of startlement; the computer's monotone mental voice seemed out of place now that he was out of the ship. He stopped, took his bearings from the rising sun, and pointed off to his right. "That way?"

"Affirmative."

He shrugged, turned, and marched on, the pouch and knife slapping his thighs, the submachine gun weighing on his shoulder.

Chapter Two

THE FOREST WAS ALMOST ENTIRELY PINE; SLANT no longer remembered the differences among the various species, but he amused himself by noting the many varieties he encountered. He paused occasionally to study types he hadn't seen before, ignoring the computer's objection to such delays. He found a few trees he suspected were not natural terrestrial species but that were similar enough that he guessed them to be mutants or hybrids rather than anything native to this planet. Given his former government's liking for enhanced-radiation weapons of various sorts, this world must have been largely a radioactive wasteland for a time; it was hardly surprising if a few viable mutations had arisen.

There was very little underbrush, due to the thick carpet of pine needles, and despite the seemingly endless rolling hills walking was easy once he had left the tall grass and entered the shade of the forest. He found himself enjoying his stroll very much and began idly humming to himself after a while, only to be hushed by a warning from the computer. It took this war game seriously; programming forbade anything that might draw unwanted attention.

Golden sunlight filtered through the trees around him, lighting earth and branch and fallen needles in several shades of brown and gray, and gradually warming the air. By noon he was glad that he hadn't found a shirt he liked in his supplies. The decision had been based on his lack of one primitive enough, but the weather was hot enough that he would have removed it anyway. He kept the fur vest open and loose, and wished he had worn shorts instead of the leather pants; he was perspiring freely, for the first time in years, and it made him feel

17

slimy and unclean. He was not used to such varying temperatures; the air aboard ship was kept within a range of five degrees.

Noon had been quick in coming; he realized the day must be well under the twenty-four hours of Old Earth's, the standard that he had almost always lived with, whether naturally on Old Earth, artificially in the underground complex on Mars, or from habit aboard ship. Either that or his time sense was further off than he had thought; perhaps his habits had gradually shifted over the years. He asked the computer, which informed him that the local day was in fact only slightly over twenty hours.

The sun was just past its zenith—which had been somewhat south of straight overhead, as he was well up in the northern hemisphere and it was midway between the summer solstice and the autumnal equinox—when he came across a road. It was reasonably broad and looked as if it might once have been paved, but only a narrow path down the center showed signs of recent use.

He looked both ways and saw nothing but more road, winding off in either direction until it was lost among the trees. Still, it was a good sign; roads invariably led somewhere, and this one, which curved northeastward off to his right, might well lead where he wanted to go.

He was tired and hot, though, and not inclined to march onward immediately; instead he sat down by the roadside, took some foodbars from his pouch, and ate lunch.

Standard procedure called for him to live off the land and use the ship's stores only in emergencies, a course he preferred anyway, in view of the taste of the processed algae he ate on board; he had, therefore, brought only a few bars. He wished he had more; he couldn't eat pine sap, and as yet he had seen not so much as a chipmunk by way of animal life. He had seen insects and various fungi and a few vines and creepers, but he had no way of knowing which were edible—even those that matched terrestrial life in appearance could be poisonous mutants. Besides, such foods weren't much more appealing than algae. Sooner or later, though, he knew he would reach an inhabited area, and anything the locals could eat, he could eat.

He was brushing the last crumbs from his lap when he first heard approaching hoofbeats.

He picked up the submachine gun and got quickly to his feet; the riders were approaching from the right, the east. He could not judge their distance well, but he could make out the jingle of harness now as well as the thudding hoofs; they could not be far. He considered taking cover but rejected the idea, as he was unsure he would have sufficient time. Furthermore, he would have to make contact with the locals eventually if he was to get anywhere with his investigation. Keeping the gun loose in his hands, he stood by the roadside and waited.

Within a few seconds half a dozen horsemen rode around the bend into view. All were big, burly warriors, clad in fur vests much like his own—he had chosen his garment well—and elaborately arranged loincloths. Each carried a sword slung on a broad metal-studded leather belt and a spear strapped to his shoulder; shields were slung at the back of each saddle. Their horses were large, sleek beasts, bay or black in color, and each carried a bulky pack as well as its rider.

The leader caught sight of the stranger by the roadside and slowed his mount from its trot. The others followed suit; the entire squad approached Slant at a slow walk and drew up in front of him.

The leading rider was a huge fellow, with heavily muscled limbs, long flowing black hair, and an immense drooping mustache; Slant guessed the man to be younger than himself. The horseman was first to speak.

"Hello, stranger!" His voice was a booming bass. "We had not expected to see anyone in this area. Whence do you come, and whither are you bound?" His speech was a degenerate form of the Anglo-Spanish pidgin spoken on many of the colony worlds; the computer relay translated it to Slant as quickly as possible, but the slight delay was enough to irritate the warrior with Slant's slowness of reply.

The reply was made in the same pidgin, twisted as closely as Slant could manage to the same form the horseman spoke, but it had been a long time since he had used any language but his own and the speech did not come readily at first.

"Hello, sir. I come from far away, a place called Tur, and have no particular destination." The name "Tur" was the first he could think of; he hoped it would be acceptable.

"Tur? I never heard of it. Where does it lie?"

Remembering that he was near the eastern edge of the continent, Slant answered, "To the west."

"I know of no such place, and I think I would remember such a short, odd name. Is it this side of Praunce?"

"No, it's beyond Praunce." He was improvising desperately; it seemed advisable to locate his supposed home as far away as possible. He wished the man weren't so interested in where he came from.

"I was unaware that there are any inhabited lands beyond Praunce."

Slant shrugged.

"How did you come here, then, if your home is so distant?"

"I walked. I am a wanderer, of no fixed abode." He recalled this last phrase from enemy documents he had read long ago; without that he would not have been able to remember an appropriate word.

"A wanderer? What sort of wanderer? What do you call yourself?" The warrior's voice held a note of distrust; Slant guessed that people did not travel much in this society.

"I am called Slant. I go where I please, for I have no family or possessions, and I was weary of Tur." The words were beginning to come more easily now, and he could hear for himself that the name of his imaginary home didn't fit the language well.

"What's that thing you're holding?" The horseman pointed at the submachine gun.

Slant shrugged. "I don't know; I found it in the forest and thought it might be valuable."

"Let me see it." He held out a hand.

Hiding his reluctance, Slant handed over the weapon; the computer silently warned him, "Surrender is not permitted," as he relinquished it.

A slight tension came over him, and he replied silently,

"Shut up! I'm not surrendering; he just wants to look at the gun. He doesn't know it's a weapon, he's just curious." He struggled to keep his outward appearance calm. "If I were surrendering I'd give him my knife, wouldn't I?" He knew that the computer would kill him if it decided he was surrendering; he hoped that the horseman would not ask for his knife.

The man did not ask for the knife; he studied the submachine gun, turning it over in his hands, being careful not to work any of the mechanisms. Finally he looked up from it and asked, "Where did you find it?"

"Back that way." Slant pointed vaguely off to the southwest.

"It looks like some of the relics at Setharipoor; I'd be very careful of it if I were you. One of those relics destroyed half a museum a few years back; old magic, very dangerous stuff." He handed the gun back and Slant accepted it gratefully, with a polite nod of his head. His relief was not outwardly evident as he told the computer, "See? I wasn't surrendering."

"Affirmative."

The horseman was studying Slant now, much as he had studied the gun. "You say you just roam about aimlessly?"

"Yes."

"How do you live?"

"I eat what I can find, do what work I can find when I need money or goods, sleep in the open." He tried to look diffident.

The warrior was studying the vest and trousers Slant wore, and the cyborg suddenly realized that both garments looked brand new; neither had ever been worn before this morning, and he had not thought to age them artificially. That would, he saw, be very suspicious indeed in a penniless wanderer. The man probably took him for a thief or some other sort of outlaw.

The horseman reached a decision. "Slant of Tur, as you call yourself, I am Huarram of Teyzha, Captain of Warriors, and I go now to serve as ambassador to Orna. These lands and to the east are under the jurisdiction of Teyzha and the Council that rules Teyzha, and I think I would be failing in my duty to the Council were I to leave you wandering about here. Therefore I will send you to the Council with an escort, and let them decide what to do with you. You have committed no crime to my knowledge, nor acted against the city, and if this is the case you need have no fear; we are a just people, and harm no one without reason. Is this acceptable to you?"

Slant shrugged. "I have no objection." He suspected that Teyzha was his intended destination anyway, and this seemed as good a way as any to get there.

"Good, since you have no choice. Perhaps the Council will be able to tell you what this relic of yours is, as well." He turned to look over his shoulder at the other horsemen and said, "Silner, take this man back to the city and present him to the Council. He is not a prisoner, so treat him with respect—but he is not a friend, so be cautious." He turned back, nodded at Slant, and without further ado turned his horse up the road and spurred it forward.

All but one of the others followed, and a moment later they were out of sight, leaving Slant facing a lone warrior.

Silner was the youngest and smallest of the party, barely out of his teens, yet taller and broader than Slant. He wore white-striped brownish fur, and a thick braid of blond hair reached halfway down his back. His face was clean-shaven; Slant, who had given up shaving more than ten years before, realized that Silner was the only one of the warriors who did not sport at least a mustache, and guessed that it was because he was too young to grow anything that looked halfway decent.

His horse was a glossy black animal; Slant looked at the creature and wondered whether he would be expected to walk while his escort rode. If Teyzha was in fact the disturbance center that the computer had been directing him toward, it was still a good distance away.

Silner settled that question by motioning for Slant to mount and holding out a hand to assist him. Slant obeyed, and found himself seated astride the horse in front of the saddle and rider. It was not a comfortable position, and it was not made any better by having to hang onto the submachine gun; he could not sling it over his shoulder without getting very much in Silner's way. Despite the awkward position, riding was, however, better than walking.

"Query: Advisability of current cooperation with native civilian."

The computer's question surprised Slant; it had failed to recognize the warriors as soldiers, apparently. Upon consideration, though, Slant realized they had no uniforms, no firearms—to a computer, operating on the assumption of a high-level technology, it was a reasonable mistake. It was also a good thing, since cooperation with an enemy soldier could be fatal.

"You want me to get close to the enemy weapons research, right? To do that, it appears I have to get into Teyzha, and this seems like the best way to do it. These people don't recognize my origin; I'm operating undercover. You heard the man say that I'm not a prisoner, and I'm still armed. Besides, riding is faster than walking."

"Affirmative. Continue action."

Slant nodded to himself, and noticed that while he had conversed with the computer Silner had turned the horse's head back toward Teyzha and that they were moving at a gentle trot. The young warrior did not deign to speak to Slant, then or for some time thereafter; it was not until they made camp that evening and it became necessary to discuss building a fire that the cyborg learned the youth had a pleasant tenor voice.

Chapter Three

AROUND NOON OF THE DAY AFTER SLANT LANDED, THE PAIR reached Teyzha.

About midmorning they had emerged from the forest into rolling farmland, but since neat rows of trees served as boundary markers and windbreaks on every side of each little patch of cultivated land, and since the road continued to wind between hills, Slant did not have a clear view of the city until they were less than a kilometer from its gates.

As he had half expected, the city was walled, with dull gray stone fortifications that stood seven or eight meters in height. From a distance bright domes and spires could be briefly glimpsed through the treetops, rising above the drab walls, but as they drew nearer the angle became impossible, and he could see nothing of the city but the gray stone.

The trees and the swaying motion of the horse had prevented close study, but those towers had looked quite elaborate and substantial. Slant was pleased to see that the planet was not still in the caves-and-mud-huts stage.

He had little chance to consider the city; sooner than he had expected they were at the gate, and Silner was stating his name, rank, and purpose to a suspicious guard. Slant's knowledge of the local dialect was still poor enough that it took a conscious effort for him to follow a conversation, and he made no effort to follow this one, but simply sat, silent and disinterested, until at last the guard pushed open one of the gates and allowed them through.

Slant's disinterest evaporated. The city was fascinating. He was slightly impressed; he had not expected much, given the drab gray walls, but it appeared the decorative domes he had glimpsed were more representative of the city than were the walls.

The streets were paved, and as if that were not remarkable enough, they were paved with stone and equipped with gutters and sidewalks, all spotlessly clean and apparently dead level. This was not at all usual on the less-civilized worlds Slant had seen. No garbage was visible anywhere, and neither his eye nor his nose could detect sewage. Could it be that this primitive culture had underground sewers? If not, at least they had something that seemed to serve about as well. It was an accepted fact on some planets he had visited that cities stank, and he had expected the same here. Teyzha was a pleasant surprise.

He sniffed the air; there was not the slightest trace of foulness, but only fresh air, the sweat of his companion and himself, the odor of their horse, and a faint whiff of incense and cooking odors from buildings nearby.

The buildings were another surprise; he had expected sagging half-timbered structures scattered more or less randomly about the streets, interspersed, perhaps, with ones of brick or wood or stone. Instead, the street before him was lined with tidy stone structures, of cut and polished blocks and trimmed with ornate carvings. The structural stone was granite, or something very similar, but the carvings, sills, cornices, and so forth were of varying materials—mostly colored marbles, but he spotted malachite adorning the windows of one house, and lapis lazuli inlays on another.

Or at least there were ornaments of stones that resembled these; he knew well enough that minerals varied from world to world, and one could never be sure just what one was seeing.

Many buildings sported such luxuries as glass windows and brass hinges—though those were scarcely universal, of course. He was quite impressed.

The truly remarkable thing about the city, though—or at least about the avenue he and Silner were riding along— was that it appeared to be the work of a single architect, built all as a unit. Every building was in harmony with its neighbors, and all were graceful and elegant, with a pleasing repetition of detail. Not that all the buildings were the same; on the contrary, they varied greatly. The variations, however, were never of style, but of detail, size, purpose, and arrangement.

If it had been the work of a single architect, Slant decided, he or she had been a singularly gifted one. He had rarely seen such a beautiful city street, even on Old Earth.

Silner and the occasional pedestrian they encountered along the avenue showed no signs of appreciating the beauty of the city; doubtless they were used to it.

Perhaps a kilometer from the gate they emerged from the broad avenue into an even broader plaza, a square paved with three colors of stone in spiral patterns, with a fountain bubbling at its center. Silner halted his horse and dismounted; Slant followed his example and swung to the ground. He discovered that he was stiff from his long ride, and that a great many parts of his body were slightly painful. He performed a curious stretching exercise he had been taught back on Mars, designed to loosen the muscles in preparation for hand-to-hand combat, and felt the tension and discomfort fade.

He noticed Silner staring at him and decided not to repeat the motion; the warrior's expression betrayed hostile astonishment, as if Slant's stretching offended him in an entirely new and original way.

When he was sure he had the stranger's attention, Silner turned and marched across the plaza to an especially large and elegant building that occupied most of one side, and up the steps that led to its entrance. Slant followed obediently, slinging the submachine gun on his shoulder as he did.

The building was adorned with rather more marble than was customary, and the cyborg guessed it to be the seat of the local government and the meeting place of the Council he had been brought to see. Silner did not hesitate upon reaching the top of the steps, but flung open the great black doors and marched across the antechamber within, and then onward into the torchlit corridor beyond.

Slant followed, thinking of nothing in particular, noticing how very dim the torches seemed after the brilliant sunlight outside. So far he was more or less letting events go as they would, taking the path of least resistance. He was aware that this was not what was expected of an IRU cyborg, so that it was no surprise when the computer said, "Cyborg unit is entering a building that must be assumed to be an enemy stronghold. Programming indicates that such an action must be considered a high-risk operation despite undercover status. All high-risk actions call for alert status, and cyborg unit should exploit all opportunities to reconnoiter enemy stronghold in detail."

"I can't reconnoiter anything; I'm not alone. This person ahead of me thinks I'm one of his own personnel from another base, per my cover story, and is taking me to the local authorities to obtain my clearance for free movement within this installation. It's advisable to cooperate completely until such clearance is obtained." That was a distortion of the truth, of course; the fact was that Slant didn't want to be bothered with a lot of military nonsense on what he was sure was a wild goose chase. He had begun to think that the gravitational disturbances were probably due to an instrument malfunction's causing a misinterpretation of some natural phenomenon on this planet; he really couldn't imagine how the disturbances could be artificial.

The computer took a second or two before replying, and he worried for an instant that it might have decided he was lying. It would probably consider that treason and kill him. He continued to march mechanically down the corridor as he waited for its response.

"Explanation accepted; continue action."

Slant exhaled, noticing for the first time that he had been holding his breath.

The computer had a final comment to add. "Cyborg unit is within area of concentration of anomalies representing enemy weapons research and approaching center of area of concentration. Extreme caution advisable."

That confirmed Slant's suspicion that Teyzha was where he'd been heading in the first place; he wondered if perhaps the ship's scanners had somehow misregistered something innocuous in the city, such as oil lamps or brain waves, as gravitational disturbances. He had no idea whether such a screw-up was possible, but it would serve to explain the matter. Whatever the situation, it appeared that he was in the right place to resolve matters.

The corridor ended in a pair of heavy wooden doors; Silner knocked upon one, then stood and waited. Slant, who had been trailing a few paces behind him, also stopped and stood.

The doors swung partway open, and a bearded face appeared between them.

"Oh, hello, Silner." The man spoke in a friendly and conversational tone, but the helmet that hid most of his curly black hair marked him as a guard of some sort. "What can I do for you?"

"Hello, Kirridin. I'm afraid I need an audience, as soon as possible. We picked up a stranger on the road, and Huarram thought the Council should see him."

"That's no problem; they're just arguing about the apprenticeship system again. Wait here, it'll only be a minute."

The head vanished and the doors closed again; Silner and Slant waited patiently.

Sure enough, a moment later the doors were opened wide and the guard announced, "Silner of Teyzha, your audience is granted." He stood aside, and Silner led Slant past him into the chamber beyond.

It was a good-sized room, circular, perhaps twenty meters in diameter; a translucent white dome covered most of the distant ceiling and admitted most of the light, but lamps gleamed from white marble walls as well. There were benches scattered along the wall. In the center of the room stood a large round table, with seven black-robed figures seated at it. All seven were turned to face the two newcomers.

Silner approached until he was two or three feet from the nearest, then went down on one knee, motioning for Slant to do likewise. After a moment's hesitation, Slant complied.

They knelt awkwardly in silence for a moment. Then one of the robed figures spoke, an old man with a long white beard, and said, "Well, Silner, explain yourself. I thought we sent you to Orna with Huarram's party." His voice was firm and robust, in contrast to his ancient and decrepit appearance.

Silner rose before replying, and Slant followed his example, since he found the kneeling posture uncomfortable.

"Yes, Councillor, you did send me with Huarram, but he sent me back, to escort this stranger, who calls himself Slant."

"Phrasing indicates possible doubt as to authenticity of your identity. Deception may be aborted."

Slant ignored the computer's comment and listened to the white-bearded Councillor, who said, "Indeed. Let the stranger present himself, then, if Huarram has sent him to us."

Slant obediently took a step forward, bringing himself even with Silner, and said, "I am called Slant, from Tur, a village beyond Pruance. I am a harmless wanderer; I happened to encounter your ambassadorial party on the road and was brought here."

"A wanderer, you say? We see very few wanderers around here."

Slant shrugged.

One of the other councillors, a young man with the light-brown hair and beard, asked, "What's that on your shoulder?"

The cyborg looked at the submachine gun as if he had forgotten it was there, and explained, "I don't know; I found it in the woods southwest of here. I thought it might be worth something, so I kept it."

A new councillor spoke, a middle-aged woman seated nearest the cyborg. "May I see that? Perhaps we can tell you what it is."

Reluctantly, Slant unslung the gun and handed it to her; she placed it on the table, where the gaze of all seven councillors fixed upon it.

A sensation like a mild electric current filled the room; Slant's skin prickled, though he could see nothing out of the ordinary. He resisted the urge to look wildly about for the source of the eerie feeling, since nobody else seemed to pay any attention to it.

The computer informed him, "Anomalous disturbance representing enemy weapons research activity occurring in immediate vicinity of cyborg unit, directly ahead, at a distance of approximately two meters. No visual confirmation received. Interference assumed. Report situation in detail."

"I can't see anything odd either, just the seven councillors looking at my gun. I thought I felt something, like an electrical discharge of some kind; did you detect anything of that sort?" Although he gave no outward sign and tried to keep his communication with the computer calm and efficient, Slant was confused and astonished. It

looked like there really was something new here, something that used no machinery that he could detect.

"No electrical discharge noted. No unusual activity detected other than anomalous disturbance representing
enemy weapons research activity."

One of the councillors looked up from the gun and
asked, "Where did you get this?"

"In the woods. What is it? What were you doing to it?"

The other councillors had turned away from the gun
now; the white-bearded old man replied, "We were just
studying it. It's a weapon, a death machine, like so many
of the relics that turn up. There's something strange about
this one, though; it's almost new, not more than twenty
years old, while all the other relics are from the Bad
Times, more than three hundred years ago. Now, will
you please tell us, truthfully, where you got it?"

"Question indicates doubt as to authenticity of cover
story. Deception may be aborted."

"Shut up!" He shouted mentally, nervous enough without the computer's interference; he was out of practice in
dealing with people, despite his training and conditioning.
"I told you, I found it in the woods southwest of here."

"Nonsense." It was the middle-aged woman who spoke.

"Perhaps not; true, it can't be a relic of the Bad Times,
but this man might not be its rightful owner," a new
speaker said, a man of indeterminate age and curly brown
hair.

"Is it yours? Tell the truth." The white-bearded man's
gaze fixed on Slant's face, and he felt a faint electric
tingle again.

"I did tell the truth; I found it in the woods!"

"Enemy officials are displaying extreme suspicion. An
immediate escape attempt may be advisable," the computer
warned.

"No, you didn't. Surely you know that a wizard can
read the truth, and that you cannot deceive any of the
seven of us. No one can fool seven wizards. There is
something very strange about you; who are you really?"

"What? Wizards?" he said aloud, simultaneously subvocalizing, "Look, computer, I . . ." Slant was becom-

ing thoroughly confused trying to carry on two vitally important conversations at the same time—particularly since the spoken conversation was in a strange language, and involved concepts he didn't understand at all. What was this talk about wizards? Had he walked into the middle of a fairy tale?

"Deception is aborted. An immediate escape attempt is advisable."

One of the councillors turned his gaze from Slant and said, "Silner, stand ready; it appears there is more to this man than is readily seen."

Silner stepped back, spreading his feet to provide a steadier base, and drew his sword.

"Listen, Slant as you call yourself, we mean you no harm. However, we . . ."

Slant did not hear the rest of the old councillor's words; instead, he heard, "Deception is aborted. Capture is imminent. An immediate escape attempt is required. Failure to attempt escape will allow termination of cyborg unit." There was an instant of panic; then he was suddenly calm as his combat personality took over, and with no conscious thought whatsoever he whirled, launching a vicious kick into Silner's belly and chopping a hand into his wrist, sending the sword clattering across the floor. With no sign that any of the councillors was armed, his next move was to dive into their midst and retrieve his weapon. He landed sitting on the table, the gun already in his hand, facing back toward the door.

Silner was doubling over but had not yet fallen; the councillors had not yet had time to react at all. The guard by the door was starting to reach for his sword.

His right hand clutching the submachine gun, Slant used his left hand to thrust himself upright and off the table; then he was running across the chamber toward the door. A sidestep and a swipe of the right forearm disposed of the guard, who sprawled backward onto the stone floor, his helmet rattling off the wall; then Slant was out of the room and running full speed down the corridor, vaguely aware of a voice calling for him to wait, the voice of the white-bearded councillor.

Chapter Four

TRAINING CALLED FOR EVASIVE ACTION. EVEN IN HIS UN-
thinking state, though, Slant knew that he might never
find his way from the city if he followed any route
other than the straight line he had entered by. There would
be plenty of time to confuse his trail once he reached open
country; for the present, his first priority was to get outside
the walls before the gates could be barred against him.
Therefore the only consideration now was speed; he ran
flat out down the avenue, gun clutched in his hand, ignoring
the townspeople he passed. They gaped but made no move
to stop him.

He reached the gate approximately two minutes after
leaving the Council chamber. It was closed, but that was
no obstacle for an IRU cyborg; the gates were just wood,
and held by a simple iron latch. There were brackets for
heavy bars, but the bars were not in place, instead, they
lay neatly stacked at one side.

A flying kick demolished the latch, and the gates, re-
bounding from the impact, swung open a half meter.
Slant landed on one foot from his kick, then spun about
and was out the gate, still running, before the astonished
gatekeeper had time to react. The man called after him,
but Slant kept running.

There was room now for evasive action, and he left
the road, ran across the fields, then looped southward.
Ten minutes later he settled onto a patch of grass amid a
small stand of trees and told the computer angrily, "Well,
now you've done it. I could have convinced them I'd
found the gun."

"Evidence was to the contrary."

"Evidence, hell! We're dealing with ordinary people—a bunch of near-savages, in fact. I could have convinced them."

The computer did not reply.

"What do you think we're doing, anyway? What's the point in having a human do your scouting if you overrule me every time I try to do something you can't?"

"Information unavailable."

"What information is unavailable?"

"Purpose of cyborg unit."

"What?" Slant was surprised out of his irritation. "You don't know what I'm for?"

"Programming provides instructions as to when to permit cyborg unit to act independently and when to override or terminate. No statement of purpose is provided."

Slant mulled that over for a moment, and was about to ask another question when he was interrupted by the sound of hoofbeats, approaching from the direction of Teyzha. In an instant he was on his feet, gun at ready, looking for cover. He ducked between two of the largest trees and waited.

"Party approaching coincides with mobile gravitational anomaly."

"Where is he?" The voice was closer than he had expected, and much closer than he liked.

"There, behind that tree. Be careful, he's got a weapon from the Bad Times."

Slant cursed under his breath; how had he been spotted? He was not visible and had made no sound; he was too well trained for that. Was this more "magic?" He also found himself annoyed at the second voice's exact words; it was the fact that his weapon apparently wasn't from the "Bad Times" that had forced him to flee.

There was no time to worry about details, though; he had to keep the element of surprise, and move too fast for the Teyzhans to organize and plan. The gun was already in his hands; he leaped from his concealment and fired a burst at the approaching party, aiming low.

The effect was shattering and gratifying; one of the half-dozen horses fell, apparently hit, throwing his rider

headlong and tripping up at least one of the other mounts.
The remaining horses, some perhaps wounded and all
terrified by the roar and flash of the gun, reared and
bucked uncontrollably, whinnying their fear and trying to
turn and flee. Their riders, scarcely less frightened themselves, struggled to control them.

Slant did not wait to see the outcome of the chaos he
had created; he turned and ran, heading for the woods.
Behind him more men lost their holds and fell, narrowly
avoiding the hoofs of their own panicked steeds; he con-
gratulated himself on choosing the flamboyant submachine gun over the silent lasers and snarks.

He did not follow a straight course, but twisted and
dodged across the outer farms and onward into the forest
beyond; he had no fear of losing himself, since the computer was always able to orient him. After a few minutes
of swift travel, he slowed to a walk; he did not dare stop
completely again. Perhaps if he kept moving the Teyzhans
would be less able to find him. He wondered how they
had found him that first time.

He also wondered what the damn computer's orders
called for now that his scouting expedition had come to
a sudden end. "Well, computer," he asked silently, "what
would you advise me to do now?"

"Recommended action is surreptitious entry and investigation of enemy stronghold for purpose of locating enemy
weapons research."

"You want me to play burglar and find whatever-it-is."

"Query: Term 'whatever-it-is' refers to gravitational
anomalies representing enemy weapons research?"

"Right."

"Reference filed."

"How am I supposed to sneak into a city with a wall
around it and guards at the gate?"

"Query: Evidence of aerial surveillance."

"There isn't any; it's a preaviation culture, at least
around here. Anyway, I think it is; it appears to be pretechnological, except for whatever-it-is."

"Recommended action is surreptitious entry by parachute or other silent aerial approach."

Slant snorted as he walked. "You want me to parachute into the middle of a city?"

"Affirmative."

"Sure, why not? I can only get killed once. I haven't used a parachute in fourteen years, you stupid machine!"

The computer made no reply; it was not programmed to worry about rusty skills.

It was, Slant reminded himself, not programmed for much of anything that related to having spent an extended time in space. The Command had not expected his mission to last that long, either because they thought the war would end quickly or because they thought he'd have gotten killed long before this.

Resigned, he asked, "Should I return to the ship, then?"

"Affirmative."

"Great," he muttered. He slung the gun over his shoulder and turned his heretofore more or less random course toward his starship. After a few moments of walking quietly, letting the gentle breeze and the crunching of pine needles calm him, he remembered the conversation that had been interrupted by his pursuers.

"Computer, you said that you don't know what I'm for."

"Affirmative."

"What are you for? Do you know?"

"Restate question."

"What's your purpose? What goal are you after?"

"That is not a single question."

"Answer both questions, then."

"Purpose of computer control complex of Independent Reconnaissance Unit two-oh-five is to provide necessary assistance to cyborg unit in piloting of starship, processing data, monitoring communications, maintenance of all units, and analysis of situation during actions; also, to assure continued loyalty and service of cyborg unit through use of override and threat of termination; also, to terminate cyborg unit in the event of service dysfunction; also, to assure that cyborg unit carries out mission orders where feasible; also, to carry out mission orders in the absence of cyborg unit or authorized human command. Goal of computer control complex of Independent Reconnaissance

Unit two-oh-five is not stated in programming, but can be determined to be termination of all unit function."

"What!" Slant stumbled in surprise.

"Restate question."

"Your goal is your own termination?"

"Affirmative."

"You want to die?"

"Affirmative."

Slant stopped walking, in order to think without distraction. "How can you terminate yourself? Under what conditions?"

"Programming provides the following termination options: Shut-down order following receipt of release code; self-destruct in the event of capture; self-destruct in the event of cyborg unit termination. Evidence indicates first option is no longer viable."

Slant was surprised; the computer was aware that their side had lost the war after all, it seemed. "You're right about that. Capture's pretty damn unlikely, too, with the war over." He had intended to say more but broke off suddenly when he realized he had just told the computer that the only way it could achieve its goal of self-destruction was to kill him—or to get him killed, at any rate.

Was that related to what had happened in Teyzha? Had the computer intentionally fouled things up and forced his flight in hopes that he'd get killed? Its programming forbade it from taking any direct action against him as long as he remained loyal, but it just might be subtle enough to try indirect action.

That might be why it wanted to parachute him into Teyzha; it might be aware that he stood a good chance of getting killed. Its orders did not allow for the passage of time, but it might know that humans could lose skills through atrophy, unlike computers; it could be using that as a loophole.

Then again, maybe it simply arrived at that as the best military option, in accordance wtih the available data.

Well, whatever the truth, he'd just have to be more careful from now on. He started walking again, mulling the situation over. For the first time in years, he began seriously considering schemes to detach himself from the computer and remove the thermite and the override from his skull; the discovery of the computer's death wish had seriously jarred his longstanding acceptance of his unhappy situation.

Approximately three hours later, as Slant was settling to the ground for a brief rest and wishing he had something to eat, the computer informed him, "Ongoing gravitational anomaly approaching cyborg unit from northeast, at an altitude of approximately twenty meters and ground speed of approximately two meters per second; distance from cyborg unit approximately one kilometer."

"More pursuit from Teyzha?"

"Information insufficient."

Slant sighed and rose to his feet unconcernedly; then the computer's exact words registered, and he asked, "Damn, did you say altitude? You mean it's flying?"

"Affirmative."

"Damn!" he said aloud.

Slant considered taking cover but decided against it; it had done no good previously. He also considered attempting to outrace whatever was pursuing him, but that, too, he rejected; the pursuit was traveling at a good speed, in clear air while he would have to dodge trees and underbrush, and there was no reason to assume that its current pace—which he could probably better—was its top speed, or that it was subject to normal fatigue. Instead he simply unslung his gun and stood waiting, watching the treetops in the direction he had just come from.

A few moments later he caught a glimpse of something gliding above the treetops and moving directly toward him. He checked the gun. It was ready, the clip still almost full; his first burst hadn't used more than half a dozen rounds.

The flying object was closing; even through the treetops he could see that it was apparently a man, moving through the air with no visible means of support. He began to wonder if wizards really existed on this strange planet.

The man, if it was a man, was slowing; he was still about twenty meters off horizontally, as well as twenty meters above the ground.

He stopped, hanging calmly in midair, and called out, "Slant of Tur! Are you down there?"

This was obviously for form's sake; Slant had no doubt that the "wizard" knew exactly where he was. He said nothing.

"I know you're there, Slant."

So much for pretense, then; Slant shouted, "Go away!"

"Slant, I mean you no harm; none of us do. Listen, please! Let me talk to you! You're possessed by a demon, a metal demon in your head; we saw it! You must come back to Teyzha so that we can remove it! Only wizards can help you!"

Slant grinned to himself. The wizards really did seem to know their business; they knew about the computer hookup and called it a demon, did they? It sounded reasonable enough.

"Well, computer, what do you suggest? Should I go back?" he asked silently.

"Negative. High probability exists that removal of 'metal demon,' proper designation unknown, would impair cyborg function and/or loyalty."

The idiot machine didn't even recognize that it was the demon, Slant realized. "I think it might be worth a try."

"Negative. Such action would constitute cooperation with the enemy."

"That's ridiculous."

"Negative. Further conversation with airborne enemy patrol must be considered counterproductive, increasing probability of enemy action against cyborg unit."

"Slant? Please, say something!" The breeze briefly parted the leaves, and Slant caught a glimpse of the flying man's face; he was a very young man, and the cyborg thought he recognized him as the youngest of the Teyzhan councillors.

"If I'm not supposed to talk with him, what should I do? Flee? He can probably follow."

"Negative. Standard procedures calls for elimination of airborne enemy patrol to prevent relay of cyborg unit location or other data."

"He's just a kid! And he's one of the wizards you wanted to know about!"

"Irrelevant. Please take proper action."

Slant recognized that phrase as one that warned of an imminent override if he continued to fail to cooperate; reluctantly, he raised the gun and fired a warning burst in front of the hovering man.

The chattering roar of the gun tore through the quiet forest; bits of shredded leaves flew in every direction like green confetti as the bullets ripped through the trees. Slant's ears rang when the roar stopped.

As the echoes faded off in the maze of trees and the machine-gunned leaves, twigs, and branches finished falling, crackling, and rustling, Slant saw the flying figure fleeing the way he had come, skimming the treetops. He started to call a sardonic farewell, but his voice caught in his throat and his body twitched convulsively as the computer tried to take control of his body. The override was far less efficient at a distance than through the direct-control cable, so for a few seconds Slant was subjected to spastic twitching, but the computer had taken him completely by surprise. Involuntarily the submachine gun was wrenched back up and the remainder of the ammunition clip fired in the direction of the departing wizard, obliterating the new silence and tearing apart more leaves.

Slant was pleased to see that there was no sign any of this renewed fire had touched the Teyzhan councillor.

The computer apparently saw the same thing; when the firing mechanism clicked after discharging the last cartridge, the override released abruptly, and a final uncoordinated jerk sent Slant sprawling awkwardly on the carpet of pine needles.

He lay there for a second, listening to echoes dying once again and watching bits of mangled leaf drift to the ground, then demanded, "What the hell was that all about?"

"Cyborg unit dysfunction; airborne enemy patrol escaping."

"What dysfunction? I didn't want to kill him. There was no reason to kill him; he wasn't going to hurt us."

"Contention unsupported by evidence. Standard procedure calls for elimination of any enemy patrol or individual discovering location of any IRU unit not operating under cover, to prevent relay of unit location or other data harmful to IRU or beneficial to enemy military intelligence."

"Don't spout orders at me! You know there are special cases, and that it's up to me to assess them, not you!"

"Affirmative. However, there is no evidence to indicate that recent action constituted a special case calling for deviation from standard procedure."

"What evidence do you want?"

"Any evidence that would indicate recent action to be a special case calling for deviation from standard procedure. Providing such evidence will modify record of cyborg unit dysfunction."

"And if I have no objective evidence, just my intuition?"

"Record of cyborg unit dysfunction will remain."

Slant wearily regained his feet.

"Warning: Cyborg unit has shown high incidence of marginal dysfunction and lack of enthusiasm for mission. Further dysfunction may allow termination without further warning."

"What?"

"Warning: Cyborg unit—"

"No, never mind, I heard you." That, he thought to himself, was just lovely; he might get his head burned off any time the computer thought he was shirking. He wondered whether this was a manifestation of the machine's death wish, and decided that it almost certainly was. He slung the submachine gun over his shoulder, remembering as he did that it was now useless until he returned the ship and reloaded it, and started to trudge south.

"It's too bad I couldn't just fly, like the Teyzhan councillor," he muttered to himself. He wondered just what he had stumbled into, and how these "wizards" worked their magic.

"You know, computer," he said thoughtfully, "for the first time on this damn mission we might actually have found something."

"Affirmative."

Slipping back into the more familiar subvocalizing, he continued, "It's almost too bad the war's over."

The computer did not answer.

Chapter Five

SLANT SPOKE ALOUD, DEMANDING ANGRILY, "YOU SERIously expect me to parachute into the middle of an unfriendly city at *night*?"

"Affirmative."

"It's been fourteen years since I used a parachute!"

"Query: Advisability of practice jumps."

"Probably . . . no, let's get it over with." He lay back on the acceleration couch, hands behind his head.

"Launch in thirty seconds."

"Fine."

"Drop will be from altitude of fifteen kilometers."

"What? Are you crazy?" He took his hands from beneath his head and sat up.

"Negative."

"Why so high?"

"Extreme altitude is advisable to lessen risk of detection."

And to increase my chances of getting killed, Slant thought. "Right. I'll need oxygen equipment, and maybe a pressure suit."

"Affirmative."

He decided he didn't dare argue further; the computer might decide he was disloyal. He had no desire to have his brain fried. He lay back down, and a moment later the ship launched itself forward and upward. He wondered how much of a mess the takeoff had made of the clearing and surrounding forest; perhaps he should have piloted it himself.

It was a little late to think of that, though; he thought of something else instead. "You know, I was wrong; this isn't exactly a preaviation culture after all. That person who found me in the woods was certainly flying, using whatever this thing is that we're after."

"Affirmative."

"Coming in by parachute might not be a good idea: they probably have 'wizards' flying a nightly sky patrol."

"There is no evidence of airborne enemy patrols."

"Maybe there aren't any aloft right now, but what if one comes along while I'm halfway down? It's pretty hard to hide while dangling in midair, even with a steerable 'chute."

"Cyborg unit will be armed; airborne enemy patrols may be eliminated. There has been no evidence of nocturnal airborne enemy patrols since planetfall."

"Oh." He could think of no further arguments, and although far from convinced, he wanted to reassure the computer of his enthusiasm. "Okay. That's fine, then."

He lay back for a moment, eyes closed, but then rebelled against this familiar position; there was no need for it. He had a new planet to look at. Unpleasant though his current situation was, there was no call to return to his habitual shipboard boredom. He opened his eyes and reached behind him for the direct-control cable. Plugging it into his neck, he called for belly-camera relay and watched as the deep green forests slid by below him, receding as the ship gained altitude. Standard procedure for a parachute drop was to approach from a very low orbit, he recalled, to dip down briefly, drop the 'chutist, and then return to orbit; presumably the computer would be doing exactly that.

"How long till drop?"

"Approximately ninety-four minutes."

That was probably two revolutions; he was sure the computer wouldn't use that high an orbit for what was, after all, almost a ground operation from its point of view. "Why so long?"

"Standard procedure calls for initial pass to evaluate weather conditions and tactical situation."

That made sense, and incidentally added a new worry to his list; he hadn't thought about weather. It hadn't been a concern during the years in space, nor underground on

Mars, and the weather had been uniformly calm and beautiful since he landed. With any luck at all, he knew, it would stay that way, and the computer would not be so reckless as to drop him into the middle of a storm should one arise—but he still had visions of falling through rain clouds.

Well, he had time to worry about it and to try to think of some way to convince the computer there was a better approach than parachuting him anywhere. He watched the land slip away as the ship's orbit took it out past the coast and over the ocean.

When the first pass brought it back over Teyzha, the computer informed him that the weather was clear and calm, that there was no sign of aerial surveillance, and that he had forty-five minutes to suit up and arm himself.

At the end of the second revolution, as the ship decelerated and dipped out of orbit, he was waiting in the airlock clad in a lightweight insulating pressure suit, black from head to toe, his black glider-chute packed on his back. The submachine gun, reloaded, was slung across his shoulders, above his chute, and a snark and a flashlight were clipped on his belt. A snug helmet and oxygen mask completed his outfit.

He had expected to be terrified when the outer door opened and he heard and felt the cold wind roaring past; jumping from the wing of a starship fifteen kilometers up was not something he was confident he could survive. Nonetheless, when the port slid aside and the computer signalled something shifted within him, and he was completely calm, moving with easy self-assurance, as he stepped from the airlock and let the wind rip him from the ship's wing. He had forgotten that he was not a normal man but a cyborg; the computer was regulating his glands, preventing the physical effects of panic, and his conditioning had brought to the fore the schizoid fragment of his psyche that had been trained in military operations of this type, a personality that knew no fear, that thought no more of a parachute jump than of riding a horse or fording a stream.

It was this fearless Slant that plummeted groundward, opening his 'chute at the most opportune moment to take advantage of the wind patterns the computer had charted on its first pass, calculating how best to maximize his chances of landing safely on target—on target meaning anywhere inside the city of Teyzha, though the Council's palace was his theoretical ground zero.

Even had he been his normal self, there would have been little for him to fear after the initial plunge; the night sky was indeed clear, the air calm, and there was no sign of airborne activity in the city below. There was very little evidence of any activity at all; by local time it was approximately an hour past midnight, and most of the population was doubtlessly long abed.

When he first looked down from freefall, with his ship still visible as a dwindling speck in the distance, it had taken him several seconds to find Teyzha at all; the city was nothing but a dot, surrounded by a small patch of paleness, colorless in the darkness, that was farmland, almost lost in the dark immensity of the forest that covered the land in all directions. That dot was now swooping up at him as the wind carried him toward it.

Although the air rushing by and the speed with which the ground approached gave him a feeling of great velocity—an accurate feeling—the fall seemed to take hours. He knew that it was actually only a few minutes between leaving his ship and seeing the city jump up at him with frightening suddenness, but it felt as if he had been hanging in space forever.

Then abruptly time was rushing by, and he had none to spare to admire the starlit scenery; he had to devote his attention to steering his rectangular web of nylon, riding the air currents over the city wall and into Teyzha.

As he passed over the parapet his 'chute caught an updraft, and the few meters that separated his feet from the battlements became a respectable distance again; he guessed that the stone buildings and pavements must still be radiating the day's accumulated heat, warming the air and creating the updraft. He hadn't counted on that; it slowed his descent and made steering much easier, so that he could choose any landing spot he liked. He wished more light were available than the feeble starshine.

Ahead of him he made out a pale, looming dome; he

could not be sure it was actually white, but it appeared to be, and he was fairly sure it must be the dome of the Council palace. The plaza before the palace would be a perfect landing spot, wide and level, and at this late hour he doubted even so public a place carried much risk of his being spotted. He steered toward it.

Unfortunately, he had more altitude than he had realized, and even in his efficient military persona he was out of practime in guiding a glider-chute, particularly in an environment with slightly less than terrestrial gravity. He passed neatly over the plaza, and before he could loop back he was descending on the roof of the palace itself. He had no choice but to make the best of it, and managed a passable landing just to the right of the dome, on a flat expanse of tile.

Still acting on programmed reflex, he stood, scanned for enemies, and seeing none hauled in his 'chute, then detached it and bundled it under one arm. That was as far as his conditioning carried him; his normal emotions slipped back, and his knees felt weak as he realized he had just survived a fifteen-kilometer fall, supported only by a couple of kilograms of nylon. He looked about, considering what to do next.

His immediate goal was to get off the roof; he was no good to anyone up there. He saw no sign of any door, hatch, trap, skylight, airshaft, vent, or other opening; he moved carefully around the dome, but there was no entry to be had anywhere.

Cautiously he approached the edge of the roof and peered over at the street that ran behind the building, a narrow lane displaying no sign of life at all, not so much as a foraging rat. If he could lower himself over the edge with the lines from his parachute, he could drop down into that alley without any undue fuss and proceed from there; he looked about for some means of anchoring the 'chute to the rooftop.

A narrow metal chimney stuck up near the edge of the dome; Slant unfolded the mass of nylon under his arm and hooked the approximate center of the 'chute around the protruding pipe. The shrouds were hopelessly tangled;

rather than try to separate them he twisted them together further, so that they served as a single thick rope. He lowered this makeshift rope over the edge of the roof.

It didn't reach anywhere near as far as he would have liked, but he thought it would do; he took a final look around to make sure he hadn't missed a trap door in the darkness, then slid backward over the eaves, his ankles wrapped around the tangled lines and his hands gripping them firmly—but not too tightly, as that could be dangerous.

Cautiously he worked his way down the rope until he was below the narrow overhang of the eaves; then he unwrapped his legs and swung them forward, planting his feet on the side of the palace, so that he wouldn't sway from side to side. Thus stabilized, he took a moment to look about.

The street was still distressingly distant; the palace was at least three, perhaps four stories high, and he had had to hook his 'chute well back from the edge, so that he had less than two meters of line left. That meant an uncomfortably long drop.

He noticed, however, that his left foot was just a few centimeters from a window, and that he saw no sign of shutters or any other serious barrier.

This was too good an opportunity to miss; he pushed himself sideways and hooked his foot on the window frame, then slid himself down and over until he was perched on the sill, one hand still clutching the shrouds to steady him as he studied the situation.

As soon as he got a good look at the window he realized he had made a mistake. Although there were no shutters on the outside, he had underestimated the thickness of the wall; thirty centimeters in, hidden by the shadows and virtually invisible in the faint light, was a casement. One of his knees was actually touching it.

He cursed silently.

"Query: Report status."

"I'm trying to break into the main government building through an upper-story window. Shut up and let me concentrate."

"Termination of communications contact between ship and cyborg unit imminent."

"Fine. Look, I'm busy; I can handle this without you. Let me know when you're back in range."

"Affirmative."

Without intending to, Slant waited for some sign that the computer really was out of range below the horizon and that he was out of radio contact with it for the first time in years. No such sign came; most of the equipment in his head and body had its own self-regulating mechanisms and was supposed to be able to run for days, coasting, without the computer's control.

When several seconds of dead silence, both mental and physical, had passed, he roused himself, telling himself that he was stupid to expect something to change just because his ship was gone. Still keeping his right hand firmly on his climbing line, he leaned forward as far as he could and felt the casement with his unencumbered left hand. The motion twisted his shoulders so that the barrel of the submachine gun clanked noisily against the stone wall; he froze but detected no activity, no evidence that anyone had heard.

Very much annoyed at his carelessness, he continued his investigation of the window.

It was simple enough; a wooden frame holding many small panes of glass, leaded together. Naturally, there was no latch on the outside, but he found the hinges on the right side, ordinary hinges, each with a pin holding two flanges together. If he could work the pins free, he could open the window. Unfortunately, he had no way of removing the pins; he hadn't thought to bring any small tools. He tried pulling one up with his fingers but with no success. He couldn't remove his gloves without letting go of the support line, and he couldn't get a good grip through the slick plastic; besides, it felt as if the pins had rusted in place.

Frustration swelled up in his chest; he found it impossible to believe that after risking his neck getting this far he was being daunted by a pair of rusty hinges. He drew his fist back, seriously considering simply smashing in the glass and forgetting any attempt at stealth.

He caught himself, stopped and unclenched his fist. He

might yet resort to that, he told himself, but first he should consider every other possibility. There appeared to be no way to open the window with just his hand; the simple experiment of tugging at the wooden frame as best he could demonstrated that it was securely latched, and he was unable to work the hinges apart—at least, he was unable to do it in his current position. He could climb back up on the rooftop, remove his gloves, then climb back down and try again, but that idea did not appeal to him at all. He didn't care for climbing, and there was no assurance he could pull the hinge pins even with his gloves off.

If he had some tool, such as a screwdriver, he could get them apart, he was sure. Mentally he reviewed his supplies, what few he had.

He had a glider-chute, consisting of several meters of fine nylon, a lot of nylon cord, and spring-loaded expanding plastic ribs that gave the 'chute its shape. The ribs might possibly be of use, but that would mean climbing back onto the roof and ripping apart the 'chute.

He was wearing a helmet and oxygen mask; the mask hung loose around his neck. There was no help in those two items.

The submachine gun was slung across his shoulders; if he could get a meter or two away, and disregard the noise, he could blow the entire window apart.

Last, there were the flashlight and snark on his belt; remembering the snark, he suddenly felt foolish.

It was clipped on the right, for easy use by his right hand; that hand was still clutching his makeshift rope, however, so that he reached awkwardly across with his left and carefully unfastened the little weapon. Moving very slowly and deliberately—it would not do to drop the thing in the alley —he brought it across his body.

It wasn't safe to be too close to anything that the snark's beam hit; he edged back off the windowsill until he hung from his right hand, his toes on the edge of the sill to steady him. Carefully, he used his thumb to turn the control setting from SAFETY to MODERATE; the power dial lit a dull red, and the needle swung to the 90 percent charge mark. He pointed it at the window and pressed the trigger, holding his breath.

The casement vanished in a puff of gray dust, sparkling in the starlight; he heard a soft hissing as powdered glass sprinkled across the windowsill.

He turned the setting back to SAFETY, then carefully clipped the snark back onto his belt. Reaching forward, he thrust his hand through the opening the weapon had made.

It had not dissolved the entire window, but it had made a hole about a quarter meter across; within Slant discovered that even had he gotten the casement open he would not have been able to just climb inside, as there had indeed been shutters. The snark's beam had gone through these as well, removing their latch; he could easily push them aside and reach across to the casement latch.

Slowly and carefully, so as not to dislodge any loosened panes of glass in what was left of the window, he swung the casement open and slid into the room beyond.

Here he had virtually no light at all, not ever the starlight; closing what remained of the shutters behind him, he took the flashlight from his belt and shone it about.

The room was, fortunately, uninhabited; that meant that he didn't have to kill anyone just yet. Had it been occupied, of course, his rattling about outside the window would probably have been heard.

Two of the four walls, ahead and to his left, were lined with books from floor to ceiling, a matter of slightly more than two meters; the Teyzhans apparently didn't bother with high ceilings everywhere as they had in the Council chamber. A third wall was papered with maps and charts and diagrams. The fourth wall, although lined with shelves, did not hold books but an amazing clutter of apparently random and bizarre objects, trinkets, and talismans, everything from mounted gems to stuffed birds to tableware. Among this display of arcana were several skulls of various kinds and innumerable flasks, jars, and vials.

The window he had entered by was in the wall of charts, as was a second window off to his left; there were two doors, one in each wall of books, directly across from him and at the left end of the room. The one at the end stood slightly ajar.

It was a good-sized room, perhaps four meters across and six meters long, and there was considerable furniture scattered about, including two heavy wooden tables of different heights, a desk, assorted chairs, and half a dozen stands or pedestals bearing strange instruments, one of which he recognized as a celestial globe. A reading stand was pushed into a corner, where the shelves of junk met bookshelves. Dozens of candles, from tall tapers to burned-out stubs, were scattered about, some in candlesticks or sconces, others just set upon whatever was handy.

Slant had encountered many similar rooms in fiction but never before in reality; he had no doubt whatsoever that he had stumbled upon a wizard's laboratory.

Since there was reason to believe that he was to investigate whatever the "wizards" used for magic, chancing upon the laboratory was an incredible stroke of luck. Right there he might find what he was looking for and be able to go his way without killing anybody or doing any further harm.

He needed more light; the flashlight wasn't suitable for anything beyond a casual glance around. A few candles would do nicely if he could find some way to light them.

The thing to do was to consider the question logically. How did the room's regular user light all these candles? If he used his so-called magic, that was no help; Slant therefore assumed, for the sake of argument, that magic was not put to such petty uses.

What, then? There was no fireplace from which a splint could be lit, nor anything he recognized as a firepot. Flint and steel, perhaps, or even matches, might well be lying around somewhere in the clutter. Matches were simple enough, just a little basic chemistry; with any luck these people used them. The thought of trying to light anything with flint and steel did not appeal to him at all; he'd tried it once or twice and knew how slow and tedious it was.

If there were matches, where would they be? They would be near the door, of course, where they could be found easily upon entering.

Sure enough, a careful search with the flashlight discovered a jar of blue-tipped splinters on the corner of a table near the door in the long wall. He soon had several candles burning brightly.

The candlelight gave the room a much warmer and homier feel; he no longer felt like a nervous burglar, sneak-

ing about in the dark. He put away his flashlight and removed his helmet and oxygen mask, laying them on the
nearest table.

Thus unencumbered, he decided that the best place to
start was with the books. The problem was that there were
so many of them. He ran his eye casually along the nearest
shelf, reading the titles.

*The Morality of Magic, Magic and Its Misuse, Profes-
sional Ethics*—none of those sounded very helpful. He
wanted an elementary general text on the subject. He
skipped down a few shelves, and found *The Book of Law:
Volume Twelve, War and Conflict*. That wasn't any better.
He moved farther down the room and found *Techniques of
Weather and Storm Control*. That still wasn't very basic, but
it sounded interesting; he lifted the volume down from the
shelf and opened it carefully.

He had half expected it to be old and dusty, in keeping
with the traditional image of a wizard's book; instead it was
fresh and clean, smelling of new leather and ink. The pages
were neatly if unevenly cut, and not at all worn, showing
not so much as a smudged thumbprint; the binding was
still stiff. It was, he saw, printed, and not hand-lettered;
the art of movable type had apparently not been lost. The
planet continued to surprise him. Still, he should have
realized that a library such as this would be extremely un-
unlikely without the printing press.

There was a title page, printed in blood red; at the bottom of the page he found a warning that read "This book
is for the use of magicians of the fifth degree or above, and
is dangerous to lesser magicians." He would have expected
such a warning to be embellished with curses and dire
threats, but perhaps that was unnecessary when the magic
actually worked. The book might well really be dangerous
to an amateur. He wondered whether these wizards actually
could influence storms and weather; if so, the upper echelon
might be capable of enforcing their decrees without resort-
ing to threats.

It seemed unlikely; probably the book was a sham.

The print was quite large throughout, he saw; he theorized that the wizards tended toward poor vision, poor
lighting, poor typemakers, or all three. In any case, it was

no strain to read even in the dim candlelight. He turned to the first page and began scanning the text.

As he read his opinion of the planet's culture improved with every page; this book was, as far as he could see, an accurate, scientific description of atmospheric behavior. He found no mystic nonsense of spirits or magical forces; instead there was a straightforward explanation of air currents, evaporation, condensation, frontal patterns, air pressure . . .

Technology might be lacking in this culture, but their knowledge of at least one science surpassed his own. He wondered whether the book was a transcription of a surviving prewar work, or whether the information had somehow been rediscovered and accumulated since. Perhaps some had been transmitted orally.

So far, however, the book had little to do with antigravity, or staring at a gun and making one's skin crawl, or locating hidden people, or flying with no visible means of propulsion. He read on.

A soft sound interrupted him; he turned and saw that a large black cat had entered the room, presumably through the open door—he didn't think he could have failed to see it had it already been in the chamber. It studied him.

The two stared at each other for a moment; then Slant returned to his book, and the cat began washing itself.

A moment later there was another interruption as the computer regained contact.

"Query: Relevance of text to present investigation."

Slant had been thoroughly absorbed in his book and took a moment before replying. "It's relevant, all right. This is an instruction manual for controlling the weather with whatever-it-is." He did not mention that so far the book had explained in great detail how weather worked and what various manipulations of the air would do without ever saying how these manipulations could be done.

"Query: Are more general texts available?"

"I haven't found any."

"Further investigation is advisable."

"Yeah, right, just a second." He closed the book and returned it to its place on the shelves, then considered where to look next. The other wall might have more general works; the area he had checked seemed to be highly specialized stuff. He crossed the room.

As he did so, the cat rose and leaped off the desk. When he lit a convenient candle and began studying titles, the animal brushed against his legs, purring.

"Quiet, cat," he whispered, as he skipped over *Basic Anatomy, The Structure of the Human Body,* and other such titles. The cat, in typical feline fashion, ignored his request and continued rubbing and purring.

"Query: Nature of small animal."

"It's a cat, a household pet; it's harmless. Don't worry about it."

"Query: Is small animal designated 'cat' a familiar?"

Slant stopped scanning titles. "A what?"

"A familiar."

"I don't know. Why do you ask? What's a familiar?"

"Term is from reference material category 'Folklore,' describing a small animal kept by witch or wizard. Natives of this planet have used term 'wizard' apparently in application to themselves. Familiars were said to carry messages. If this small animal is a familiar it may pose a detection risk."

"I wouldn't worry about it; that's just a myth. It's just an ordinary cat. Why are you concerned about folklore, anyway? I thought you knew that stuff was inoperative." He looked down at the cat, which looked up to meet his gaze, and for an instant wondered whether the computer might be right. That was nonsense; these so-called wizards were just scientists, he was sure, using some new gimmick they had discovered.

"Standard procedure calls for checking available data on all new terminology. Term 'wizard' is listed in reference material category 'Folklore.' "

"Oh. That makes sense, I guess. Look, I'm not sure, but I think that these people use the term 'wizard' to refer to persons participating in development and use of whatever it is we're after, and possibly to scientists in general. I don't think they're really wizards."

"Opinion noted."

That seemed to end the discussion; the cat went on trying to coax him into petting it, and he went on reading titles: *On Raising Palaces, The Conjuration of Shelter, Protection by Magic*. That last might be worth checking out, he thought, if he found nothing better.

The next shelf and the two that followed were in a different language, one that Slant didn't recognize; below that he found an assortment of languages, a few volumes on magical interpretation, and a collection of dictionaries. He moved on to the next section, which showed promise, as there were texts on levitation and flying, which he was sure must be fairly basic skills for a wizard; he was choosing a text to study when the cat, which had been gently pawing at his leg, suddenly tensed, driving its claws through his thin pressure suit and into the flesh beneath.

He stifled a yell and looked down just as the computer informed him, "Minor gravitational anomaly occurring in immediate vicinity of cyborg unit. Investigate immediately."

"Hah?" He looked wildly about, then back at the cat. There was no one else in the room, nor any sign of anything out of the ordinary—except that the cat was motionless, its claws still digging into him, its eyes wide and staring, its tail puffed up like a bottle brush and the hairs on its back raised.

"Damn, it *is* a familiar," he thought. "I have to get out of here."

He reached down to pry the cat away, but before his hand touched it it freed itself and ran off, yowling, through the open door.

"Immediate departure is advisable," the computer agreed.

He started toward the window he had entered through, but then paused, as he remembered the long drop to the street. Could he go up to the roof? That would leave him stranded and provide little protection, since the wizards could fly and he could not. He looked instead at the two doors and in desperation asked, "Please advise."

"Departure from building not recommended; enemy would presumably expect such a course of action, and investigation is not complete. Eluding pursuit is facilitated by unexpected action."

"Right, I stay in the building; it's big enough that I should be able to hide. Which door do I try?"

"Standard pursuit assumes quarry will follow path of least resistance; therefore it is advisable to follow path of greater difficulty, avoiding open doors, clear corridors, and so forth."

There were times, Slant thought, when the computer could be helpful; that advice seemed very sensible. He tried the latch on the closed door and found it unlocked.

Beyond the door was a small, unlit chamber; he crossed that and found another door. This one led into a corridor, which was wonderfully empty. He started to turn right, but the computer stopped him. "Human psychology tends to prefer turning right; therefore evasive tactics include preference for turning left."

He turned left, moved a few feet down the darkened passage, and picked a door at random. It was locked. He moved farther and found a staircase. There was a light at the bottom, and he heard footsteps somewhere below; that was out of the question. He backed up and tried another door.

It opened easily, and he stepped through into the room beyond. Like everywhere else he had seen since entering the palace, it was dark; he took the flashlight from his belt, closed the door carefully behind him, then turned on the light and looked about.

He was in a lavish bedchamber, the walls covered with embroidered hangings, the marble floor piled thick with rugs, furs, and pillows. A chest of drawers topped with five mirrors at different angles was against one wall; an upholstered divan was opposite it. Two doors in the far wall apparently led into other rooms in the suite. In the center, of course, there was the bed, a great canopied thing, its white velvet curtains drawn.

He saw no sign of occupants. There was a key in the door he had just closed, which he turned, locking it; that would delay anyone's attempting to come in after him. Thus protected, he relaxed slightly. A conditioned reflex thrust him forward, though, and he found himself checking the other two doors. One led into a magnificent marble-and-fur bathroom, with a huge sunken tub and other fixtures that made it plain this culture had indoor plumbing. He began to wonder whether they had in fact lost anything beside electricity and space flight; it was obviously not the stone-age society he had first thought it to be. There was no other entrance to the bathroom, so that was safe. He turned to the other door, but his hand never reached the latch; he was distracted by a head peering out through the bed-curtains at him.

Chapter Six

I T WAS A YOUNG FEMALE HEAD, WITH LONG BLOND HAIR, big blue eyes, a long nose, and a shocked expression; an accompanying hand held a small oil lamp.

"Who are you? What are you doing in here?" she demanded.

Forgetting for the moment about the other door, Slant dove for her. To do so was not a conscious decision; his training had taken over again, and he had been trained to use physical restraint in this sort of situation. In an instant he had knocked her back on the bed, one hand over her mouth, the other pinning one of her arms, while his body pinned the other and his legs locked around hers. Miraculously, the lamp neither spilled nor went out. His reasonably neat programmed maneuver was complicated by the bed curtains, which had caught on both ends of the sub-machine gun he still wore strapped to his shoulders; one hanging was ripped half off its rings and remained wrapped around the gunstock, pinched between the stock and strap. Another had been flung forward, and wound up tangled around one of his legs.

The curtains were not a serious problem, but they were an inconvenience; when Slant was capable of conscious action again, he whispered in the girl's ear, "One sound, one move, and you're dead; do you understand?"

She nodded; he could tell from her eyes that she was on the verge of panic but thought she would probably keep quiet. He loosened his hold and untangled the hangings, keeping the girl partially pinned. That done, he set the lamp on a convenient nightstand, where it lit the entire room dimly. She remained silent, watching, wide-eyed and unmoving.

The submachine gun, even untangled, remained an inconvenience; he unstrapped it and set it aside, well out of his captive's reach. The snark remained on his belt, easily accessible; he was scarcely leaving himself unarmed.

That taken care of, he looked her over, assessing the situation. She wore a thin cotton robe, doubtlessly the local equivalent of a nightgown. It was black, which struck him as a very odd color for a young woman to wear to bed alone; had it been lace or satin he might not have thought so, but it was unadorned and made of cheap fabric. He was reminded of the black robes worn by the councillors, and considered where he was.

"Are you a wizard?" he demanded in a whisper.

She tried to speak, realized she couldn't with his hand over her mouth, and nodded, then apparently changed her mind and shook her head instead.

"Make up your mind!"

She shook her head no.

"You better not be. Or if you are, you better not call for help, because I can kill you before they can kill me."

She tried to squeal, her eyes widening still further and her muscles tensing. Slant took no notice but silently asked the computer, "Now what do I do?"

"Continue action. Wait for cessation of pursuit."

"How am I supposed to know when they stop looking for me?"

"By cessation of gravitational anomalies in vicinity of cyborg unit."

"What?"

"By cessation of gravitational anomalies in vicinity of cyborg unit."

"You mean they're looking for me with whatever-it-is, the way they did before?"

"Affirmative."

"Oh, that's just lovely. They found me twice before; they'll probably find me this time, too."

"Information insufficient."

"Great. All right, notify me if it appears they've given up."

"Affirmative."

That settled, he turned his attention to the girl and whispered, "Listen we're going to lie right here until they stop looking for me, or until they find me. It shouldn't be too long. You just keep quiet and do what I tell you and I won't hurt you. Understand?"

She nodded. They lay quietly for a moment; then something occurred to him, and he asked the computer, "When I was moving around just now, why did I have to ask you what to do? Wasn't I trained for eluding pursuit indoors?"

"Affirmative. Cyborg unit training included evasive tactics. Reason for training dysfunction unknown."

That was worrisome. Without his conditioning he wasn't much more than an ordinary human being—stronger and faster than anyone normal, but that alone didn't mean much. Was his programming wearing out with age and disuse, or was there something suppressing it? He had no idea, and no way to tell. He didn't even understand the mechanism whereby his supercompetent specialized schizoid personalities took over in the first place.

He lay quiet, thinking about his situation without reaching any sort of conclusion; his captive shifted occasionally, trying to get comfortable. Several long minutes passed; with a brief warning, the computer slipped below the horizon and out of contact again.

There was a sudden pounding on the door; he lay still, his hand tight on the girl's mouth.

The pounding stopped, and he heard the sound of a key turning.

That wasn't right; the key was on the inside of the door, still in the lock. He'd used it and left it there himself. It couldn't be a duplicate key, as that would have pushed the one on the inside out, and he would have heard it hit the floor. Could it be a different door? No, it was from the direction of the door he had entered by.

Keeping one hand on the girl, he lifted himself up and back, and peered around the torn bed curtain at the door.

The key was turning itself in the lock; as he watched it completed its turn, the lock opening with a click. The key then lifted itself from the keyhole and dropped to the floor.

He didn't need the computer to tell him that this was more antigravity magic. He leaped to his feet, his automatic combat persona taking over, the snark in his hand. His conscious self, which was now a passive observer, asked whether taking the young woman hostage would be a viable tactic; he thought back that he didn't know, having no idea how much respect the people of this society had for individual lives.

He flashed across the room, snatching up the submachine gun at the same instant that he fired the snark at the door and put enough distance between the girl and himself to minimize the risk of her interference with his actions.

The panels of the door vanished in a cloud of brown powder; the range was close to the maximum, so that the beam did not penetrate completely, leaving a large oval scar of rough raw wood. The drifting dust served to darken the already dim room still further, and Slant used the darkness to cover his movements as he shifted his weapons between hands, so that the snark, strictly a short-range weapon and with a severely limited power supply, was in his left, while the more primitive but effective submachine gun was held ready in his right. He released the gun's safety but did not fire; he had no idea what he was up against, so it would be foolhardy to try shooting his way out immediately.

The darkness was abruptly dispelled by a vivid yellow glow from the door; it swung open, revealing a black-robed figure holding a staff aloft. The light came from the head of the staff, and Slant felt an electric tingle in his skin, identical to that he had felt in the Council chamber. Behind the wizard—there could be no doubt that this was a wizard—were three other men, clad like the Council chamber guard, holding drawn swords.

Slant groped for the latch of the door he had not had time to investigate properly; he stood near it but dared not turn his gaze from his foes to see what he was doing.

"Slant, as you call yourself," said the wizard, "please surrender. We wish you no harm. There is no need for bloodshed."

"I can't surrender, damn it. Stay away, or I'll have to kill you." It was his conscious self that spoke, but the combat persona maintained control of his limbs in a curiously uncomfortable way. Two fingers of his left hand found the latch, but he could not easily work it while holding the snark.

"Please, we can help you, I'm sure we can."

"Stay away from me. In fact, get out of this room, and close the door behind you. And take the girl with you."

"Listen, you don't—"

The wizard's plea was cut off short by the roar of the gun as Slant fired a warning burst into the ceiling. "Get out of here!"

It occurred to him that the computer might object to his chasing them away rather than killing them; he hoped that it would give him time to explain that killing them would just bring more enemies down on him.

The wizard stepped back, moving his staff oddly, and Slant thought for a moment that the four Teyzhans were actually departing; then the wizard said, "Take him," and Slant realized that he had simply been getting out of the way of the three swordsmen.

The warriors marched forward—a mistake, Slant's training told him, as a quick charge would have been their best tactic here. His finger squeezed the trigger, and the gun's roar filled the room again. He watched a dozen rounds richochet off his attackers' bare faces; more magic was at work.

The wizard's voice sounded over the echoes as he stopped his useless fire. "We have protective spells. You're helpless."

The submachine gun might have been countered, but these people had not seen the snark in use before tonight. Could a protective spell stop something other than solid matter? He brought up his left hand and pressed the trigger in a single motion.

The foremost attacker was just a single pace away; his blood spattered Slant from throat to ankle as the beam cut into the warrior's chest. The man fell forward, gasping in agony, to lie in a pool of his own blood; his companions froze. There was a moment of dead silence when the victim's breath stopped, a moment in which none of them moved; Slant held the snark at ready, his finger on the trigger.

From the side, where she sat on the bed, the girl suddenly screamed as her horror overcame her initial shock; startled, Slant whirled toward her, pressing the trigger, cutting a narrow slice of destruction that ended in the girl's upraised wrist as she lifted her hand to cover her eyes. Another fountain of blood gushed forth, and Slant had time for an instant of revulsion before the pommel of a sword landed on his skull and knocked him to the floor, unconscious.

Chapter Seven

THERE WAS A SHATTERING ROAR OF WHITE NOISE IN HIS head, and the computer's monotone calling "MAYDAY! MAYDAY! MAYDAY!"

"Shut up!" he screamed.

An abrupt mental and physical silence descended; then the computer said, "Waking cyborg unit deemed imperative. Termination of communications contact between ship and cyborg imminent. Immediate evaluation of status and condition of cyborg unit required."

At that particular moment, Slant knew almost as little about his condition as the computer did; taking into account that everything he saw was relayed to the ship, there was no need to belabor such obvious facts as that he was lying on his back on a hard, thin mattress staring at the ceiling of a stone cell. Cautiously, he sat up and put his feet on the floor.

The back of his head hurt considerably, but upon investigating with his fingers he felt no blood, either fresh or clotted. There was a perceptible lump. He hoped there was no concussion.

Naturally, his weapons were gone. His pressure suit and his gloves remained—or had been replaced, as the suit seemed to be twisted about on his body and even less comfortable than he remembered.

The cell, he noticed, had a metal door with a small barred aperture in it; he noticed this when a bearded face peered through the opening and a voice asked, "Who were you shouting at?"

"My personal demon."

The man paused and considered that, then asked, "Are you all right?"

"Yes, I'm fine, thanks, except that my head hurts."

"You were shouting."

"Never mind my shouting."

"All right. I'll tell the Council that you're awake." The face vanished again, affording a view of another blank stone ceiling, presumably that of a corridor.

Slant looked around the cell, which was perhaps two meters in every dimension, and told the computer, "Other than being unarmed and in captivity, I seem to be all right. Escape may well be possible, so I suggest you hold off on terminating me."

"Affirmative. Termination of communications contact."

Slant wasn't sure if he was pleased or not that he was out of touch with the computer; it meant it wouldn't be able to kill him for nearly half an hour, but on the other hand it might have been useful.

Or it might have been an idiotic nuisance, as it had been when he spoke to the Council.

He had very little time to consider the matter, as a face appeared in the aperture, a different face, though still bearded. Seeing the prisoner seated quietly on the far side of the cell, this newcomer said, "The Council will see you now." There was a scrape as a key turned, and the door swung open.

This was not yet the time to make a break, though Slant was quite sure he could easily handle a single guard. He did not yet know where in the palace he was; he did know where the Council's chamber was, assuming this audience was to be in the same place. Furthermore, he might gain useful information from an interview, or even an interrogation; questions could be as revealing as answers. And finally, he had hopes of finding his weapons; he did not like the idea of leaving them in the possession of the Teyzhan wizards, who just might be capable of duplicating and mass-producing them.

Therefore he followed the guard meekly. Once out of the cell and in the passage beyond, they were joined by two more guards carrying drawn swords and a young man in a black robe, presumably a wizard; they were taking no chances with their dangerous prisoner. Rather, they thought they were taking no chances; the part of Slant's mind concerned with personal combat tactics informed him that the right sort of assault would make the blades an encumbrance rather than a help by removing the intended target and substituting the swordsmen's allies, enabling him to concentrate on a quick killing of the wizard and a speedy escape. It was quite possible, better than a fifty-fifty chance.

The time, however, was still not right. He wanted to see the Council.

As he had suspected, his cell was underground; he and his escort ascended two short flights of torchlit stairs and wound through a series of corridors before arriving in the white-domed chamber. The dome was illuminated by daylight; he had been unconscious for hours. He wondered how, even when distracted, he had been so careless as to allow himself to be knocked out.

As before, the seven councillors were seated around their wooden table. He approached and nodded politely, but did not kneel; it seemed inappropriate for a prisoner of war.

There was a moment of silence, and Slant felt his skin prickling and crawling. He saw nothing that indicated where magic was being used, and guessed, since the sensation seemed more intense than on previous occasions, that he was being studied as his submachine gun had been before.

The silence was broken by the white-bearded old councillor, who said, "Hello, Slant, as you call yourself. You spoke to us before and lied; will you speak the truth this time?"

"That depends on many things."

"Foremost, it depends upon the metal demon in your head, I think. Would you like to be rid of it?"

Slant considered this. He knew that the Council expected him to say yes; he knew also that the computer would not be happy with any answer that smacked of disloyalty or cooperation with the enemy. It would have a record of his words when it came back into contact. He was unsure whether the computer would be able to figure out that it was the demon in question, but it had already made plain it didn't want enemy personnel messing around in Slant's skull. He might be able to convince it that he was playing along, awaiting an opportunity for escape.

Whatever he answered, the councillors claimed to be able to tell when he lied, so if he lied, they would know it and know his true answer.

Or would they? The truth, he realized, was that he wasn't sure what he wanted. He hated the computer's interference with his actions and the constant threat of execution—but he had come to depend on the machine. It was his only contact with his lost home and had been his only companion for fourteen years. Its removal would cut him off from his past.

Was that any real loss? He could start anew and build himself a life based on reality, not on a long-lost war.

The Council was waiting for an answer. "Yes," he said, "I would." He said to himself, in such a way that he hoped it would register on the computer's records when contact was reestablished, "I'm just playing along, keeping them happy."

"You speak the truth, I see. Do you not fear the demon's anger?"

"The demon is ever vigilant, always watching me; it watches at this very minute." Slant noticed that his command of the language seemed to have returned with practice; he had no trouble at all with it.

"Why do you lie?" The old man looked wary.

"The demon keeps a record of everything I say and do."

"Ah, that I see is the truth. I think I understand. Listen, Slant, we are very interested in you; nothing like you has been seen in Teyzha in all our history. However, you cannot speak or act freely, and we cannot deal with you, while you are possessed. That is why I ask only about this thing in your head. If we free you, will you cooperate with us?"

Automatically, self-preservation his first concern, he answered, "No; I am loyal to Old Earth and will not aid those who seek her destruction."

"What?" The wizard's confusion showed on his face.

The middle-aged woman whom he had shown the submachine gun at his first audience asked, "What's this about Old Earth?"

"Never mind, it's not important," said the old man.

"But—"

"We can ask about that later. Our first concern is to remove the demon that controls this man. Slant, is the demon watching you now?"

"I think so." He was quite sure that the wizards would spot the lie, as they had others.

"Have you any idea when it does and doesn't control you?"

"No."

It occurred to Slant to wonder how the truth-detecting mechanism worked; it was not simply a variation on the polygraph, because his body was regulated so that lying did not affect his pulse or respiration. This was another mystery of this wizardly "magic." He wondered where their machines were hidden; in the table, perhaps, or under those flowing black robes.

"Will it return soon?"

Slant estimated the time elapsed since he had lost contact and answered truthfully, "In about ten minutes."

The old man turned to his compatriots, and they whispered briefly among themselves. He turned back, and said, "It is our consensus that that is not sufficient time for a proper and careful exorcism; let use therefore deal with other matters."

Slant was surprised at his own disappointment; had he really thought that these people might free him so quickly? He said nothing.

"What is the demon's name?"

That seemed a very peculiar but harmless question. "Computer Control Complex, Independent Reconnaissance Unit Two-oh-five," he replied in his own language.

"So long? And in a strange tongue? Unfortunate. Is that its true name, or its calling name?"

Slant considered that, and suddenly realized that the question might not be peculiar or harmless; it might have been very important, had he been able to give the answer the councillor wanted. "That's its calling name. I don't know its release code—what you'd call its true name."

"That's unfortunate."

Slant shrugged. If he knew the release code, he wouldn't need any wizards in the first place.

"You killed a man this morning."

The abrupt change of subject caught him by surprise. "I'm sorry." He remembered the bloody disaster in the top-floor bedchamber, and asked, "What about the girl? Will she live?"

"She will live, but she lost her hand, and we are unsure it can be repaired."

"I'm sorry about that, too. Really."

"Where did you get that weapon you used? We have never heard of such a thing."

"Until I came here I'd never seen real magic."

"You have not answered the question."

"I brought it with me." He wasn't about to get killed for cooperating with the enemy at this point; it would do him no good to answer such questions, where questions about the computer might have led to his freedom.

His interviewer changed tack. "Why did you come here?"

"Where?"

"To Teyzha."

An answer to this might possibly be of use in dealing with the computer, so he replied, "The demon sent me to learn about magic."

"Why?"

"I don't know."

The councillor turned back for another session of whispering; Slant watched, and showed no outward reaction when the computer said, "Query: Report status."

"I'm in what I believe to be the center of local government, being questioned by a governing council. I hope I can learn more about the gravitational disturbances from the framing of their questions."

"This is not a recommended approach. Advisable course of action would be escape followed by further investigation in another area showing gravitational anomalies representing enemy weapons research."

"What? Where?"

"Appropriate subject locations may be found in several places on this planet. Eleven have been identified."

"I don't know; we've already spent so much time here." He really didn't want to start all over, particularly since wizards in other places might be less eager to exorcise his particular demon. He tried to think of a convincing reason for staying that wouldn't put his loyalty in question.

"Prepare to attempt escape. Ship will land near you and provide covering fire."

"What, inside the city?"

"Affirmative."

"That'll do a lot of damage; is it necessary?"

"Why is the demon interested in our magic?" The whispering session was over.

"Affirmative. Maximum possible destruction has high distraction and deterrence value, and is in accordance with standard procedure."

"I don't know," he said aloud; at the same time he asked the computer telepathically, "May I warn these people? It would have high propaganda value as a humanitarian gesture."

"Is our magic that much different from its own?" the wizard asked.

"Affirmative," the computer answered his request.

"Listen, in a couple of minutes my ship is going to rescue me and destroy anything that gets in its way; it could wreck the entire city. I suggest you get out of here and take shelter." He shouted this warning, loudly and slowly and clearly, so that everyone in the room would hear and understand despite the stir it created.

His guards stepped forward and tried to grab him; one called, "We'll hold him! He won't get away this time!"

The guard had miscalculated, however; he had assumed

Slant was an ordinary human, and that it took a perceptible time for him to react. The human nervous system has synapses that transmit impulses from one nerve cell to the next, and serve to slow down messages to and from the brain; Slant's nervous system had been completely rewired, and the synapses bridged or eliminated, so that his reaction time was measured in millionths of a second instead of hundredths. In an ordinary human this would put intolerable strains on the body, as the brain would not be able to regulate itself at such a pace, but in Slant's computer-assisted system, with his steel-braced skeleton and restructured muscles, there were no such problems. In less time than it would take a normal man to register that something had been said, let alone to interpret or react to it, Slant had turned control over to his combat persona and was in motion, moving with blurring speed.

The edge of his right hand caught one man in the belly, causing serious and possibly fatal internal injuries; one heel struck out to his left, catching a second guard in the crotch. This motion served to spin Slant around, so that he faced the third and final member of the trio of guards who had accompanied him from his cell. This individual was reacting to the sudden assault reflexively, in the way he had been conditioned to react; he was reaching for his sword. That meant Slant could deal with him in any number of ways; the right hand reaching across for the sword hilt was out of action and served to block the motion of the left, so that the entire right half of the man's body was unprotected. Vaguely aware that his dominant personality did not want to kill unnecessarily, he passed up several fatal or crippling blows and instead brought the heel of his left hand against the side of the guard's head; the man went down immediately, almost certainly unconscious, but unless he fell wrong he could expect to survive with nothing worse than a mild concussion.

There were two other guards in the room, at the door to the entrance corridor, and eight wizards. None were making threatening moves in his direction—at least, not yet.

Without any conscious thought, he knew that his next priorities were weapons and flight. His own weapons were not in evidence, nor did any of his enemies have any firearms visible; he had not been trained in archaic weaponry and therefore did not choose to acquire a sword. A knife, garrote, or other device used in modern espionage would have been far more to his liking.

Flight was called for, but he did not yet know where his ship would be landing, or exactly when. It might be a good idea to try and get out of the building, in case the ship brought down the ceiling.

That meant leaving the room through the guarded door, which meant getting past the two guards. They were too far away to take by hand, by surprise; even he couldn't cross the intevening distance that fast. If he tried it, one might get him while he took care of the other. He needed a missile, or a distraction.

First, he had to get away from the three downed guards and the wizards; they might get in his way. He followed through on his left-handed head blow, having thought this out before it landed, and used the momentum to give him a start in his dash not for the door but for the nearest wall. The wooden benches that stood along the sides of the room would do for weaponry in lieu of better, and the oil lamps would be useful if flung, as either missiles or diversions.

He never reached the bench he was aiming for; he stumbled halfway there, though he saw nothing that could have tripped him, and fell. He caught himself before he hit the floor and landed in a crouch, but when he tried to rise and continue his run he found himself unable to do so. Something invisible was holding him down.

That was the wizards' doing, of course; he knew that immediately. He would have to eliminate them—all of them—if he was to escape unhampered. He considered methods of doing that.

Unable to move as he was, he could not attack them directly, and he was still too far away to help; he needed something he could throw. He tried to figure out where the energy field holding him originated; he could not see or hear any machinery at all, though he felt that now-familiar electric tingle all over his body. He assessed his resources.

He wore a thin pressure suit of insulating plastic, from neck to ankle. An equipment belt, with no equipment attached, was around his waist. He had gloves and boots, and nothing else. The boots and belt might be useful armament; he tried to release the catch on his belt but discovered that he could no longer move at all.

The warrior was stymied. There was no simple tactical solution, except to wait until the ship arrived to rescue him. There was no need for combat training if all he had to do was wait. Therefore, his combat personality shut itself off, abdicating control, and Slant was himself again, held immobile in an awkward crouch in the middle of the marble floor by the wizards' magic while the three guards he had incapacitated lay unconscious a few meters away.

The remaining two guards were just now becoming aware of what had happened; they drew their swords and looked hesitantly from Slant to the Council and back.

"We have him; stay where you are," said the middle-aged woman.

Slant was still reorienting himself; his more specialized personalities often operated at such high speed that time seemed to distort. It took him a moment to realize that the warrior persona had only been in control for about ten seconds and that it would still be a few minutes before his ship reached the city.

When his head was clear, he shouted at the councillors, "Let me go and get out of here! This place is going to be destroyed in a few minutes!"

They looked at one another, and a ripple of current seemed to flicker across his skin, but no one answered, and he still couldn't move.

"Listen, I'm sorry about the guards, but it was self-defense. Get out of here! If you don't take shelter you'll be killed!"

"I don't understand," said the white-bearded old man. "What will destroy this place? We see no one but you, and we've taken your weapons."

"My ship! It'll be here any minute now!"

He still saw only blank incomprehension.

"Look, you can see I'm not lying! It's a starship, don't you know what that means? It's from the Bad Times, the same kind of ship that almost wiped out your entire world three hundred years ago!"

"A sky machine, you mean?"

"Yes, a sky machine, a death machine."

The wizards looked at one another; another ripple ran through the field holding him.

"One minute to impact."

"Wait, they've got me restrained somehow."

"Fire will be directed toward possible power sources as they are detected. Destruction of power supply should remove restraining field."

"But the power source may be right near me! I've seen no sign of any major power sources; I think they're all small portable units."

"No preferable course of action is known to be available."

"You've got less than a minute! Run for cover!" This final yell seemed to register; the invisible hold on him was gone, and he was up and running. His training in evasion was in control; before the guards could react, he was past them and out the door, racing down the corridor. Somehow, his normal self managed to communicate even while suppressed, saying "I'm free; you don't have to shoot up power sources, they let me go."

The only reply was a screaming roar that drowned out his footsteps on the marble floor; there was a thunderous booming crash, a vivid flash that was visible through the crack around the door a few feet in front of him, and the entire building shook around him.

He skidded to a stop, half a meter from the door, waiting for the roar to subside. The sound did not subside but merely changed form; the initial howl of the ship's approach became the shattering crash of its impact on the place in less than a second, and that first great explosion had not yet faded when a series of lesser but still earth-shaking explosions began. The ship was firing its main armament.

There was a roar of falling masonry somewhere behind him, barely audible over the sound of the ship's weapons; sunlight spilled into the corridor behind him, lighting clouds of drifting dust that he knew must be powdered stone. He wondered whether any of the people in the Council chamber were still alive.

He also wondered whether he himself would survive; the computer seemed to be getting careless, shooting closer to him than necessary, and he remembered that it wanted him dead.

He heard a human voice; someone was screaming, sounding like the faint call of a distant bird over the cacophony of the starship's assault.

He opened the palace door and moved out into the plaza, with the broken zigzag run that he had been taught for battlefield use.

The square was already strewn with rubble, ranging from marble dust and gravel to a chunk of wall several meters across that leaned up against the side of the palace. To his left he saw the glint of metal; he turned and saw his ship lying across a huge heap of debris, its nose thrust up over the ruins of the palace, its tail resting on the plaza pavement. The air rippled around it from the heat of the hull, and the main drive exhaust was invisible in a fog of vaporized stone. The explosions continued, mostly up around the nose, as the computer fired off everything from antipersonnel missiles to snark-type blasters.

"Well, here I am; how do you suggest I get aboard, with the ship at that angle?"

"Climb service ladder."

The service ladder, intended for use in space, was, like the rest of the ship, at about a forty degree angle. Its tail end was a good four meters off the ground. Slant took a running start and leaped for it, catching hold with one hand and hauling himself up, trying to keep his bare head as far from the hot metal of the hull as he could. The insulated gloves, boots, and suit made it bearable for the rest of his body as he clambered his way up the side of the ship.

"Open up," he demanded as he neared the hatch, "and stop shooting. You're wasting power and ammunition."

"Affirmative." The explosions stopped, leaving only the sounds of crumbling walls and falling debris and the hiss of the airlock door opening.

As soon as he was aboard he ordered the computer to open the inner lock door immediately, rather than wait for the full cycle. It opened; he strode through, went straight to the control cabin, and climbed onto the acceleration couch. He reached back for the direct-control cable and told the computer, "Get us out of here."

Immediately he was smashed back into the couch by the crushing acceleration of a full-power launch, and he knew that anything that had still stood in the immediate area of the plaza was gone. Besides the blast itself there would be fires from the heat, and nobody around to fight them. The pressure of acceleration overcame him, and he blacked out.

Chapter Eight

WHEN HE CAME TO, THE DIRECT-CONTROL CABLE WAS still in his hand, though he had not managed to plug himself in. He lay still for a moment, gathering his wits, looking about the cabin at the familiar tapestries and fur-covered walls he hadn't gotten around to changing from white. He idly turned them light blue and asked, "Where are we?"

"In low elliptical orbit around planet; no surface references available."

"Was the ship damaged in the landing?"

"Minor abrasion of hull occurred on impact; no other known damage."

"What about Teyzha?"

"Restate question."

"How much damage did the city receive?"

"Exact information unavailable. Estimate severe damage to central area, ten percent of area within walls; light or moderate damage to further twenty percent of area within walls. Probable enemy losses between one hundred and three thousand dead."

"That's a pretty damn wide range." He hoped that the

lower end was more nearly correct. He noticed the direct-control cable he still held and fitted it into the back of his neck. "Play the tapes of the landing." He closed his eyes and waited.

He was tearing down through the sky toward Teyzha at an incredible speed; the tape had been made through a camera mounted below the nose of the ship, so that his vision was cut off at the top by an arc of metal but wide open below. The camera and tape were extreme wide-angle, wider than human vision, but for his convenience he was shown only the central portion in normal perspective, with the option of turning his view in any direction to the limits of the lens.

The city rushed up at him, hundreds of times faster than it had when he parachuted in; he felt a moment of vertigo. Then his plunge was slowing; a full-speed impact would have vaporized the ship and probably the entire city as well. Still, he flinched mentally as the image of the palace came up and seemed to smash into him.

There was something about the last few seconds that bothered him. "Back it up, then come forward at quarter speed," he ordered the computer.

Obediently, the view pulled back, so that he was again hanging in midair, approaching the city. This time the speed was much less, and he was able to make out more detail instead of just a blur. Something flickered at the bottom of his field of vision as he neared the city wall; then again.

"Stop a minute."

The computer obeyed; the forward motion stopped, and the flicker became a short line of golden light, frozen immobile in the air over Teyzha's ramparts.

"I'd like some magnification; zoom in slowly."

He kept his gaze fixed on that yellow line as the image enlarged; it was tipped with silver. The silver tip was in turn tipped with glowing red.

It was a missile; the ship had gone in shooting, as well as providing covering fire on the ground.

"What is that?"

"Restate question."

"Identify that missile I'm looking at."

"Ordnance model MHE-fifteen, serial number one-one-seven-zero-one-five. High-explosive warhead, shrapnel-loaded, antipersonnel type. Impact fuse. Range—"

"That's enough. Why'd you fire it?"

"Enemy personnel on thoroughfare provided target of opportunity."

"Run the tape from the belly camera, one-quarter speed."

He was looking straight down, the ground sweeping by underneath, as the ship once more approached the city. He watched as a barrage of missiles ripped the city wall apart; that had been the first flicker. A string of antipersonnel missiles then laced the main avenue, and incendiaries sprayed into flame atop the surrounding buildings. Heavy lasers flashed across the streets, cutting through softer materials and igniting anything flammable.

He continued to watch as the plaza swept underneath and the shattered wall of the palace cut off vision upon impact; he switched back to the nose camera and watched as the blasters came into play. He wondered how much damage they would have done if they had a range of more than twenty meters. Finally there came the sound of his own voice, the launch, and the ground falling away again.

"Shut it off." He opened his eyes and glared at the blue chameleon fur. "Why did you do so much damage?" He suspected that, if anything, the computer's damage estimate was low—perhaps very low. It assumed that buildings had steel frames rather than stone arches, and that people knew enough to take shelter—and had somewhere they could go to take shelter.

"Standard procedure for assault on enemy position."

"Why didn't you just nuke the city and have done with it?"

"Use of nuclear weapons would have aborted rescue of cyborg unit and resulted in termination of cyborg unit without justification."

"Well, that's something, anyway."

"Query: Advisability of resuming attack, using nuclear weapons."

"I don't think so. It'd be a waste of a warhead, and we haven't got very many. They can't do us any more harm. Besides, it would negate any propaganda value my warning had, and it's possible that we might want to try dealing with them again later, when they've had time to clean up." He was getting better at making up excuses for not killing people, he thought.

"Affirmative."

An idea occurred to him. "Hey, did anything out of the ordinary happen during that attack? Any systems malfunction, or inexplicable diversions from course?"

"Negative. No resistance of any sort encountered."

Then the wizards hadn't been able to do anything against the starship. He wondered if they'd had the chance to try. "Not even small-arms fire?"

"Negative."

They hadn't even used his submachine gun. His ship had been shooting at completely defenseless people. He was not at all happy about that. The war was over; he shouldn't be killing anybody.

After a moment's consideration, he asked, "Now what? On to the next system?"

"Negative. Gravitational anomalies representing enemy weapons research not yet fully investigated."

That was what he had feared. "We can't go back to Teyzha for a while; I'd be killed on sight."

"Affirmative."

"Do we just wait here in orbit, then?"

"Negative. Other locations show similar levels of gravitational disturbance."

"Then why did you pick on Teyzha?"

"Level of gravitational disturbance was marginally higher."

"Oh." That was perfectly reasonable, actually. The computer had never said that there was anything special about Teyzha, and he hadn't asked; thinking back, he remembered that the little sparkles he had seen in the planet's gravitational field had been scattered all across its land area, not concentrated in Teyzha. "Wonderful. So we go somewhere else and try again?"

"Affirmative."

"Where?"

"Cyborg unit discretion permitted."

"I get to choose?"

"Affirmative."

The cable was still plugged into his neck; he closed his eyes and said, "Okay, give me a map."

The computer displayed in his mind a topographical map of the planet in cylindrical projection, with glowing red indicating areas of gravitational disturbance—concentrations of magic, presumably. Teyzha was marked with a yellow glow.

Slant picked a bright spot on the same continent as Teyzha, but far to the west, on the edge of a broad plain. "What about here?"

"Acceptable."

"Let's go, then."

"Affirmative. Landing in twenty-three minutes."

"No, wait; let me take a nap and get myself organized first. I don't want to screw up again."

"Affirmative. Notify when ready to land."

"Right." Slant detached the cable from his neck and lay back on the couch; a moment later he was asleep.

Chapter Nine

"HELLO, STRANGER."

The farmer looked up from the whetstone he had been using to sharpen a scythe and squinted sideways at Slant from beneath his wide-brimmed straw hat. He said nothing.

"What city is that ahead?"

The farmer put down the scythe and studied Slant from head to toe, staring critically at his fur vest and the loincloth he'd made from spare fabric. At last he said, in a new and unfamiliar accent, "That's Awlmei."

"Thank you." Slant bobbed his head politely and turned to continue toward the city.

"Hey!"

Slant turned back toward the farmer.

"What do you want around here?"

Slant was terse in his reply, as the man showed no trace of courtesy himself, and said simply, "Food and shelter."

"You speak strangely. Where are you from?"

"Teyzha." He was glad that he didn't have to try inventing a name this time.

The farmer stared at him for a moment longer, then declared, "You don't concern me. Go on, then."

Slant nodded again and continued toward the city. He made an effort to remember as exactly as possible the farmer's accent; there was no need to draw attention to the fact that he was a foreigner. Had the man been friendlier or more talkative he might have stayed and spoken for a while, to pick up the local dialect better.

It seemed that a distrust of strangers was widespread on this planet, and not just a local aberration near Teyzha. Perhaps it resulted from the events of the so-called Bad Times; the destruction of the local civilization must have led to a period of chaos, and probably considerable lawlessness.

He wondered whether there had been a city or other settlement on the site of Awlmei before the war; it seemed like a good location, with several small streams flowing down from the hills nearby and watering the plain, making it excellent farmland, and then merging into a river that wound off northward.

He had landed several kilometers to the south, well out of sight of the city in a stretch of uncultivated grassland, where the ship had concealed itself in a small gully. He had then slipped out at dawn, wearing the vest and loincloth and a pair of sandals—which were more comfortable than boots and perfectly adequate on the gentler terrain of the region. Not wishing to repeat his earlier mistake, he had not replaced his lost submachine gun with a duplicate from the ship's armory; instead he had sewn several sturdy pockets into the lining of the vest, which now held a snark, a general-purpose hand laser, and an automatic pistol he hoped would be loud and impressive enough to serve much the same purpose as the submachine gun had in frightening people. A casual inspection would reveal nothing extraordinary about him. The submachine gun, useful as it was, had been a mistake, attracting far too much attention.

This time he hoped to get by without attracting any attention at all. Now that he had some idea what he was dealing with, he had devised a plan of action and cleared it with the computer, rather than just blundering in—not that he had had much choice before. There was no way to learn enough about a society to blend into it without seeing it close up firsthand. Now he had seen Teyzha close up, and hoped that Awlmei was similar enough for him to get by.

Since the wizards seemed to be an elite group by virtue of their magic, and apparently kept the workings of that magic a secret from the rest of the populace, he would obviously have to find a wizard. This time, though, he was not about to put up with any Council audiences; he would get a wizard alone and interrogate him, trying first bribery and then threats should he prove uncooperative.

He hoped that all the wizards knew the basics of whatever mysterious devices they used, and that there wasn't an elite within the elite that kept that information secret; such a complication could be very annoying indeed.

It was still at least half an hour before noon when he reached the city gates. The walls here weren't the cut stone that Teyzha used, but adobe; still, they stood a good five meters high and looked sturdy and formidable. Guards could be seen occasionally as they patrolled the ramparts.

There were several gates, but Slant saw no reason to prefer one over another and chose to follow the road to the nearest. It was a wide pair of heavy wooden doors, guarded by an aging soldier wearing an outfit of thick leather and leaning lazily against the wall. As Slant walked up, this person stood upright and put a hand to his sword hilt.

"Hello, stranger," the guard said. "What brings you to Awlmei?"

"Personal business." Slant saw no reason to say any more than necessary; he didn't care to draw attention to his accent, which he was sure remained very alien.

"What sort of business?"

"That's none of your concern."

"I don't recognize you; you're foreign, aren't you?"

Reluctantly, Slant admitted, "Yes."

"Do you have any kin in Awlmei?"

"No."

"What's your name, then, and where are you from?"

"I'm called Slant. I've come from Teyzha."

"I never heard of it."

Slant shrugged.

"Where is it?" The guard did not take the shrug as Slant had hoped he would.

"Far to the east."

"I still never heard of it."

"It's there."

There was a moment of silence as Slant and the guard considered one another. The guard ended it by saying "You won't state your business?"

Slant reconsidered; there was no reason not to tell the guard something, and it would apparently facilitate his entrance. These people tended toward the suspicious, and a refusal to speak would just add to the guard's suspicions. Besides, the man might be of help.

"I'm looking for a good wizard. I need some magic done."

"What sort of magic?"

"That's a personal matter. I've heard that there are several wizards in Awlmei; might you know the best way to approach one?"

"There are several with shops; pick any of them."

Awlmei was set up differently from Teyzha, Slant realized. He had assumed that the wizards were the ruling class everywhere on the planet, but here they had apparently preferred economic exploitation to political use of their abilities. "Thank you. May I enter the city, then?"

The guard gave him a final inspection, looking him over from head to heel, and when he had satisfied himself that Slant could not have a sword or other familiar weapon more dangerous than a knife on him, he stepped back and rapped on the gate. He did not touch the cyborg and failed to detect the devices inside his vest.

A voice answered the knock from beyond the doors, but Slant could not catch the words; the guard replied with a nonsense phrase involving a green dog, and there was a rattling of latches being drawn aside. The gates swung open and Slant stepped through, finding himself on a narrow street that wound its way between low adobe buildings.

Beside him, closing the gate, was a youth clad in a ragged tunic. He held out a palm and said, "It's customary to pay the gatekeeper something."

"I'm sorry," Slant replied, "I have no local currency. Perhaps when I leave I'll have something for you."

The lad shrugged and turned away, saying "It was worth a try."

Slant walked on, then paused when he was out of sight of the gate and took a look about him.

This city was much more what he had expected of a barbaric planet; it had none of Teyzha's splendor and ornament. The buildings were all a drab sun-baked yellow, and many had projecting beam ends visible. The streets were unpaved and dusty—but just as free of sewage and refuse as the avenues of Teyzha, for which he was grateful.

A small plaza lay ahead, crowded with pedestrians, and people hurried along every street he could see, with an occasional horse or ox cart interspersed among them. Slant made his way into the square, dodging the larger gatherings and listening to the speech of those he passed; he hoped to improve his accent.

He looked about, hoping to spot something that was obviously a wizard's shop, but was disappointed. He was able to recognize shops because they had open doors and visible windows, while residences were thoroughly closed off and presumably had courtyards to let in light and air, like the houses of ancient Rome. There were buildings that could be entered through broad open arches but that were windowless and arranged around courtyards; he was not sure what these were.

The shops, however, were identified by signboards bearing unfamiliar symbols. He could figure out some, such as a stylized boot that must represent a shoemaker, but most were so simplified as to be unrecognizable. The natives undoubtedly knew them all from long exposure; they had probably originally been detailed pictures that were gradually stripped down over the years into quick and easy trademarks.

He left the square and began strolling the street that appeared to have the highest percentage of shops, peering into the display windows and trying to figure out the signboards. A symbol halfway between a cross and a swastika he realized represented scissors, and indicated a tailor, apparently. A thing with two uprights and a low crossbar meant a blacksmith's forge. He passed several shops with windows that displayed nothing but were curtained off instead, any one of which could have been a wizard's; they bore different signs, however, and might have been anything from laundries to brothels. He did not care to venture into one at random.

A couple of dozen meters from the square he came across one of the buildings with an open archway, and saw that a signboard hung over the arch; it was definitely a commercial establishment, then. Its symbol was a curlicue with an inverted trapezoid at each end.

He peered through the arch and saw that the central court held several tables. He looked at the signboard again; he could imagine no way that the symbol could represent a restaurant or an inn, but it might possibly be intended for a still, indicating a tavern or a distillery. Such a place might be a good location to pick up a little information—such as how a wizard might be found.

"I'm going to inquire in here; any objections or advice?" he asked telepathically.

"Course of action appears advisable."

If it was a tavern, there was a secondary purpose for stopping in, Slant decided as he strolled through the arch; he was thirsty from the morning's long walk. He'd brought some Old Earth coins; he hoped they'd be accepted.

The courtyard was small but pleasant; a fountain splashed in one corner, its spray serving both to cool the air and keep down the dust, services very welcome, as the day was warm and dry. Half a dozen tables were scattered about, with varying numbers of chairs at each.

A few green plants struggled feebly to survive in tubs of black earth.

The sides of the yard were open arcades; more tables stood in their shady interiors. One side was lined with large barrels, ranged on their sides ready for tapping. A large blond man, presumably the proprietor, leaned against one barrel; the only three customers were huddled around a small table at the back.

Slant looked appraisingly at the blond fellow, who returned his gaze in kind. The man looked friendly enough; Slant crossed the yard and said, "I could use a drink."

The blond nodded and asked, "What'll you have?"

"Something cool, if you have it; I'm thirsty."

"Beer?"

"That would be fine."

"Red or black?"

That gave him a moment's pause; no beer he was familiar with was either color. "Red," he ventured.

The proprietor took a mug down from an overhead hook —Slant noticed for the first time that the rafters were lined with them—and filled it from one of the barrels. The liquid was a light reddish brown in color and bubbled forth messily, spilling as much on the man's arm and the ground beneath as went in the mug.

When a reasonable amount had found its way into the vessel he closed the tap and held out his free hand, retaining the mug. "That'll be four bits," he said.

"I don't have any local currency; will this do?" Slant reached into a pocket in his vest, fished out a small gold coin, and held it forth.

The tavernkeeper looked at it dubiously. "What is it?"

"It's an old gold piece I found. I give you my word, it's real gold."

The man took the coin, studied it, then shrugged and handed Slant the mug. "It'll do, I guess," he said.

Slant took a gulp of beer and discovered that it was thick, and not as cold as he might like, but cool and perfectly drinkable. "Do I get any change? That was real gold."

"I don't work that way. You've got a few more drinks coming, though, if you don't get rowdy." The barman leaned forward, trying to look threatening; Slant automatically assessed his actual danger—virtually none—but made an effort to look appropriately intimidated. After all, the fellow was a good ten centimeters taller than himself, probably just about two meters even, and fifteen kilos heavier at a minimum. To an untrained person that could make a very big difference.

When the blond was satisfied that Slant was not going to make a fuss over this minor extortion, he leaned back against his barrel once more. Slant, in turn, leaned against one of the pillars supporting the arcade and sipped his beer.

After a moment, when he judged the proprietor was at ease again, he asked, "Could I have some information instead of some of that beer I've got coming?"

The barman, who had been contemplating the sky above the far side of the courtyard, looked at him and replied, "That depends what it is."

"It's nothing much. I'm just looking for a wizard, and I can't read the signs."

"You're a foreigner, then? I thought you spoke strangely. What do you want a wizard for?"

"It's a personal matter."

"Well, I can't tell you which wizard might be best if I don't know what you want done."

"Just tell me where the nearest one is, then."

"The nearest? That would be old Kurao, just up the street."

"Where?"

"It's just a few shops up that way." He pointed. "The symbol's like this." He scratched a sign in the dirt with his heel; Slant thought it might have been derived from a pair of eyes.

"Thank you." Slant leaned back against the pillar and finished his beer; the beverage felt good going down. It occurred to him that it was the first alcohol he'd drunk in four years or more, since an earlier planetfall. He hoped he hadn't lost his tolerance.

He stayed for one more drink, which he consumed while seated at a table near the arch, giving his feet a rest. When that was gone he rose, thanked the proprietor, and departed. He was dismayed to notice that he was slightly unsteady; either the beer here was far more potent than he had realized, or he was in bad shape physically.

He told the computer, "The alcohol's affecting me, I think."

"Affirmative."

"Can you do something?"

"Affirmative."

"Do it, then."

Something seemed to grab the inside of his chest; he staggered, and leaned against the nearest wall. He could feel his heart pounding, and blood thundered in his ear. He thought for a moment that he would black out. Then it passed, and he stood erect once more.

"What was that?" he demanded.

"Standard procedure for removing toxins from cyborg unit bloodstream."

"Oh." He decided against asking for a detailed description; he could guess well enough that the computer had pumped all the blood in his body through some filter the doctors and technicians had installed.

He looked about, spotted the sign the barman had sketched for him, and strode up the street; he realized as he did that he felt better than he had in hours. The detoxication process apparently cleared out more than just alcohol and poisons. Either that, or he had been going about half-poisoned without knowing it.

Chapter Ten

THE WIZARD'S SHOP WAS SMALL AND CLUTTERED; THE windows were draped with black, and a curtain of red beads hung in the doorway. He stepped inside. The interior was dim and smelled of incense and wax.

"Is anyone here?" he called.

A velvet drapery at the back was pulled aside, and the wizard emerged; he was tall and thin but stooped with age, with a neatly trimmed fringe of white beard around his face and a completely bald head. He wore a simple black robe, very much like those worn in Teyzha.

"May I help you?" he inquired politely.

"Are you Kurao?"

"I am."

"I want to learn about magic."

"I already have an apprentice; I'm sorry I can't help you." The wizard started to turn away.

"No, wait, that's not what I mean," Slant said; the mage paused and turned back. "I don't want to become a wizard; I just want to learn something about magic, perhaps a few little tricks."

Kurao looked him over carefully, but Slant felt no warning tingle and hoped that the old man was relying on his natural perceptions alone.

"What for?" he asked at last.

"That's my business."

"What will you pay?"

"I have gold. It's not local currency, but it's good."

"How much?"

Slant pulled a large coin from his pocket and handed it to the wizard. Kurao looked at it disdainfully.

Slant added another.

The two coins vanished into the wizard's robe somewhere, and Kurao said, "I think that will do for a downpayment; we'll discuss the rest of the money later. What exactly did you want to know?"

"Is there somewhere more private we could talk?" He gestured toward the open door and the bead curtain.

"Certainly; follow me." The old man led the way past the velvet drapery to a small back room lit by a skylight and cluttered with the same sort of arcane miscellany as the laboratory Slant had found in Teyzha; the major furnishings were a table, three rough wooden stools, and an immense black metal cauldron hanging from a tripod over a small brazier. The walls were lined with shelves, and table and shelves were crammed with mystical apparatus:

skulls, stuffed lizards, jars of powders and potions, carved sticks, polished stones, and other such things. There were very few books, in marked contrast to the Teyzhan equivalent.

Kurao perched himself atop one of the stools and motioned for Slant to do the same. The cyborg seated himself across the table from the wizard and considered where to begin.

"What exactly do you want to know?" Kurao asked.

"I want to know about magic. I'm from far away, where there are no wizards and magic is unknown; I don't understand it at all."

"Query: Advisability of direct questioning."

"It's definitely advisable. He thinks I'm a native of this planet, one of his own people, and has no reason not to trust me."

"Continue action."

"I scarcely know where to begin," the old man said as Slant and the computer conversed silently. "Magic is basically very simple. Anyone can be given the gift of wizardry, but it takes much time and effort to master it, so that it is passed on only to apprentices who study for years. Because it can be so dangerous, we wizards are very careful in choosing our apprentices."

It was not the social structure that interested Slant. "You haven't told me what it is," he said.

"I don't understand."

"You haven't told me what magic is," he said. "I don't understand its basic nature. I have seen a wizard fly; I know wizards can tell when someone is lying. How do they do these things? What force is at work?"

"I'm afraid that's impossible to explain. A wizard learns to see things that ordinary people cannot, and by seeing them in this manner he learns to affect them without touching them in the normal sense."

Slant was not at all satisfied by this explanation. "You're being vague."

"Your questions are vague."

"Let me be specific, then. How does a wizard fly?"

"That is actually a difficult feat. He must learn to see the force that holds us to the ground, and to move around it; I cannot explain it more clearly than that to anyone who does not have the wizard sight."

"Interrogation by friendly methods appears unproductive," the computer said.

"I was noticing that myself. He does seem to be talking about gravity, though." He looked at Kurao's bland face and wished he could tell when a wizard was lying as easily as wizards could tell when he was.

"It's all dependent upon this wizard sight, then?"

"You might say so."

"And you say that's impossible to explain to someone who hasn't got it?"

"That's right."

"But it's really very simple, except it takes years to learn."

"It really is very simple, but learning to use it correctly and safely takes years."

"Does this sound like double-talk to you?" Slant asked the computer.

"Affirmative."

"I don't think he's going to cooperate much more, but I don't want to resort to violence yet. Any suggestions?"

"It is possible subject cannot explain gravitational disturbances. Query: How certain is identification of this subject as enemy weapons researcher?"

"That's a good point; I haven't seen him use any magic."

Kurao sat silently through what appeared to him a moment of contemplation on Slant's part; his gaze was beginning to wander idly about the room when Slant asked, "Could you demonstrate your magic for me?"

"Certainly; it will cost another three of those coins, though."

That did not surprise Slant in the least; he passed two coins across the table. "Start with those; I'll give you two more if I'm pleased with the demonstration."

Kurao shrugged and slipped the coins out of sight. "What sort of demonstration would you like?" he asked.

"What can you do?"

"I can do a great many things. Usually I am called on to sell aphrodisiacs and automata, but I know many wizardly arts; I can fly, and make rain, and all the usual stunts."

"Automata?"

"Yes; you know, artificial creatures. They can be very useful. People use them to spy on one another, or to carry messages—"

"I don't know what you're talking about. You can make these things?"

"Yes, exactly; I make them, and bring them to life."

"That sounds like a good demonstration."

"You'll have to pay for the materials."

"Haven't I paid enough already?" He was beginning to tire of the wizard's greed.

"Oh, well. . . ."

Slant passed another coin across the table.

Kurao smiled. "I'll start right away." He stood and crossed to the shelves; after poking about for several minutes, he turned back toward Slant, holding up a large stuffed lizard. "Will this do?"

Slant shrugged. "I suppose it will." He had no idea what the wizard was talking about.

Nodding absently, Kurao wandered from shelf to shelf, collecting various jars and other objects; at last, his arms full, he returned to the table and dumped his assortment of junk in front of the cyborg. "I don't really need all of this," he admitted apologetically, "but it helps."

Slant still didn't know what he was talking about; he said nothing. The computer was less agreeable. "Recommend subject be restricted to necessary elements of demonstration."

"Oh, shut up. If this other stuff will help him with his nonsense, it doesn't matter."

"Recommend subject be required to provide step-by-step explanation."

"That's a good idea." Kurao was sorting out his collection; Slant got his attention with a gesture and said, "Would you mind explaining as you go along?"

"Well . . . suppose, instead, you ask questions. I may be too busy."

"Is that acceptable?"

"Affirmative."

"All right. Go ahead."

"Thank you." Kurao took a pouch of yellow powder

from the heap on the table, stooped beside the hanging
cauldron, and blew on the coals in the brazier. They
flared up redly; Slant had not realized they were lit. The
wizard poured the contents of the pouch on the burning
coals. A thin wisp of smoke arose, and a sweet smell
reached Slant's nose.

"What is that?"

"Powdered tree bark."

"What's it for?"

"It burns cleanly, smells pleasant; it's a good thing to
start a spell with."

"Is it necessary?"

"No, it's mostly for effect. It helps set the proper mood."
He fanned the brazier, and another curl of smoke drifted
upward. "You must have pleasant surroundings, as the least
distraction or irritation is likely to make you miss something."

He rose, returned to the table, and pulled out the stuffed
lizard. "The object you plan to animate must have the
proper shape, you understand. It has to be a shape that
can do whatever the automaton is supposed to do. If you
want it to talk, it has to have a mouth and throat; if you
want it to walk it has to have legs; if you want it to fly
it must have wings. If you want it to write it has to have
hands and fingers; paws won't do. You might be able to
add legs and whatever later, but they'll never work right
if they weren't there from the beginning. You understand?"

"It seems clear."

"Explanation is ambiguous and unclear."

"Shut up."

"Now, since even the simplest automaton is alive, more
or less, it needs much the same things inside as you or I or
any other animal. A stuffed lizard like this hasn't any
digestive tract or anything except a gut full of sawdust,
so you need the proper materials. Transmutation would
take too long; if you tried to make what you need out of
the sawdust the part you made first would rot before you
were finished, and the poor thing would die by pieces. You
need these." He pulled several jars out of the heap, calling
off their contents as he did. "Dried bones; dried blood;
liver paste—I'd intended to eat that sometime, but it's go-

ing bad; powdered newts—very handy stuff—it has all the trace elements you'll need; bird's wings for the muscles, nice and compact; hydrochloric acid for the digestion. . . ." The list went on for quite some time, as Slant merely stared. What was the old fool talking about? Was he claiming he would *build* a live lizard?

"Ordinarily I don't explain this, I just do it; it's harder when I have to think about it." He picked up the jar of dried bones. "These are from a lizard about this size." He opened the jar and pulled out a handful of thin white objects that reminded Slant of chicken bones; the wizard's face went slack for an instant, then taut, his lips compressed into a thin line, his beard bristling, as Slant felt again the electric prickle of nearby magic.

The wizard placed the bones quickly, one by one, atop the stuffed lizard; Slant stared in amazement as they sank into the green hide, vanishing completely, apparently sucked through the scaly skin as if it were water. He paid no attention to the computer's statement, "Gravitational anomaly representing enemy weapons research occurring in immediate vicinity of cyborg unit."

"What did you do? How did you do that?"

Kurao apparently didn't hear him; he was concentrating his entire attention on his work. When he had finished with the bones, he opened the jar of pigeon wings and began arranging those carefully on the lizard; as he did they fell to pieces, feathers and bones scattering and rattling on the table, the muscles and cartilage vanishing, like the dried bones, into the skin.

"Wait! Stop and tell me what you're doing!"

"Can't." Dried blood was next, disappearing as soon as it touched the scales.

"You've got to explain!"

"Can't; it'll die." More ingredients were absorbed without a sound, leaving no sign they had ever been.

"It's already dead!"

"Visual input incomprehensible. Please verify."

Slant was too agitated to obey immediately; he watched as water and acid were spooned out, to vanish in midair even before touching the lizard's hide.

"Please verify."

"I don't understand it either; the stuff is disappearing."

Kurao continued to concentrate on the lizard; when he had put into it all the ingredients he had gathered, he still stared at it. Slant continued to demand an explanation.

He stopped talking abruptly when he saw the lizard's foot-long tail twitch.

A moment later Kurao slumped back on his stool, and the lizard turned its head to stare at Slant through green glass eyes.

"Gravitational anomalies representing enemy weapons research have subsided to steady low level; visual anomalies continue."

Slant stared back at the lizard for several seconds. "Is that really alive?"

"Information insufficient."

"No, not really. It lives only as long as I want it to. If I want, it'll be nothing but skin and sawdust and garbage again."

"What did you do? You rearranged those things until it had all its internal organs again?"

"Hligosh, no; am I a god? It's nowhere near as complex as a real lizard. It has no nervous system, no muscles except legs, neck, tail, and heart; it has to eat predigested mush. With everything I can do it probably won't live a week. It's a plaything, really. People like to have them as novelties. They're good for going places people can't fit—cleaning blocked drains and finding lost jewelry and so forth. I'll be glad to sell you this one. It'll do whatever I want it to, unless I turn it over to someone else; then it will obey its new master. If you buy it it will be as much under your control as your own hand—except that it hasn't got any nervous system, so it can't feel anything."

"Can it see?"

"I can see through its eyes, if I close my own; not very well even then, I'm afraid, and I can't transfer that. I've always had trouble with eyes."

Slant stared at the motionless lizard in awe. He still didn't understand the source or type of energy the locals used, or how they used it, but it was undeniably impressive. The lizard lashed its tail, and turned its head back and forth. He could see that it wasn't truly a lizard; its tongue hung limp and unmoving from its mouth and it never blinked. Still, it moved as if alive.

"Require further explanation," the computer told him.

"How did you do that?"

"How did I do what?"

"Bring it to life."

"By wizardry, of course."

"What machines did you use?"

"None; you saw me." Kurao was surprised by the question.

"Subject is apparently lying."

Slant wasn't so certain of that any more, and made no reply.

"Suggest interrogation by threat."

Reluctantly, Slant agreed. "You may be right. Let me try one more thing first." He looked from the lizard to Kurao and asked, "What if I want to learn some simple wizardry? Just enough to do a few stunts?"

"You can't do that. You're either a wizard or you're not, you see."

"What if I want you to make me a wizard?"

"I won't do it. It's forbidden, unless I take you on as an apprentice, and I already have an apprentice."

"What if I force you to do it?"

"You can't force me. I'm a wizard, and you're not even armed."

"How do you make someone a wizard?"

"By magic, of course." Kurao smiled.

Slant conceded to himself that he was getting nowhere, reached under his vest, and brought out his snark. Kurao looked at it curiously.

"This is a weapon from the Bad Times. I know how to use it, and protective spells don't stop it. It can kill you very quickly and messily. I really don't want to use it, but I may have to if you don't start cooperating more fully. Don't move suddenly, don't call out, and don't try using any magic on me. If you do as I say, I won't hurt you; I'll even pay you the other two coins I promised. Understand?" Slant delivered this speech slowly and clearly; Kurao listened intently.

"Yes, I understand."

Slant felt a very faint tingle; the computer informed him, "Minor gravitional anomaly occurring in immediate vicinity of cyborg unit."

"I know; shut up." To Kurao he said, "Stop it."

"I'm not doing anything."

Slant pointed the snark at the cauldron and pressed the trigger; black dust puffed out. The vessel rang dully as a hole a quarter meter across appeared in its side and the far side of the interior began to bubble like melting cheese.

He coughed from the dust once as he took the pressure off the trigger and pointed the weapon at the wizard. "Stop it, I said."

"Gravitational anomaly has ceased."

"That's better."

Kurao stared at the mouth of the snark but said nothing.

"Now, I want to know about magic. Are there any machines or devices used?"

"No, I swear, there is nothing concealed. There's no need to hide anything, because nonwizards couldn't do anything anyway."

"Query: Reliability of statement."

"I don't know; hold on a moment." He reached out with his free left hand and took hold of Kurao's right wrist. "Let me ask again; do you use any hidden machines or devices?" His thumb located the wizard's pulse.

"No."

"No detectable variation in pulse or respiration."

"I think he's telling the truth."

"Query: Possibility of antiinterrogation conditioning."

"Extremely remote."

"Continue action."

"If there are no devices, then what does a wizard use to work magic? What does he need?"

"Nothing."

There was still no change in Kurao's pulse. "What makes a wizard different? Why can he do things ordinary people cannot?"

"He's been changed by another wizard."

"What's been changed?"

"The structure of the brain."

"Explain that a bit more."

"Well . . . you know, the brain is where all thought and emotion occur, where the personality is."

"Yes, I know that."

"The human brain is made up of millions of smaller parts—"

"I know all this; I don't need a lecture on anatomy."

"You know that everything is controlled by the connections between the cells of the brain?"

"Yes."

"Well, a person becomes a wizard when another wizard rearranges those connections in a particular way; it allows one to use wizard sight, to see the underlying forces of the world and to manipulate them."

"What do you think?"

"Explanation tentatively satisfactory. Term 'magic' would apply to theoretical concept 'psionics.' "

"Good. Can we get out of here, then?"

"Negative. Orders require capture of enemy weapons research if possible, destruction of enemy capability if capture is not possible."

"How do we capture psi powers?"

"Require detailed description of modification of human brain required to induce psionic capability."

"Right." He shifted his grip on Kurao's wrist. "Tell me exactly what you have to change, which connections you rearrange."

"I can't explain in words."

"Could you explain if you had a diagram of a brain?"

"I don't think so."

"You do know how to make someone a wizard?"

"Of course; I've trained three apprentices."

"Why can't you explain it, then?"

"I don't know; I just can't. It's a matter of feel. I just feel what has to be changed."

"You became a wizard the same way, yourself?"

"Of course."

"And the wizard who trained you?"

"He had his master, too."

"It must have started somewhere."

"Oh, there are legends about a first, original wizard; she was said to have come from somewhere near Setharipoor. That was right after the Bad Times, when things were still pretty much of a mess, so the stories are vague. I don't know much about her."

"The legends give no explanation of how she acquired the ability?"

"No. I suppose it was just natural, something she was born with."

"Any comment?"

"The possibility of psionic capability as a result of induced mutation has been theorized."

"You think this first wizard was a mutant? Wouldn't some of her children have inherited the trait, then? There would be hereditary wizards as well as the apprenticed ones."

"There is no evidence to indicate that the theoretical first wizard produced offspring."

"Oh. That's true." Some mutants were sterile, after all; that might have been the case here, he thought, or perhaps she simply hadn't bothered with children. He considered for a moment. "Have there ever been any such mutations reported?"

"Negative. No evidence of practical psionic capability has been reported prior to detection of gravitational anomalies on this planet."

"That's what I thought. What now?"

"If no detailed plans or explanations are available, orders call for the capture of a working model of each new weapon, to be analyzed."

Slant looked at the almost-lizard. He would like to be able to do such things, he realized, and the best way to capture this new weapon was to carry it back in his own head. "Could you make me a wizard?" he asked Kurao.

"Anyone can become a wizard—but I won't do it. It's dangerous and forbidden."

Slant tapped the snark's plastic case on the tabletop. "I think you should reconsider," he said.

Kurao looked at the weapon and said nothing.

"Take a look at my brain, then, and see if it would be possible." It had occurred to him that the local population might be a variation on human stock incompatible with his own.

The familiar electric tingle returned, and Slant forestalled the computer by reporting, "I know, I know; he's using magic."

The eerie sensation stopped, and Kurao asked, "What are you?" His eyes were wide. "I thought you'd just found that thing, but you're all wrong inside; there's metal all through you, and something strange in your head, and your nervous system is put together wrong."

"I'm a weapon from the Bad Times, just as much as the snark. Can you make me a wizard?"

"I'm not sure. I think so, but it would take hours; your brain is full of blocks and traps, and some connections are spliced together with metal."

"How long does it usually take?"

"About a quarter of an hour."

"If I insist," Slant asked, lifting the snark, "would you make me a wizard?"

Kurao looked at the weapon again. "I wish I knew how to ruin that thing without making it explode."

"Well?"

"Yes, I'll make you a wizard—at least, I'll try."

"Good. *Shall I have him start? If he makes me a wizard, I'll have the weapon in my head.*"

"*Negative.*"

"What? Why not?"

"*Exact nature of neurological modification unknown. Risk of impairment of cyborg unit functioning, loyalty, intelligence, and/or conditioning precludes any such experimental modification. Furthermore, this procedure would require the cooperation of untrustworthy enemy personnel.*"

"What do you want, then?"

"*Capture and analysis of working model.*"

"How am I supposed to do that?"

"*Exact nature of neurological modification must be analyzed.*"

"You said that; how am I supposed to do it?"

"*Dissection of working model designated 'Kurao' would be most efficient.*"

"The hell it would!" Slant exclaimed aloud.

"What? What are you talking about? I didn't say anything." Confusion was plain on Kurao's face.

"He's a human being, not a weapon!"

"Who are you talking to?"

"Subject is both human being and weapon. There is no contradiction."

Slant could not argue with that, having just referred to himself as a weapon. *"I can't dissect him!"* He started to protest further but caught himself, remembering the computer's warning about further dysfunction; he groped about for something to say.

"Primary cyborg personality will not be required to perform actions suited to medical programming."

Slant started to frame another objection, something about antagonizing neutral natives, when he felt the familiar crawling of his skin; there was a moment of confusion, as he slipped between possible reactions. The stimulus was not one that any of his specialized personae were conditioned to respond to. Instead, the computer's override cut in, and he twisted jerkily, his finger pressing the snark's trigger convulsively; the wizard's mouth flew open in shock and pain as the beam cut into his chest, and blood spewed out across the table and the twitching body of the newly animated lizard.

Chapter Eleven

THE BEAM TORE AT THE WIZARD, THEN THROUGH HIM and at the far wall, showering dust across the smear of blood on the floor, burning for a long, long moment before Slant could resume control and release the pressure of his finger on the trigger.

He looked with disgust at the mangled corpse and the blood that drenched the table. "Was that necessary?"

"Termination of enemy personnel seemed advisable. Gravitational anomaly representing enemy weapons research activity posed possible threat to cyborg unit and success of mission."

"You didn't have to be so thorough! Look at this mess!"

"Control of cyborg unit by override through relay is imprecise. Margin of error must be compensated for."

"Oh, hell." Slant slumped on his stool, staring at the motionless lizard, its green hide spattered with darkening red.

"Delay inadvisable."

"What am I supposed to be doing, then?"

"Transportation of corpse to ship is recommended action."

"What's the hurry?"

"Risk of discovery increases with time. Also, brain tissue may deteriorate."

"Oh, that's just wonderful. How am I supposed to get this bloody mess out of the city?"

"Possible course of action: Ship lands in city, destroying resistance and interference, allowing cyborg unit to transport corpse to ship without interference. Possible course of action: Cyborg unit departs city on foot, destroying resistance and interference with available weapons. Possible course of action: Cyborg unit conceals corpse and departs city on foot."

"The first two are stupid."

"First and second courses of action require loss of mission secrecy and involve open combat. Third course of action has lowest probability of success."

"It does? Why?"

"High probability of detection by guard at checkpoint in city wall."

It took Slant a second to realize the computer was referring to the city gate. "Even if he detected me, though, I could just shoot him and run for it."

"Affirmative."

"Then that's the best thing to do, right?"

"Affirmative."

"Sometimes you're pretty stupid."

The computer didn't answer.

Slant rose and began looking around the shop for something he could use to conceal Kurao's body. He considered, but dismissed, the velvet draperies; he doubted that someone carrying a large bundle wrapped in velvet would go unnoticed. After a few moments of searching, he found a roll of something like canvas at the back of one shelf; if there were enough of the stuff, it would be perfect.

He unrolled it on a part of the floor that had not received much of the spraying blood, and decided that the size might be adequate. It was fortunate that Kurao hadn't been any larger than he was.

Slant walked behind the corpse, which had fallen forward against the table, and then froze; he had heard a noise from the front of the shop, as if someone had entered through the bead curtain.

He waited, motionless. If someone was in the shop, he or she would call out for the proprietor, and when no answer was forthcoming, do one of two things: leave, or look in the back. If the newcomer left, there was no problem; if he looked in the back, Slant might have to kill him. He waited for the call for Kurao.

It didn't come, and Slant decided that either he had imagined the sound or someone had brushed the bead curtain without entering. He stopped and pulled Kurao's body back upright; it took an effort, as the drying blood had adhered to the table, and the old man had been heavier than he looked. He started to pick the body up by the armpits, to dump it onto the canvas.

The velvet draperies swung aside and a young woman entered.

She took a step into the room, then saw a stranger holding Kurao's dead body and stopped; her mouth opened, but she did not scream. Instead a small gasping squeak emerged.

Recovering his composure first, and wanting the psychological advantage of being the first to speak, Slant demanded, "What are you doing here?"

As he spoke, he looked her over; she was small, both short and thin, wearing a gray robe, with light-brown hair and wide-set green eyes in a heart-shaped face. He could almost certainly kill her with a single blow if necessary;

she looked frail, delicate, and gentle. He knew that appearances could be deceptive but was quite sure she posed no threat other than the possibility of screaming and attracting more dangerous foes. Her expression was childlike, more surprised and confused than horrified by the sight of the bloody corpse.

"I-I live here."

"Who are you?"

"I'm Ahnao; I'm Kurao's apprentice." Her gaze had moved down from Slant's face to Kurao's, and on down to the gaping hole in the wizard's chest; her expression was gradually changing from surprise to shock and horror.

"Don't scream," Slant ordered her.

She looked up at his face again, away from the wound. "He's dead, isn't he?"

"Yes."

"What happened?"

"I don't know; I thought you might be able to tell me." She shook her head. "Who are you?"

"My name is Slant. I came in and found him like this."

There was a moment's silence; Ahnao looked down at the corpse again, then automatically looked away. Her expression had change to horror and disgust; Slant watched carefully. The danger of a scream seemed to have passed.

Then her expression changed yet again, to simple surprise. "What's that lizard doing?" she asked.

Slant looked down at the table; the newly animated lizard was moving, walking jerkily across the table, nodding as it went. "I don't know," he said, "Is it yours?"

"No. It's an automaton, a new one. He must have just finished it."

"But wouldn't it die when he did?" Slant was genuinely surprised and curious.

"Unless he'd turned it over to someone, I think it would. I wonder whose it is? No one's ordered a lizard recently—not that I know of, anyway."

"When did you leave?"

"Oh, around noon, I think."

"Someone might have come in who wanted one in a hurry."

"I suppose. What's it doing?"

Slant looked at the lizard again, and saw that it was scratching a groove in the dried blood with its lower jaw. A wave of uneasiness washed over him; he suspected that he was about to be identified as Kurao's murderer, but if he took any action to prevent it, that would also be sure to condemn him.

The lizard shaped a single shaky letter, then stumbled and collapsed. The letter was F.

Slant did not understand that at all; he had expected an S.

"Query: Automaton's intelligence."

"Hell, I don't know. What does F stand for?"

"Information insufficient."

The girl was looking at the letter curiously. "F," she said. "Do you mean Furinar?"

The lizard moved its head, as if trying to nod.

"Query: Meaning of term 'Furinar.'"

"I don't know, either." Aloud, he asked Ahnao, "What's Furinar?"

"He's a friend of ours. Do you think I should try to contact him?"

"Is he a wizard?"

"Yes."

"Maybe he's the killer."

"Oh, I don't think so!"

"Recommend termination of subject 'Ahnao.' Further delay inadvisable."

"No, wait a minute; I want to find out more about this Furinar. He might be a threat. Also, do we really want to leave another corpse around to attract attention? And what about this damn lizard?"

"Continue action."

"Why don't you think he's the killer? Why else would the lizard do that?"

"I don't know. Maybe you're right. Let me contact him." Her eyes suddenly became unfocused, gazing off into infinity; Slant reached for his snark, then changed his mind. It might already be too late. He guessed that she was using some sort of telepathic communication.

"Gravitational anomaly representing enemy weapons research activity occurring in immediate vicinity of cyborg unit. Recommend immediate termination of subject 'Ahnao.' "

"No, wait; she's not attacking us, and I still want to find out what's going on. Besides, by now she may have alerted this Furinar character. She might be useful as a hostage."

"Continue action."

The computer was being unusually agreeable, Slant thought; that worried him.

The girl came out of her apparent trance and immediately turned as if to run; Slant moved faster, however, and grabbed her wrist before she could take a step. She struggled, and he threw his other arm around her neck, restraining her effectively.

"What's going on?" he asked. "Why did you try to leave?"

"Furinar says you killed Kurao!"

As Slant had suspected, wizards apparently were telepathic. "How does he know? Was he here?"

"No, Kurao sent him a message; you were threatening him with a death machine from the Bad Times, and you killed him!"

"Why did the lizard write an F?"

"Kurao turned it over to Furinar just before he died; Furinar wanted to contact me, but I wasn't listening, so he used the lizard."

"Where is Furinar now?"

"He's on his way here; he'll be here any minute. Let me go!"

"Damn!"

"Recommend immediate evasive action."

"No, they can track me, the way they did in Teyzha. I can use the girl as a hostage, though."

"Affirmative. Query: Possibility of handling corpse in addition to hostage."

"Oh, hell. I'd forgotten about that." The girl twisted in his grip, trying to free herself; he tightened his hold, not because that made it any more secure but as a warning. "Hold still. You were right, you know, I did kill Kurao; if you don't do exactly what you're told, I'll kill you, too. Do you understand?"

She nodded.

"Good." He looked at the corpse and decided there was no way he could possibly carry it while holding Ahnao and a weapon. If he didn't get it back to the ship, though, he would have to kill another wizard for the computer to dissect. An idea struck him. "Do you need the whole corpse? Would just the brain do?"

"Information insufficient; however, brain alone would probably be sufficient. Furthermore, brain and corpse are expendable, as others are available."

"Good." He loosened his hold on Ahnao and informed her, "I'm going to let go of you. Don't run away, don't do anything suspicious, and I won't hurt you. Remember, I'm much faster and stronger than you are, and I have weapons from the Bad Times. Do you understand?"

She nodded again, and he released her. She stood, trembling, just where she was, her head turned to watch him.

He took the snark from his pocket and grabbed a firm hold on Kurao's ear with his free hand; he wished the old man had had hair, as it would have provided a better grip. Then, with the snark set on a fine beam, he cut through the cadaver's neck, leaving the severed head hanging from his hand by its ear.

Ahnao moaned and sank to her knees. Slant ignored her as she vomited onto the floor; he understood her reaction, as he felt none too well himself. He had no time to be sick, however, as he wrapped the head in canvas, making as neat a parcel as he could, being careful not to get blood on the outside of the wrapping. He found string on a nearby shelf and tied the bundle closed as best he could manage. Just as he finished he heard footsteps and the rattle of the bead curtain; in an instant he had dragged Ahnao to her feet, one arm around her neck, holding the package by the string, and his other hand pointing the snark at her head. She cringed, trying to back away from the bundle and simultaneously avoid the snark.

The drapes parted, and a tall, thin man wearing the black robe of a wizard appeared. Gray hair reached to his shoulders, and he gazed at the cyborg from watery blue eyes.

"Hello, Slant," the newcomer said.

"Hello, Furinar. Stay where you are. If you take another step toward me, I will kill Ahnao."

"You have a hostage."

"Yes."

"You told Kurao that protective spells can't stop that weapon."

"That's right. I can tell when you're using magic, too; if you try any, I'll kill her."

There was a moment of silence; the computer said, "Recommend immediate departure. Additional enemy personnel may be nearby."

"Just a moment." He looked Furinar in the eye and said, "You wizards can tell truth from lies. Listen, then. It's possible that you could kill me, one way or another, but I suggest that you not try it. If I die, the demon that possesses me, a relic of the Bad Times, will destroy your entire city. If I reach my ship safely, with this package, I will let the girl go, unharmed, and I hope that I will be able to leave your world forever without harming anyone else."

"The package holds Kurao's head."

"That's right."

"What do you want it for?"

"The demon wants to learn how a wizard's brain differs from an ordinary one; it doesn't care if the wizard is alive or dead. Once it knows how magic works, we can leave here. Now let me go."

"I cannot stop you." The wizard stood aside, holding back the velvet drapery so that Slant could pass unhindered.

He prodded Ahnao forward with the snark, and the two of them marched past Furinar. When they reached the door of the shop, Slant took his arm from her neck and moved the snark to point at her back, making sure she knew it was still there. None of the three said anything further, and the two of them walked out onto the street.

No one interfered as they made their way through the city streets; at the gate the watch simply stood aside and let them pass. Slant guessed that Furinar had contacted them somehow, perhaps through another wizard, and told them to do nothing that might have unpleasant results.

Once they were out of the city Slant relaxed slightly; he

did not put the snark away, but carried it loose in his hand instead of keeping it pointed at the girl. Neither of them spoke; they had nothing to say to one another. Ahnao cast occasional wary glances at Slant, and several times he thought she was going to say something, perhaps ask a question, but she never did. She made no complaint as they walked, though she was obviously not accustomed to traveling such a distance on foot.

When they were a few kilometers from the city Slant glanced back and noticed specks hanging in the sky, following them; the computer confirmed his suspicion that Furinar had recruited other wizards, six in all, and that the seven were following him at a distance. The seven were moving gravitational anomalies to the computer, of course, but Slant knew they were wizards.

They stayed well back, however, and Slant paid them no heed beyond glancing back every few moments to make sure they kept their distance.

Their presence did not seem to worry the computer, either; it made no suggestions or complaints.

Well after dark they arrived at the edge of the gully that hid the ship. Slant could not see it; he realized that the computer must have applied camouflage after he left. Either that or he had misjudged his own route.

"Where are you?" he asked.

There was a sudden blaze of light off to his right; the ship had turned on floodlights, illuminating the inside of its plastic covering. It had not used artificial vines this time, but a translucent plastic sheet the approximate color of young grass; with the floodlights on, it appeared as a huge irregular mass glowing an eerie green.

Ahnao gasped at the sight and stopped dead in her tracks. "What is it?"

"That's my ship."

"I thought it would be wood or metal; why is it green?"

"It's not, really; that's just the covering. I'll show you." He led the way down to the vessel, and after a little groping found an opening in the camouflage cover. He pulled the plastic aside, and white light poured out across the grass and sand of the gully's side.

Ahnao peered past him at the gleaming metal of the

ship's wing, lit silver and green by the floodlight and the reflection from the plastic; she stared in wonder but balked when Slant urged her forward.

"I'm not going in there!"

Slant was annoyed but thought better of immediate argument. Instead, he asked the computer, "What's our situation?"

"Seven gravitational anomalies representing enemy action are approaching at an altitude of twenty meters at an approximate ground speed of five kilometers per hour. No other enemy activity detected in immediate area of ship. No overt hostile actions in progress."

"Do we still need a hostage?"

"Negative."

"Good." He let go of Ahnao's wrist, which he had grabbed when she stepped back from the opening, and told her, "All right, you can go."

"Query: Advisability of releasing hostage."

"You just said we don't need her!"

"Affirmative. Standard procedure calls for termination of enemy personnel in immediate vicinity of ship."

"Idiot machine! We're being watched by seven enemy wizards of unknown capabilities, and you want to antagonize them by killing a civilian and breaking my word?" Even as he said it, he realized that the computer might want exactly that; he had forgotten that it wanted to die. Perhaps it had allowed him to overrule so many suggestions lately because it hoped he'd get himself killed by taking less than optimal courses of action; perhaps, on the other hand, it had made stupid suggestions hoping to get him killed when he followed them, and was forced to concede when presented with better options.

"Negative. Continue action."

"Right." He started toward the airlock but was stopped by Ahnao's voice.

"May I see inside?"

Exasperated, he turned back and said, "A moment ago you wouldn't go near it!"

"I changed my mind."

"Enemy personnel are not permitted aboard."

"I know that!" He almost spoke that aloud but caught

himself in time, and kept his voice calm as he said, "No, I'm sorry, you may not see inside. Go home now."

"But it's dark!"

"What of it? You're a grown woman and an apprentice wizard, and there are seven of your friends a kilometer up the road. Now go away."

She said nothing further, but the expression on her face was that of a chastised puppy, hurt and sorrowful. Slant watched as she turned and walked a few paces back up the side of the gully, then turned himself, closing the plastic cover behind him, and climbed up onto the wing. The airlock slid open as he approached, lit from inside, and the floodlights shut off, plunging everything but the open port into darkness.

He entered the ship and tucked the snark into his vest pocket, safety on, glad to have the thing out of his hand at last. At the entrance to the control cabin he turned briefly aside and got the ship's surgical kit out of the medical locker; he also found a plastic dropcloth in a nearby supply cabinet.

In the control cabin he spread the dropcloth across the acceleration couch, then dumped the bundle he had carried from Awlmei on it. Blood had soaked through the canvas at the bottom, making a messy brownish stain.

"Prepare for launch."

The computer's interruption caught Slant by surprise. "Wait a minute," he said, "Are you sure that's a good idea?"

"Enemy personnel of unknown capabilities are in immediate vicinity of ship."

"Yes, but what will the acceleration do to this damn brain you made me bring back? Besides, what can they do to us without heavy weapons?"

"Information insufficient."

"What would acceleration do to ordinary unprotected brain tissue?"

"Damage would be minimal. However, advisability of launch doubtful."

"Good. That's what I thought. Let's just stay here for the moment, then, and get this dissection over with, all right?"

"Affirmative."

"I just hope the damn thing hasn't already deteriorated too much." He unwrapped the bundle, revealing Kurao's severed head; a momentary revulsion overcame him, and he stepped back. When he had recovered, he opened the surgical kit, laid it out neatly, then found the direct-control cable and plugged it into his neck.

"Go ahead," he said.

The override came on; for once he didn't fight it. Instead, he watched disinterestedly from a semitrance as the computer and his own hypnopedic medical training jointly controlled his hands, neatly removing the scalp and the top of the skull, and systematically disassembling and analyzing the brain within.

The process took a very long time; it was complicated enough to begin with, and was further slowed by the necessity of using both Slant's eyes and a high-magnification camera, as his eyes were no use at microscopic scale and the camera was not suitable for guiding his hands directly. The dissection was less than half completed when the first faltering took place; the scalpel slipped, destroying several cells.

Had Slant been fully conscious and under his own control, he couldn't have detected the error; it was microscopic. To the computer, however, working through the camera, it was glaringly obvious. A slip of that magnitude could be catastrophic in other situations. The override shut off.

Slant found himself holding a greasy scalpel, staring at a grisly gray and red mess. "What's wrong? Why did you stop?" he asked.

"An error was made. Query: Was any action taken by cyborg unit primary personality?"

"No, of course not; I couldn't have done anything if I wanted to, you know that. Hell, I couldn't even want to!"

"Affirmative. Warning: Evidence of computer malfunction. Request emergency maintenance check."

"Right." Frightened, Slant unplugged the cable from his neck and started toward the door of the cabin; the access panel for the computer's test circuits was in the main airlock to facilitate an emergency exit if something dangerously wrong should be found. Though the computer was a constant annoyance, he did not want it to fail; he depended on it, could not run the ship without it. Furthermore, if it was not seriously damaged, it might still be erratic and make mistakes, which might well mean that his life expectancy was nil.

He had not yet reached the door when an alarm beeped somewhere, and the computer informed him, "Main drive has been shut down."

"What did you do that for?"

"There is no record of shut-down procedure for main drive on any inboard system. Possible explanations are spontaneous system failure or enemy action. There is no evidence of system failure."

"Oh, God," Slant muttered. The ship was going mad; there was something seriously wrong with it. No other explanation made sense. He wondered whether it was worth the trouble to run a systems check, but no other course of action came to mind.

"Power drain is higher than normal. Reserve power level dropping."

That didn't make sense; even with the fusion drive shut down, the ship's energy cells should be fully charged and sufficient to run all systems for months—assuming there was no call for the ship's blasters and no attempt to restart the drive, as either of those would consume incredible amounts of power. "Are you sure? Double-check that."

"Affirmative. Reserve power level dropping."

Energy couldn't just disappear; it had to be going somewhere. "Trace the drain; something must be malfunctioning. Are the lasers in the drive drawing any power?" Even as he asked, he was almost to the airlock. He was fairly certain that part of the computer's regulating machinery must have gone berserk and lost contact with the main system; the test circuits should let him locate the problem. He hoped it wasn't too extensive.

The corridor lights dimmed. "Emergency power conservation measures in effect."

He reached the inner door of the lock; it did not slide out of his way. He realized that that must be part of the emergency measures, and began to crank it open manually.

"Power drain located. Power is being diverted from

number three fusion-core laser through gravitational anomaly."

"What? Why didn't you spot that before?" He kept cranking; even if it was the wizards' doing, he had no better course of action, and the sudden belated discovery of enemy action could well be a further malfunction rather than an accurate analysis.

"Information insufficient. There is evidence that sensor circuits have been tampered with."

"Can you stop the drain?"

"Negative. Ship is not equipped with gravitational manipulation."

"Where are the wizards?" The lock was open; he stepped in and found the test circuit access panel. It was held in place with plastic clamps; he slid them to the unlocked position and discovered that there were also three Phillips-head screws that the clamps had been hiding.

"Enemy personnel are approximately eighty meters north by northwest."

"They're on the ground?" There was a tool kit somewhere, he knew there was.

"Affirmative."

"Can you open fire on them?" He found the tool cabinet; it had plastic clamps holding it shut, but fortunately no screws. He opened it.

"Negative. All weapons are below rim of depression. No line of sight to enemy personnel above rim of depression is possible."

"What about missiles? Throw something at them, anything!" He had the screwdriver.

"All anti-personnel missiles are located on underside of ship, and intended for air-to-ground use."

"What about incendiaries?" He had one screw out.

"All incendiary missiles are located on underside of ship, and intended for air-to-ground use."

"Don't we have any air-to-air or ground-to-air or ground-to-ground?" The second screw came free.

"Affirmative. Air-to-air missiles are armor-piercing, located on underside of ship. Ground-to-air missiles are magnetically guided high explosive. Ground-to-ground are nuclear. Ship is well within blast area of nuclear arms."

That was no help at all. The third screw came loose and fell to the floor of the airlock.

"Power levels critical."

He flipped the switch that activated the testing mechanism; a red light reading INSUFFICIENT POWER immediately came on.

"Termination of communications contact with cyborg unit to conserve power."

"No, wait!" There was no response.

He looked at the test panel, trying to decide what to do; the lights in the passageway went out completely, and he was in total darkness except for the red glow labeled INSUFFICIENT POWER.

He knew there was emergency lighting somewhere; he could not see well enough to locate it. Aloud, he shouted, "Give me some light!"

There was no answer; the darkness remained.

A new light appeared, a yellow glow from the test panel; it was a warning light that read SYSTEMS FAILURE. He stared at it.

An instant later it winked out, and a new, larger, red light came on, reading ALL SYSTEMS OFF.

There had to be a flashlight in the tool kit; he groped for it in the dark and found it as even the red warning lights began to dim.

There was a click, and a whir, and the hiss of recording tape came from a speaker near his head; he froze and listened with a mix of fear and anticipation. Was the computer back in service? The red light reading ALL SYSTEMS OFF still glowed faintly. A voice spoke, the first other than his own to be heard aboard the ship for fourteen years.

"Independent Reconnaissance Unit two-oh-five, this is a recorded message from the Command, activated by the failure of your shipboard computer systems and/or power supply.

"We, of course, know nothing of your current situation, so this message cannot address itself to specifics. It is a safe assumption, however, that the systems failure is the result of enemy action, and we can offer a little general advice.

"We suggest you make planetfall immediately, if you

have not done so, and get away from your ship as fast as possible, taking whatever supplies seem appropriate. Your ship can make an emergency landing without computer assistance under the right circumstances. Once away from the ship, try to blend with the local population, if any; a single person is harder to find in a crowd than in a wilderness. Avoid local capitals and military installations. Your situation has been reported by emergency relay to all units in your area, and assistance will be sent as soon as possible; we do not consider IRU personnel expendable.

"Since you must be prepared for all eventualities, and there may arise situations in which the maintenance of your status as an IRU is counterproductive, you may need the release code for your computer and yourself. This is simply your civilian name, spoken aloud three times; it can be retrieved from your memory by any person with a rudimentary knowledge of hypnosis, or if necessary through self-hypnosis. We do not recommend that you use it lightly, and certainly not immediately; it will erase your conditioning and block your memory of all militarily sensitive subjects and training.

"Remember, help is on the way. Good luck."

Blank tape hissed, then stopped; the dim red of the warning light died, and he was alone in the dark.

Chapter Twelve

THE FLASHLIGHT WAS A SORT THAT COULD BE RECHARGED by pumping a generator handle, so that even though its original charge had long ago dribbled away during fourteen years of disuse and its automatic recharging had failed along with everything else dependent upon ship's power, he was able to use it to find his way around the ship. It was a strange experience to be prowling through the darkened ship; the old familiar passageways and compartments were new and different, as he had never before seen them completely unlit.

He was primarily interested in obtaining supplies from the storage lockers, but could not resist taking a glance at the control cabin. He was surprised to see that the chameleon fur was now an unpleasant, murkily iridescent gray; he had never known how the stuff worked, and had not realized it required electricity to keep its color. Kurao's ruined head still lay on the couch where he had left it.

He considered taking a few of his favorite books from the bookcase on the forward bulkhead but decided against it; unnecessary weight would be a mistake. He was unsure where he would be going and what he would be doing, and therefore did not know what he might need; he planned to cover as many possibilities as he could.

The lockers were shut, of course, and could not be commanded to open; instead he had to work each individual emergency door release. The magnetic equipment clamps still held; apparently they were ordinary magnets, and not dependent upon electricity.

The snark in his vest pocket was down well below half charge; he replaced it with another, fully charged, that had been disconnected from the recharging circuit when the power failed and therefore hadn't drained back. He kept the laser, as a tool with any number of uses. He considered various firearms.

He did not want anything big and cumbersome; that let out anything heavier than a submachine gun. He thought about the fuss his lost gun had caused in Teyzha and decided he wanted something small enough to conceal, which let out most of the rifles, shotguns, and automatic weapons.

It occurred to him he might take more than one, but he quickly rejected the idea; it would be too much weight to too little purpose. He did want at least one loud and frightening weapon that wouldn't go dead in half a dozen uses as a snark would—but only one such weapon.

Finally he settled on a machine-pistol, light and compact; it did not have the range or impact of the heavy automatic he had taken to Awlmei, and was not as easily hidden, but the rapid fire might be useful. A good-sized knife and a dozen clips of ammunition for the machine-pistol completed his armament.

Rope had any number of uses, so he took a coil of nylon line. He was unsure about money and food, and cleared out the ship's store of gold coins and all the food he could carry.

When he felt that he had everything he needed, including a few extra garments and a stout pair of boots, he made his way back to the airlock, leaving the lockers standing open. He knew of no way that the ship's power could be restored without electricity and doubted there was enough generated power on the entire planet to restart the fusion drive, so the ship was useless to him; he intended to abandon it permanently, and he knew that locker doors wouldn't stop anyone who was determined to loot the vessel.

Airlock doors might be a bit more daunting, however, and he might someday want to replenish his supplies, so he did crank shut the inner door of the airlock.

He paused before taking the next step. Outside the ship somewhere were the wizards of Awlmei. They might well be waiting for him, to execute him for Kurao's murder. He wouldn't blame them if they were; however, he intended to survive. He hadn't killed Kurao, the damn computer had.

He wished he could open the door with a weapon in hand, but it wasn't possible; he needed one hand to hold the flashlight and the other to work the lock. He would have to rely on his superhuman speed to avoid any traps that might have been set.

He worked the door's mechanism, and it slid aside; he paused and peered out.

It was very nearly as dark outside as it was in the ship; dawn was still a couple of hours away. What little starlight there might be was completely blocked by the camouflage cover. In short, he couldn't see a thing.

He stepped out onto the ship's wing and cranked the airlock shut, working by the light of the flashlight. Once the door was securely closed, he kept the light in one hand and drew the machine-pistol with the other. He felt slightly safer now that he was armed again.

He stood where he was for a moment, listening; he heard nothing except the wind in the grass. Perhaps the wizards had gone. Perhaps they had not been responsible for the ship's failure; the computer might actually have gone mad and killed itself, as it had admitted wanting to.

He shone the light on the camouflage cover, then stopped and turned it downward again; that was stupid. It revealed his position without doing him any good. He knew where the opening in the plastic was and didn't need the flashlight to find it. He climbed off the wing and made his way cautiously up the slope of the gully and out into the open night beyond the plastic.

The wizards were waiting for him at the gully's rim, standing motionless in the darkness, their robes blowing slightly in the night wind.

He came out of the plastic, took three steps toward them, then stopped, face to face. There was a moment of silence as each sized up the other.

Slant turned off the flashlight, and let his eyes adjust to the dim starlight. The wizards still said nothing.

At last, Slant broke the silence, saying, "I hope one of you saw Ahnao safely home."

"The girl is safe, and none of your concern." It was the tallest of the seven who spoke, a man about his own age; Slant was mildly surprised that Furinar did not serve as spokesman.

"Was it you who shut down the drive?"

"We stopped the machines, yes. Now get out of here."

"What?"

"Get out of here."

"I don't understand."

"We are banishing you from Awlmei."

"Why? It was the computer that killed Kurao; you've killed the computer, and justice is done. I mean you no harm." Slant was honestly surprised; he had expected either a trial and attempt at execution or a friendly reception as a freed slave.

"You are a dangerous, evil person, and although you may not have killed our comrade of your own free will, you are nonetheless not welcome in Awlmei. Return here, and we will kill you. Is that clear?"

"Completely clear." He could hardly blame them for such an attitude. "Step aside, then, and I'll go."

To his surprise, the wizards did just that, stepping back from the edge of the gully and allowing him to scramble up onto the flat plain. He looked about; the wizards were again motionless and silent.

It took very little thought to decide where to go, with Awlmei forbidden to him; he would head east, into the hills. Every other direction led only to open prairie, so far as he could tell. He had one final question. "What are you going to do with my ship?"

"Nothing. It is as tainted with the evil of the Bad Times as you are, and will lie where it is until it rusts."

That was fine with him; it meant that he might be able to sneak back and replenish his supplies should the need arise. He said nothing further, but instead walked off eastward into the darkness.

A few moments later he glanced back; the wizards were no longer standing by the gully, but after a moment's searching he spotted them well on their way back to Awlmei. He could return to his ship now, if he chose, but there was no reason to; instead he turned back toward the hills and continued walking.

He had not yet decided what to do with himself. He had, in fact, not given it any thought yet, being far more concerned with his immediate survival.

He knew now what his release code was, but he dismissed quickly the thought of using it; on a planet as backward as this, he might well need every bit of his combat training, even though such other abilities as piloting were now useless. Should he ever settle down somewhere into a peaceful and stable life, he might reconsider. He wondered whether the release from his conditioning would have any effect on his accelerated reflexes and added strength; those, after all, were the result of the restructuring of his body rather than his mind.

The only way he could find out would be to use his release code, and that experiment seemed a little too final; one thing he was quite sure of was that it would be irreversible.

He found himself wanting to ask the computer's advice,

to inquire what course of action it recommended, to use its vast stores of information; it was very strange not being able to. Without meaning to, he found himself phrasing his thoughts for the computer to understand, wording questions that went unanswered. It was the first time in fourteen years that he had been out of touch with the machine for more than an hour, and the unbroken mental silence grew gradually more oppressive with every passing minute.

He had never liked the computer; he had often hated it and feared it. He was discovering now that he had also come to depend upon it much more than he liked to admit.

As he walked on across the plain and the dawn soared up out of the hills ahead of him, he found himself thinking about nothing else except his ship, the computer, and his release code. That was not good. Those things were past—or at least, two were past, the third not to be used. He had left the ship and the computer was dead; he needed something else to think about.

That brought up the question of what he was to do with himself. He was not in the habit of planning for the future—that had always been left up to the computer's interpretation of their orders rather than his own discretion. It took a concerted effort to consider it for himself rather than to wait for the computer to present him with options he might choose from.

There was obviously no point in continuing with his mission of investigating wizards—but what else was he to do?

Survival was his first priority, of course, and it began to sink in that he no longer had the ship's armaments to protect him, the hydroponic banks to feed him, the hull to shelter him. He would have to fend entirely for himself, without an emergency reserve.

He could forage in the forests that covered the hills, but that wouldn't be much of a life, if it was even possible. The forests he had seen couldn't support a man at anything above subsistence level, if that.

He could take to theft, living off whatever he could

steal from unguarded farms or shops; that was what he had been taught to do. That was for short-term use, however, and as he thought it over he realized it would be a very poor way to live for an extended period, moral questions aside. He would be on this planet forever, for the rest of his life; he was not leaving. This was not a mission, to be finished up and left behind; this was his life.

It was a new concept, and not a particularly appealing one. He had never before had to plan for the long term. Even in his civilian identity, those many years ago, he hadn't planned for the long term; he had attended school because it was expected, joined the military for lack of a better course of action, never worrying about what came afterward in any but the vaguest terms. He had thought that he'd serve his term and then see what happened.

Now, abruptly, his military service was at long last done.

If he was no longer in military service, then he was a civilian again, despite his retention of his military training and cyborg nature. What did civilians do?

Long ago, he had planned on a career in art; he had never taken the trouble to decide what sort of a career. Could he now pursue that?

Somehow, he doubted that he could; this planet did not appear to be a place where an art historian would have much of a life.

Was he actually stuck on this planet? The taped message from the command had said help would be sent. He felt a moment of foolish optimism before telling himself that no help would come. That message had been recorded more than three hundred years ago, by a government destroyed shortly thereafter; the only way it might conceivably bring aid would be if it reached a military unit somewhere that, as he himself had been, was still fighting a lost war, sailing through the stars and the centuries at near-light speeds. Even if there were such ships out there—and it was possible there were—the odds were that they were nowhere near him. If one were cruising even the nearest star system to this, his cry for help would take more than three years to be picked up, and no ship could reach him in less than another four—and that only if it were a fast ship already headed in approximately the right direction.

He knew that no other ships had been detectable within this system when he landed; if there was help out there, it would be years before it reached him. He might die of old age before a ship could arrive from just a few stars away.

Could he get off this planet himself?

There was no way he could build a starship, that was very obvious. The only other possibilities were repairing his own or finding another left from before the war.

The possibility of finding an intact ship more than three hundred years old was even slimmer than that of help reaching him.

Could he repair his ship?

Although he had at first dismissed the idea, it might be possible; the ship was intact, except for the complete loss of power, so far as he knew. If he could pour enough electricity into the lasers to restart the fusion reaction, he'd be back exactly where he was before the wizards shut it down.

Even on a planet as primitive as this, it should be possible to generate electricity. It might take years, but it could be done. With the starship serviceable, his options would be greatly increased.

There were problems, however. The wizards of Awlmei weren't likely to let him hook a generator up to his ship. He would have to deal with them somehow.

There was also the matter of the computer. If he restarted the drive, it would come back on line and insist on his continuing the mission. He didn't want that. He could use the release code—but then he couldn't fly the ship. He was quite sure that an ordinary human being was incapable of piloting the thing.

Could he start the drive without reviving the computer?

No, it was hooked directly into the drive, as it was essential for controlling the fusion reaction. Besides, even a fully operational cyborg couldn't pilot the ship without the computer. The tape had said an emergency landing was possible without it; it might be, but he doubted it, and was sure that nothing else could be done.

What he had to do, therefore, was to find some way of removing the computer's hold on him without using his release code, and then restart the drive.

He'd been trying for years to remove the computer's hold on him, of course; there was a crucial difference this time, however, in that he was currently free. He could do as he pleased.

If he were to have the override mechanism and the thermite removed from his head, then the computer would be unable to harm him; he could use the ship as he pleased. That, then, was the thing to do.

The wizards of Teyzha had said they could free him of his demon; perhaps he should take them up on their offer now that he could. He thought they would understand that the computer had destroyed their city, and that he had done his best to warn them; if any had survived the attack, they could remove the bomb and override. He would be glad to do whatever he could in exchange, perhaps make up in some small part for the damage he had done them.

By midmorning, he had decided that he would definitely head for Teyzha. He thought his supply of money and food would be adequate for most of the trip; he would have to manage as best he could, perhaps hunt or find odd jobs along the way. He did not know the exact distance, of course; he told himself he might be grossly underestimating the length of the journey.

He had all the time in the world, though. He was into the first low hills now, and paused atop a rise to look back at his ship.

He couldn't see it; he could not even be sure that he was looking toward the right gully. He shrugged and turned east again.

Under the green plastic camouflage, something whirred softly. A service robot, its batteries finally sufficiently charged by draining the last trickle of electricity from the others, rolled out of its storage compartment and set about its programmed task.

Chapter Thirteen

I T WAS MIDAFTERNOON WHEN SLANT HAPPENED ACROSS A
road. It ran east by southeast, which was very nearly his
own direction, so he followed it. It could scarcely be
worse than cross-country, he told himself. His feet were beginning to hurt; he'd done a lot of walking yesterday, from
the ship to Awlmei and back, and had been walking since
well before dawn on his present course, without any sleep
in between. His body was equipped with regulating mechanisms, run off microminiature batteries or his own body
heat or heartbeat, so that the lack of sleep did not need to
bother him unless it extended beyond about a hundred
hours—a limit he had no intention of reaching—and his
endurance was in general fairly remarkable, but the wear
and tear on his feet was still painful. They were unaccus-
tomed to heavy boots and rough walking after years of a
passive existence surrounded by chameleon fur carpet and
metal decks. He was grateful that the local gravity wasn't
any heavier than it was.

The plain had been left behind long ago, and he was
once again in a forest; this one was not pine but a mix
of deciduous trees, oak, maple, aspen, alder, and others he
couldn't identify. The leaves had not yet begun to turn,
and the south side of the road was therefore shady while
the north was in full sunlight; it had been the line of
bright light penetrating the leaf cover that he first recognized as being a road.

The highway had once been paved; occasional patches
of something smooth, hard, and black still showed here
and there. The rest of the surface was hard-packed dirt.
He was glad it wasn't gravel, or anything else that might
chew up the soles of his boots, and hoped that it wouldn't
be too muddy in the event of rain.

Besides saving wear and tear on boots and feet, there was another obvious advantage to following a road; roads led somewhere. This one, he was sure, led to some sort of human habitation; it was not overgrown, which meant it was still in use. If he found people, he would be able to replenish his supplies, one way or another, and perhaps acquire transportation other than his feet. It was even possible he might obtain directions for reaching Teyzha; so far he was dependent entirely upon his memory of the map of the continent the computer had shown him, which told him only that the city lay somewhere far to the east.

He did not reach whatever the road led to that day, nor did he encounter anyone along the way. At sunset he stopped, ate a small meal, washed it down with water from a brook that ran parallel to the highway for a few kilometers, and found himself a soft place to lie, just out of sight of the road, on a pile of old leaves. That was enough of a camp; the weather was still warm, and he needed no fire. After having stayed awake and active the entire preceding night, it was no trouble at all for him to go to sleep while the western sky was still light.

It was so easy, in fact, that he gave no thought at all to anything beyond falling asleep. His hypnotic conditioning had included learning how to wake at any predetermined hour, but he had not bothered to determine when he wanted to arise; therefore, he slept uninterrupted until the morning sun stood halfway up the sky, when a sound other than the normal noise of the local minor fauna jarred him out of his slumber.

Instantly he was fully alert again; he lay where he was, to avoid revealing his presence to anyone who might notice a movement, and considered. From the angle of the light he knew the time; the sound he recognized as the jingle of stirrups and harness and the dull thud of hoofbeats.

Alert he might be, but that did not mean he was entirely awake; he wasted several seconds wondering why the computer hadn't roused him sooner, and trying to ask it for its evaluation of the situation. Finally the lack of response and his returning memory brought back the knowledge that the computer was gone, shut down by the wizards of Awlmei, and he had to rely entirely on his own resources.

The hoofbeats came quite close, then receded again; the rider, whoever it was, had passed without seeing him. With a brief effort he reoriented himself, and knew that the passerby was heading westward, the opposite direction from him.

He relaxed; there was no danger. He did not even need to worry about encountering whoever it was later on.

When the hoofbeats had faded in the distance he sat up, stretched, and reached for his boots. The action served to draw attention to his feet, and he realized they still hurt slightly. He pulled the first boot on anyway, and winced at the sting when the bottom of his foot hit the bottom of the boot. The second was no better.

He sat for a moment, hoping that the discomfort would pass. It didn't. He asked himself if he really wanted to do any walking.

No, he didn't want to do any walking, but he did want to get to Teyzha—or at least to somewhere. He was in the middle of nowhere at present.

Might he do better to settle in the first village that would take him? Teyzha was still halfway across the continent, however far that was. What made Teyzha worth the trip?

The thermite charge in his skull was certainly a major consideration. Even if he never got the drive restarted and the computer back in operation, he didn't much care to go through life with a bomb in his head. There was also the possibility that he might somehow help the Teyzhans, and make amends for a little of the damage he had done. He really did want to go to Teyzha.

He remembered the sound of hoofs and harness; a horse would be a very good thing to have for such a trip, he thought. Perhaps he should pursue the rider, kill him, and take his horse.

No, he should do nothing of the sort. He had no right to kill anyone without the computer forcing him to; it would be murder. He knew that—but old habits die hard, and he knew that the computer would have sent him after the horseman without a second thought. He would have gone, too, without much protest. It had been very easy to do what was expedient regardless of right when he had the computer for a scapegoat.

He might be able to buy a horse somewhere. That was a much better idea. He would look into it at the first opportunity.

For the present, though, he was on foot, and might as well make the best of it. He got to his feet, gathered up his supplies, and made his way back onto the highway. Once he was moving his feet seemed less painful, he noticed.

The short day passed quickly; he took frequent rests, as he had not the day before. He knew that his feet would tighten up with time and travel, and he saw no need to batter them unnecessarily while the toughening was just starting. He passed two forks and a crossroads, each time taking the most nearly eastward course. He glimpsed a wooden palisade off to the side at one point but did not actually encounter any human habitation. Four times he was passed by other travelers, one party of three westbound and the others—two individuals and a fair-sized group—eastward bound. All were on horseback; the eastbound group was accompanied by two large canvas-draped wagons. All glanced at him curiously, but none spoke. He also stayed silent; he preferred not to draw attention to himself.

When the sun reddened and began to slip below the trees behind him, he again stopped for the night. As before, he found a comfortable pile of dead leaves, but this time he did not bother to get out of sight of the highway. Everyone he had seen so far had been, if not friendly, at least not hostile.

It was an unpleasant surprise, therefore, to be awakened shortly before sunrise, when the eastern sky was warmly pink, by the prodding of a spear-point at his side.

As always, he was instantly alert. The spear was held by a large black-haired man with a long drooping mustache; behind him were two other men, mounted on two of three horses. Slant did not take time to study details. This was not quite a combat situation, but he could feel his warrior personality ready in his mind, prepared to take over instantly.

"What do you want?" he asked.

"What have you got?" The spear-holder grinned broadly; his mustache twitched as he did.

"Nothing of any value."

"I don't believe that."

"It's true."

"I think we'll look for ourselves—and I don't much care whether you help or whether I search your corpse. Corpses are heavy and awkward, but they don't argue."

"You'll kill me if I don't cooperate?"

"That's right." The bandit poked him lightly with the spear to emphasize his statement.

Slant let his fighting persona take over; immediately, he was rolling away from the bandit and the spear. By the time he had completed a full revolution the machine-pistol was in his hand, and before his attacker had time to react he had fired twice, with a sharp double crack.

He was not familiar with the gun; the first shot missed. He had adjusted his aim for the second, however, and it caught the man in the throat, sending him staggering backward with a choking gurgle. Blood spattered the dead leaves as Slant flicked the switch to rapid fire, and as the man fell Slant emptied the clip of ammunition in a spray toward his two mounted comrades.

One man twisted back and went down, falling awkwardly sideways from his horse as the gun's chatter stopped and the faint echoes died in the surrounding trees. The other dropped his horse's reins and grabbed at his shoulder but did not fall. He also made no aggressive move, and therefore stayed alive.

The horses tossed their heads, making uneasy noises, but did not flee; the machine-pistol was much quieter than the submachine gun, and perhaps these animals were accustomed to loud noises, such as screams and clashing steel.

Still moving entirely automatically, Slant snapped the empty clip out of the machine pistol and flung it aside, then shoved the gun back into his vest and pulled out the snark. He moved forward, cautiously approaching the downed spearman; one foot held down the man's right wrist as he looked the bandit over, carefully casting a glance at the other two every few seconds.

There was no hope for the bandit, and no further danger; the bullet had gone through his throat and hit his spine. He was in shock and had lost a great deal of blood, and had no chance of survival without immediate hospitalization—which he wasn't going to receive out in the woods of a backwater planet. His eyes were wide and staring, his breath labored and bubbling with blood; Slant stepped away. There was nothing to be done for him except perhaps to finish him quickly, and he didn't want to take the time for that just now, while there were two more enemies to attend to.

He turned to the horses. The man who had stayed astride stared at him, still clutching his shoulder, and Slant ordered him, "Don't move. Just stay right where you are and I won't hurt you."

The man nodded, but Slant was still careful to stay well out of reach and keep him under observation as he moved around the horses to where the other man had fallen.

A lucky shot had gotten him through the heart; he was already dead. Slant pried the reins from his hand, then made a quick scan of the surrounding forest, peering up the road in both directions and seeing nothing. There was no sign of further reinforcements, and these three were defeated, two dead and one prisoner; the battle was over. He turned back toward the lone survivor, snark in hand, and allowed the primary personality to return to control.

Slant studied his captive briefly but saw nothing unusual. The man wore leather breeches and a sleeveless canvas shirt; he was short, of medium build, with greasy brown hair and beard.

The only thing out of the ordinary was the trickle of blood that was seeping past his fingers and staining the fabric of his shirt. "Are you all right?" Slant asked.

The man's expression changed from wary apprehension to astonishment. "What?" he asked.

"Are you all right? How bad is that wound?"

The bandit looked at the blood. "I don't know." Cautiously, he took his hand away; there was no gush of red. "It doesn't look too bad; I don't think the artery has been cut."

"Have you got any bandages?"

"No."

"We'll have to improvise, then." He fitted actions to his words, rummaging through a pack strapped behind an empty saddle until he found something made of a suitable fabric. He hacked off a strip, partly tearing it and partly cutting with his knife, and passed it to the bandit.

He took it but said, "I can't bandage it myself; I can't reach it with both hands."

"Oh. All right, get off the horse and I'll help you."

He was unable to dismount unassisted, as well, and Slant helped him to the ground, then tied the rough bandage in place.

When it was on as well as the two of them could manage, the bandit seated himself on a pile of leaves, looked up at Slant, and said, "Thank you."

"You're welcome."

"I thought you were going to kill me."

"If you'd tried to attack me I would have had to kill you, as I did your companions."

The bandit thought that that was phrased rather oddly but let it pass. "What are you going to do with me now?"

Slant sat down and said, after a pause, "I haven't decided."

"You aren't going to kill me?"

"No, of course not. I don't like killing people. I don't do it if I can help it."

"Are you going to let me go?"

"I suppose I am; I don't want to keep you a prisoner forever." He looked at the three animals quietly cropping grass at the roadside, and added, "I'll keep your horse, though, and any money you've got."

"Why? What do you need with three horses? You can take the other two, but why take mine?"

"I'm making a rather long trip, and I don't have money of my own; I'll probably have to sell one or two of the horses to buy supplies along the way."

"What's to become of me, then?"

"I haven't the faintest idea."

"How can I be a bandit without a horse?"

Slant looked at him curiously. "You plan to go on as a bandit?"

"What else can I do? It's the only job I've ever had."

"What happens if you run into somebody else with a gun?"

"A what?"

"A gun, a weapon from the Bad Times. I can't be the only person on the planet who has one."

"I never saw one before."

"That doesn't mean there aren't any. If you had seen one you might well be dead by now." He gestured at the two corpses. "They are, after running into me."

"I'll just have to take my chances. I did before. I always knew being a bandit was dangerous work."

"Why do it, then? Why not find an honest job?"

"What sort of a job? I don't know how to do anything but steal."

"You could learn. Find a position as an apprentice somewhere."

"I suppose I could."

"Besides, could you make it as a bandit by yourself? Your companions won't be around to help you any more."

"That's true. I never saw anyone move as fast as you did; you probably could have killed us all even without that gah, or guh, or whatever you called it."

"It's a gun. Yes, I probably could have killed you without it."

"If you are taking my horse, are you going to just leave me here?"

"I hadn't thought about it. If you like you can ride along as far east as the next village."

"That would be Arbauru; if I go there they'll probably hang me."

"They know you there?"

"I've robbed a lot of traders from Arbauru."

"Would they recognize you?"

"I don't know."

"Is there anywhere that you could go where you haven't robbed anyone?"

"Nowhere this side of Praunce, I'm afraid."

"Then you'll just have to take your chances in Arbauru, or else stay here."

The bandit considered for a moment. "They might not know me; the others always did the talking. If I stay here I'll probably starve to death."

"You're coming to Arbauru then?"

"Yes."

"How far is it?"

"Oh, about four hours' ride."

"Good." Slant rose. "Let's go, then."

Chapter Fourteen

R IDING WAS BETTER THAN WALKING, SLANT DECIDED, BUT neither was really a good way to pass the day. His feet stopped hurting, for the most part, though the stirrups banged against his arches, but other parts of his anatomy now took a beating. He had never been an expert rider, or even merely a good one; his training had been based on the assumption that he would only visit civilized planets, where most travel was mechanized. He had been taught the rudiments one afternoon, just in case, but that one day more than fourteen years ago and his brief jaunt with Silner had scarcely been adequate preparation for anything but the gentlest of rides.

Fortunately, the bandits' horses were fairly placid and perfectly willing to plod along at a slow walk, which he could handle. With the passage of time and distance he began to get the hang of coordinating his own movement with that of the horse, minimizing the bruises he had been getting every time his mount stepped over a rock or otherwise deviated from a slow dead-level course. The little he had been taught began to come back—it had been taught consciously, rather than through hypnotic conditioning, since it was considered unimportant—and he picked up a few points from the bandit, who had been riding since infancy.

The bandit's name was Thurrel, Slant learned, and he was eager to talk; he seemed to be very lonely, or perhaps it was a reaction to the deaths of his two comrades. Slant let him talk, and occasionally asked questions, as it seemed a good way to pick up more information about the world he found himself in.

Thurrel had grown up the third son of a blacksmith in a village called Duar, which lay to the northwest of the road they were currently traveling; Duar had become an outpost of the growing nation of Praunce when he was fifteen, and he had run away from home as the result of an argument with his father about whether the new government was a good thing. His father had maintained that it was a very fine thing indeed, as it meant the village would be safe from the raids by bandits and wars with other villages that had plagued it. Trade would flourish and there would be peace and plenty.

Thurrel had disagreed; he didn't like Prauncers because one had cheated him at dice, and he considered them to be thieves and scoundrels who would tax the village into poverty. When he had loudly proclaimed his opinion it led to shouting and eventually to blows, and he had left the village and become a bandit. He had no prospects anyway, being the third son, and thievery seemed as good a life as any other he was likely to find.

Slant asked, out of idle curiosity, who had been right about the rule of Praunce. Thurrel admitted that his father had been closer to the truth—but neither was fully correct. No heavy taxes had been levied nor other great burdens, and trade had improved considerably—which was one reason Thurrel had been able to survive as a bandit—but peace was still a long way off. The towns and villages that had not yet joined Praunce continued to launch raids against those that had, and Praunce's small army could not be everywhere at once. The border was gradually being pushed back, and fewer raids penetrated as far as Duar now.

It sounded to Slant rather as if Praunce, with its empire-

building, was putting an end to the era of city-states on
this planet, much as Rome had on Old Earth three thousand years earlier. If that was the case, the city of Praunce
itself would probably be a major center economically as
well as politically, and would attract people from all over
the continent. Those people would include wizards, probably the best wizards around; there might be some who
were capable of removing the bomb and override from
his skull.

He asked Thurrel how far it was to Praunce, and how
far it was to Teyzha.

Thurrel replied that Praunce was three days' ride to the
east, and he had never heard of Teyzha.

That implied that Teyzha was still a very long way off,
and Praunce a good deal closer. It might be wise to visit
Praunce. Even if he couldn't find a wizard there who
could remove the thermite, he could at least replenish his
supplies, learn more about the local culture, and perhaps
obtain directions to Teyzha. If he simply headed east indefinitely he would eventually find someplace where it
was known, but he might be several hundred kilometers
out of his way by then. Praunce, as a center of trade—
Thurrel assured him it was a center of trade—would be a
likely place to find maps and route information.

"Tell me about Praunce," he said.

"I've never been there, actually. I've heard about it,
of course. It was built on the ruins of a great city, and
began as a city-state like any other, but now its borders
cannot be seen from atop its highest tower—and it has
the highest towers on Dest."

"Are there many wizards there?"

"Not that I know of, but I told you, I've never been
there."

A thought occurred to Slant. "Are there any wizards in
Arbauru?"

"No. I've never seen a wizard. I've heard stories about
them, of course."

Slant dismissed that and returned to his former subject.
"Is there anything special about Praunce? I heard it men-
tioned in Teyzha, yet here you have never heard of
Teyzha, which is a good-sized city itself."

"Praunce is very large, and rules more lands than any other city, as I have said. It's built on ruins, so of course there are a lot of freaks and monsters and stillbirths. There are even said to be dragons about; perhaps that's why it's never been attacked."

"Dragons?"

"So they say."

That interested Slant; were dragons a revived myth, or was there some sort of large indigenous beast that had been given the name?

"What does a dragon look like?"

"I've never seen one."

"What are they said to look like, then?"

"Descriptions vary—and there aren't all that many descriptions, since most people who encounter a dragon up close don't live to describe it. They all agree that they're big and dangerous and they kill people."

"How big are they?"

"The smallest claim I ever heard was twice the size of a horse. Of course, tale-tellers exaggerate."

Slant was well aware of that, and guessed that the described size was closer to an average than a minimum. He said nothing further on the subject, but asked more questions about Praunce instead.

By the time they arrived at the gates of Arbauru, he had detailed instructions for reaching the city and was fairly certain that Thurrel could provide no further useful information about it.

The village was located at the confluence of two good-sized streams, which provided water, transport, and defense on two sides of a triangle. The third side was blocked off by a sturdy wooden palisade. Slant wondered where the village got its food, since there were no surrounding farms and the rivers didn't appear large enough to provide sufficient trade, but then he noticed nets strung across the water. The fishing must be very good indeed, he decided.

The gate was open; a bored guard rhetorically asked their business, and Thurrel replied they sought food and shelter. The guard waved them through, and they rode on into the village.

Slant immediately noticed another source of food; small gardens were everywhere. The streets were narrow paths leading from building to building through a maze of vegetables and fruit trees. Such an arrangement certainly simplified withstanding a siege, he decided, but it was very inconvenient in other regards. What would happen when the population of the village began to crowd out the gardens? The wall had been built across a narrow point between the two streams, just before they diverged widely; it could not easily be moved or extended.

Perhaps they had some method of controlling the size of the population. It was no concern of his, in any case.

Thurrel spotted an inn, where they bought themselves a good and filling meal of fish and fruit. Slant had relented of his original intention of leaving Thurrel penniless, and had instead swapped three of his gold Imperials for the contents of the bandit's purse, a collection of three dozen coins of a dozen different kinds, mostly copper, a few silver. Either gold had more value here than in Awlmei or he had been cheated much worse than he had realized before, because a single gold coin paid for a lavish meal for the both of them and brought a few bits of silver in change. He remarked to Thurrel that the locals seemed to have no objection to foreign currency.

Thurrel shrugged. "Why should they? Money is money. Gold is good anywhere."

"That doesn't seem to be the attitude in Awlmei."

"Then they're fools in Awlmei."

"It must be a nuisance converting the different currencies, though."

"What converting?"

"They don't use the same units everywhere, do they?"

"No, but the weights don't change. They just weigh the coin—or raw metal, if you prefer to pay that way. The problem with raw metal is that you can't be sure it's pure."

"Are all the coins pure?"

"Certainly. See there?" He held out a copper coin, and Slant looked closely at the writing on it. There was an emblem resembling a coronet around a tower, surrounded by the legend "Certified in Praunce to be pure copper." There was no mention of any number of units, no government motto. The other side of the coin was blank except for a single letter *P*.

He looked through other coins and found the names and seals of various cities and towns, but all simply announced the coins to be pure metal. He discovered that with a little effort he could bend any of them. His Imperials, of course, were not absolutely pure; he wondered if he should mention that fact but decided against it, and went on eating his meal without further comment.

When he had finished he sat back for a moment, gazing out the window of the inn at the fruit trees that shaded it. He felt good, contented and relaxed; it was an unfamiliar sensation. He relished it for a moment, then reminded himself that he still had a long way to travel, even if he was only going to Praunce instead of Teyzha, and that there was no sense in wasting the few remaining hours of daylight. He had no intention of staying the night at the inn in Arbauru; that would cost money. He would find somewhere to camp again. He felt himself quite capable of dealing with anything he might run across, be it bad weather, more bandits, or even a dragon—whatever dragons were.

"I'll be going now, Thurrel." He noticed the bandage on the man's shoulder and remarked, "You should have that wound looked at by someone who knows about such things; it's not a very serious injury, but it could get infected."

Thurrel glanced at his shoulder and replied, "I will. Thank you for treating me with such kindness; it's more than I could have expected."

"Will you be staying here, or do you still think you may go back to your old occupation?"

"I don't know. This looks like a pleasant enough place, I have to admit; I'll give it a try."

"Good." Slant rose and left the inn, feeling pleased that he had not had to kill Thurrel and that he had apparently convinced the man to give up banditry, perhaps saving other lives. He mounted his chosen horse, the largest of the three, and rode out the gate, leading the other two.

Before he had gone half a dozen kilometers he found himself wishing Thurrel were still with him. The bandit was the first human being he had been able to hold a casual conversation with since he left Mars, and he had enjoyed it far more than he had realized; for the first time in years he was aware how lonely his life was, since he finally had something to compare it to.

There were supposed to be things that prevented him from feeling lonely, he reminded himself; his body chemistry was carefully regulated, his mind controlled by hypnotic suggestion. He was not supposed to need or want human companionship.

Assuring himself of that seemed to relieve a little of the sadness he felt, and he told himself that he had only thought he felt lonely, that he had only remembered what loneliness was like rather than actually experiencing it.

It occurred to him that perhaps the mechanisms that controlled his emotions were beginning to break down; he knew they were not designed to last forever. He had been able to remember his name any number of times, and there had been that suspicious failure of his training while attempting to evade pursuit in the Teyzhan palace—though that might have had something to do with wizardry, one way or another.

It didn't really matter, anyway; after all, with the computer down, he no longer needed to be lonely. He could make friends if he chose, live among ordinary people.

Of course, that assumed he couldn't get the starship back into usable shape. Or did it? Perhaps he could take others with him if and when he left this planet. It might be difficult finding people who wanted to go, though, and he was unsure how many people the ship could support. It could certainly handle two, as he knew it was equipped for taking and escorting a prisoner if necessary.

He tried to imagine what it would be like to be back aboard ship, with himself setting the course instead of the computer, with someone else aboard.

He was still trying to imagine it, and failing, as he made camp and settled down for the night two hours later.

Chapter Fifteen

H E HAD REMEMBERED TO SET HIMSELF A TIME WHEN going to sleep, and therefore woke at dawn, just in time to see the first light of morning find its way, green and gold and pink, through the leafy treetops.

The morning was just a trifle cooler than the morning before, which had been cooler than its predecessor; he was unsure if this was simply a quirk of the weather or if the summer was really ending. It made very little difference. He could handle a little cold weather, especially now that he had the horses and supplies he had taken from the bandits. The only thing that would even slow him up measurably would be a real snowstorm, an event that must surely still be weeks, if not months, away—and even if a snowstorm struck, he would just take shelter in a village or city. He had all the time he needed. Without the computer hounding him, he could wait out anything. He was still young, despite the fourteen years—fifteen, including basic training and so forth—spent in the military.

It might almost turn out that his wandering damnation had been worth the years it cost; after all, he was free now, and alive, which might well not have been had he stayed on Old Earth. Leaving aside the three-century time difference—obviously he would not have lived three hundred years—it was extremely unlikely he would have survived to his current physiological age of thirty-three. If the D-series itself hadn't gotten him, the inevitable aftermath of the collapse of civilization might have.

Instead, he was alive and well, albeit on a backward and alien planet, and possessed of several valuable resources: his strength, speed, and training; the horses and supplies that he had acquired; and a starship that might be available someday for his own personal use.

It was going to be a good day, he decided. He ran through the stretching exercises taught him on Mars fourteen years ago, as he had almost every time he awoke aboard his ship, then mounted and headed east. Praunce was less than three days away; in seventy-two hours—no, sixty hours, with the shorter days—he might no longer have that infernal thermite bomb in his skull. That was a truly wonderful thought, and he savored it at length.

He paused briefly at midday, and ate a good-sized meal of dried fruit and salted meat from the supplies that had been in the bandits' packs; he knew that his ship's stores would keep indefinitely, while this other food might not, so he was using it up first. Besides, it tasted better.

He had finished and was about to remount his horse when a distant cry distracted him; he turned and looked westward in time to see a dark shape plummet from the sky and vanish amid the trees.

Some sort of large bird, he decided, probably a bird of prey attacking something he hadn't seen. It was nothing that concerned him. He swung into the saddle and rode on.

Approximately twenty minutes later his horse slowed its gait, unbidden; Slant was instantly wary. Had it detected something ahead it didn't like? Had it smelled something, perhaps? He had no idea what might lurk in these woods; just because he had not yet encountered any predators except humans, that didn't mean there weren't any.

His mount tried to stop completely, but Slant would not allow that; he urged it forward, giving an encouraging yank to the other horses' lead ropes as well. He drew his machine-pistol from his pocket, holding it loosely in his right hand while his left held the reins.

The stretch of road he was on described a reverse curve, turning first right and then back toward the left before the next straight section, and as he rounded the second bend he saw the thing asleep beside the road, on the right, its tail curling halfway across the highway. He guessed immediately that this was one of the "dragons" Thurrel had spoken of.

The beast was immense; Slant could not see its full size, curled up as it was, but its unmoving head appeared to be a good two meters from the base of the skull to the tip of the snout. Its body did not seem quite as large, proportionately, but was certainly large enough to deserve extremes of caution and respect.

It was the size that convinced Slant it was a dragon, nothing else, because the creature was not reptilian at all. It resembled a cat of some kind, save that its mottled hide was almost hairless; it had fangs that would do justice to a saber-tooth tiger. The shape of its head was distinctly feline, but it had no visible ears, which gave it a certain wrongness. Its black-spotted pink-and-brown skin had a raw, unhealthy look.

He wondered how such a thing could exist, even on a planet like this one, and remembered that Thurrel had spoken of freaks, monsters, and stillbirths as commonplace in Praunce, which had been built on ruins. The ruins must have been left after a nuclear attack, saturated with hard radiation; how could people have been foolish enough to live in such a place?

Furthermore, how much lingering radioactivity could there still be after three hundred years? He refused to believe that a thing like this dragon was an actual viable mutation, breeding true after three centuries; what could the first of its kind have bred with? He knew enough genetics to be certain that the odds against two such creatures occurring at once and both being fertile were absolutely astronomical. And nothing so nearly feline could reproduce asexually. Besides, Thurrel had spoken of strange births as a continuing phenomenon. There must still be a very high level of radiation.

He vaguely recalled a briefing on enhanced radiation weapons and government policy toward enemy territory, and decided that he shouldn't have been surprised. He began wondering about the local life expectancy, fertility levels, and cancer rates—and about his own life expectancy if he stayed around. He wished he had the computer available to measure just how much radiation he was exposing himself to. He knew that the equipment in his body included radiation counters, but the data were only accessible through the computer.

His horse did not want to go closer to the dragon; it made this known by planting its hoofs firmly and refusing to take another step. He could hear its breathing, rough and harsh, and sensed that it was on the verge of panic. Fortunately, even in its terror it had enough sense not to make unnecessary noise—or perhaps it was frightened beyond being able to make noise.

That was inconvenient. He had been lucky enough to come across the creature while it was asleep, and his best chance for safely continuing his journey was to go around it before it awoke. If it had the habits of lesser felines, it could wake up at any moment. Therefore, every delay increased the risk.

He wore no spurs, and his mount refused to respond to his boot heels; he managed to twist the stirrups so that the bottom inside corners dug in as well, and thereby coaxed the horse into taking a few more steps before it froze again.

He considered dismounting and leading the three horses past, but he was unsure he could hold and control them. If he stayed astride, he would not lose all three, at any rate; the other two might flee, but wherever the first went he would go as well.

He wondered whether he might do better to backtrack and loop around the dragon or wait until it departed on its own, but he rejected both ideas. He did not know the way well enough to risk leaving the road, and the dragon might not leave for a good long time—or it might smell his horses wherever he chose to wait, and pursue them.

He reached back with his right hand and slapped the horse's rump with the butt of his machine-pistol, and it took another few hesitant steps. He was encouraged; he might coax it past yet. He directed his mount well to the left, along the verge of the highway, and managed to work it along until he was about even with the monster, almost directly across the highway from it, less than five meters away, but within two meters of its tail.

He looked the creature over while waiting for his mount to calm enough for another prodding. The great size, lack of fur and external ears, and oversized fangs were not the only changes from more ordinary felines; even curled up as it was, Slant could see that the creaure's proportions were wrong, its head too large for its body, its legs thick and awkward. He wondered what it would look like in motion but was not foolish enough to risk waking it. He glanced back at the other two horses, which had so far followed without much resistance; as he did, he heard a call from somewhere overhead.

"Slant of Teyzha! Is that you? Are you there? Slant?"

It was a woman's voice, high-pitched and piercing. He made no effort to recognize it and paid no attention at all to what it said; he was too busy watching the dragon, which began to stir.

He gave his mount a sharp, sudden slap on the rump with the trailing ends of the reins; the frightened animal responded by rearing up, then plunging forward and charging down the road at full gallop, past the dragon and away. Slant did not mind in the least that he found himself clinging for his life, jarred violently up and down. Several items fell from his pockets as the horse leaped a fallen branch and came down still running, but he did not worry about what he had lost. He was gratified to hear the galloping hoofs of the other two horses close behind, and to see that the lead-ropes were still secured to the back of his saddle.

Somewhere behind him he heard tree branches breaking; he assumed it was the dragon's doing until the woman's voice called again.

"Help! Slant, help me!"

Cursing in three languages, Slant struggled to rein in his mount. He had no idea what was going on behind him, and couldn't get a good look while the horse was galloping.

The horse was in no mood to slow down, but eventually it gave in to his brutal yanking on the bit and came to an uneasy halt, allowing Slant to look back up the road.

A girl was lying on her back in the middle of the road, the dragon standing over her, looking at her curiously. Slant was tempted to turn and flee, it being none of his business, but he recognized the girl as Ahnao, the wizard's apprentice he had taken hostage in Awlmei. That explained how she knew his name. It did not explain what she was doing there. Had something happened to his ship? Had the wizards of Awlmei reconsidered their sentence? Was his banishment voided, or had they perhaps decided to kill him after all?

He had to know what was going on; the machine-pistol still in his hand, he dismounted and ran at the monster, shouting.

The dragon, or the cat, or whatever it was, had been watching the girl, waiting for her to make a move. Had she moved, it would doubtlessly have pounced, in the tradition of cats everywhere, or perhaps just batted at her with a paw. Even a tap from a paw would put an end to any attempt at flight; it would probably mash her flat. Slant's shouting distracted it only momentarily; it glanced in his direction, apparently decided he was harmless, and then, intent on its chosen prey, turned back to Ahnao.

As he came within range, Slant raised his pistol and fired, still running. The single shot hit the dragon squarely in the head.

That distracted it from Ahnao but did little else; either the bullet had failed to penetrate the skull or it was too small to do any significant damage once it had penetrated. A small dribble of blood appeared, but that did not seem to inconvenience the monster as it glanced up again at this new annoyance. Except for its head, it did not move; Ahnao did not move at all.

Slant was only a few meters away now; he took aim and emptied the rest of the clip across the dragon's head and chest, in a diagonal from the right eye to where he estimated the heart to be.

The monster did not ignore that; it screamed, more like a bird of prey than any cat, and rose from its crouch as blood seeped from a dozen wounds. Ahnao was carelessly kicked aside as it charged toward its attacker.

The instant it became clear that the thing was attacking him, Slant slipped easily into his warrior self. He watched calmly as the monster came at him, and at the optimum moment he dove sideways out of its path.

It whirled with incredible speed, froze for an instant, and prepared to pounce. Slant got a good clear look at its thick, short legs and long, heavy body, and the blood streaking its hide and dripping from the neat dotted line across its face and chest. One bullet had damaged an eye but not ruined it; it could apparently see as well as ever, though the injury must have stung. Other bullets had torn into its muzzle, its lower jaw, and its chest; none had touched its neck. The neck might prove a vulnerable spot, then, Slant told himself.

He rolled out of the path of its second lunge, easily avoiding it by watching the tension in its leg muscles, so that he began moving at the same instant it did. It was obvious by now that the machine-pistol was not the optimal weapon against the creature, even had he cared to take the time to reload; he thrust the gun into its pocket and reached for his snark.

It wasn't there.

He had dropped it, probably during that mad gallop. His best weapon was gone. The dragon was turning, lashing its tail, preparing for another lunge; he did not have time to reload the machine-pistol. He found the hand laser, still securely in its place, and drew that instead.

The creature did behave like a cat in several ways, but it did not move like a cat; it was not quick and graceful, but slow and lumbering for the most part, though it showed occasional flashes of surprising speed, particularly in stopping and turning. Its charges were more reminiscent of a rhino or an elephant than of a cat's pounce; the short, thick legs it needed to support its great weight made that inevitable.

The third attack came, and he dove aside again. He had no desire to keep this up for very long, however, as he had no idea whether the monster would tire before he did. Rather than stop and wait for the next attack, he kept moving and leaped for a low-hanging limb of a nearby maple tree. A thing of that size and bulk could not possibly climb or jump well in a gravity so close to that of Old Earth.

He had chosen the maple from the several trees within reach because it looked sturdy and easy to climb. In general, he recalled from both basic training and a chance fragment of childhood memory, maples were good climbing trees once you got started.

This one was no exception; he made his way upward easily, clambering from branch to branch, until he was about ten meters off the ground. The monster had located him again and watched his ascent.

A cat, Slant knew, would sit back on its haunches and consider the situation; he watched with satisfaction as the monster sank to the ground and stared contemplatively up at him. It was not designed for sitting, its legs were far too short in proportion to its body; it measured perhaps two meters from shoulder to paw, and at least eight meters from shoulder to tail.

It settled itself comfortably and tried to wash its wounds between wary glances at its treed quarry; the washing was not a success, as its stubby paws could not reach far enough. Still, it went through the instinctive motions.

Slant used this brief respite to reload his gun, check over the laser, and study the situation below. Ahnao lay unmoving at the roadside thirty meters away; that accidental blow of the dragon's paw must have knocked her unconscious, Slant thought, or at least dazed her badly. More than a hundred meters in the opposite direction his horses were milling about uncertainly, but the dragon paid them no attention; probably they were too far away to interest it. The creature itself was directly beneath him, waiting for him to come down.

Halfway between the tree and his horses he saw sunlight glinting on metal; that was undoubtedly his lost snark.

The laser was in good working order; he tested it by cutting through a branch near the one he was perched on. It took several seconds to cut the limb free; when at last it fell, it struck the dragon full on the head and bounced harmlessly to one side. The creature looked up at him accusingly. Its face was very expressive, easily as expressive as any housecat's, despite its huge and hairless head.

This presented a target, and Slant did not miss the opportunity. He fired the laser at full intensity directly into the monster's already damaged right eye. It howled, a sound that hurt Slant's ears, and turned its head away. He changed his target accordingly and focused the beam on the back of its neck.

There was a faint smell of cooking meat; the dragon growled and turned back, fangs bared, and the beam caught it in the eye again. It tried to close the eye, but the beam cut through the eyelid. It backed off a few steps, while Slant kept the laser aimed directly at the center of the eye.

He could see a wound now, and thin fluid dribbled from it, mixing with blood from the bullet wounds. The creature had lost a great deal of blood, he noticed; it formed puddles on the road and was caked in the corners of eye, nose, and mouth.

It continued to back slowly away, then paused, at about what Slant judged to be the limit of the laser's effective range. He guessed that the right eye must be almost completely useless by this time in any case, and switched the beam to the left. Although he doubted it would do much damage at this distance, he hoped to blind the creature at least temporarily and perhaps drive it away.

The monster screamed, the same bird-of-prey cry it had used before, and charged forward at full speed, slamming its several tons against the base of the tree.

The blow shook the tree, and Slant clutched at neighboring branches in an instinctive reaction far more basic than any conditioning he had had; in doing so he lost his grip on the laser. It slammed against a limb, then fell, bouncing from branch to branch, before lodging in a crotch a few meters below, in easy reach of the enraged monster. Slant immediately dismissed any thought of retrieving it.

He had now lost two of his weapons, laser and snark, though both were in plain sight. That left the machine-pistol, which had already proven ineffective. Nonetheless he drew it, rammed in another clip, and fired three quick shots at the dragon.

As before, the bullets did little but anger the creature; it smashed at the trunk of the tree with a forepaw. This time Slant was more nearly ready, and kept hold of the gun.

He continued firing, emptying the rest of the clip; he succeeded in wounding the monster, leaving streams of blood all over its back as well as its face and chest, but not in deterring it. It was now absolutely determined to get him, one way or another. He released and dropped the spent clip, and reached in his pocket for more ammunition.

He found none. He checked other pockets; all were equally unhelpful, and he recalled that more than one object had been dropped when he lost the snark.

He was unarmed. At least, he was unarmed by his standards. He did still have a large knife on his belt. He drew it and looked at it carefully.

It was a good knife, a steel blade more than twenty centimeters long and a short, heavy hilt. It was not intended for slaying dragons, but it was all he had.

He looked down. The dragon was beginning to look unsteady; it was backing away from the tree, squinting upward through its one good—or relatively good, as the laser might have done some damage before he lost it—eye. There was no point in waiting. He pushed out through the leaves and leaped from his branch, landing full on the monster's back.

The creature, one-eyed, weak from loss of blood, and half mad with pain and rage, immediately whirled, trying to reach back with its claws or teeth to dislodge him. He avoided being flung headlong by plunging the knife into the dragon's side with one hand and grabbing a handful of rough, loose skin with the other.

The beast screamed with pain as the knife went in; it paused in its frantic movement, as if trying to think, and Slant took the opportunity to pull the knife free and to plunge it into the monster's neck. There was a gout of blood from the first wound when the blade came free, and as it sank into the creature's neck the dragon went into convulsions. Slant had no chance of holding on; he was flung aside, leaving the knife where it was.

He managed to land rolling, so that he was not seriously injured, but the left side of his body from shoulder to ankle was bruised by the impact. He had missed a tree by less than a meter.

When he stopped rolling he lay motionless for a moment, feeling his body, making certain no permanent damage had been done; then he turned and watched the dragon.

It was thrashing about, trying to get claws or teeth onto the hilt of the knife embedded in its neck. As he watched its struggles grew steadily weaker. Blood was seeping from the wound in ever-increasing streams as the creature's twisting enlarged the opening made by the blade. Slant pitied the poor thing; it had been following its instincts, nothing more.

He rose carefully to his feet; the dragon paid no attention. If it could see him at all, it was more interested in its own injuries.

His body hurt where he had fallen, and his fingers and forearms stung from the shock of being wrenched away from his hold on the beast's back, but he was otherwise intact. He moved around the dragon in a wide circle, toward his snark; he did not like being unarmed. If the thing did attack him again he wanted to be able to defend himself, and if it settled down again he wanted to be able to put it out of its misery. He did not like seeing it suffer and was reasonably certain that it could not survive the wounds he had inflicted.

The thrashing stopped; the monster lay still on one side, panting heavily. It had finally managed to dislodge the knife from its throat, and blood poured from the open gash the blade had left. Its good eye, a baleful green-gold orb, stared at Slant, but the creature was obviously unable to do him further harm. The other eye was an oozing ruin.

Slant reached the fallen branches his horse had jumped and found his snark and several clips of pistol ammunition scattered about; he retrieved all he could find, then looked back at the dragon. It was lying almost still, moved only by shallow breathing; it had tried to close its eyes, and the good one was shut, but the lid of the ruined one had been stopped by clotted blood and torn tissue while still halfway open.

He tested the snark on nearby leaves; it still worked, raising a cloud of dust and leaving a hole.

Cautiously, he approached the dying dragon. It showed no sign that it was aware of him as he positioned himself a little over a meter from its head and used the snark to cut a bloody hole through its skull and well into its brain.

The dragon was unquestionably dead.

The sound of clapping came from somewhere to one side; Ahnao's voice exclaimed, "That was wonderful!"

Chapter Sixteen

SLANT STARED AT HER FOR A MOMENT. SHE WAS STILL lying at the roadside where the monster had knocked her, applauding enthusiastically.

"It was wonderful!" she repeated.

"No, it wasn't," Slant replied. "It was hideous. What are you doing here?" He did not move from where he stood, the snark ready in his hand, as the girl rose and ran up to him.

She reached out as though to embrace him; he raised the snark threateningly, and she stopped a couple of meters away. Her expression was surprised and hurt.

"What are you doing here?" he demanded again.

"I followed you."

"That's obvious. Why?"

"Why what?"

"Why did you follow me? Why did you wake the dragon?"

"I'm sorry; I didn't see it." She looked genuinely contrite. "I didn't mean to endanger you."

"You forced me to kill it to save you."

"I'm sorry, really. I didn't mean any harm."

"Why did you follow me?"

"I . . . I didn't know what else to do. With my uncle Kurao dead, there was no one to take care of me in Awlmei."

"What about Furinar?"

"He doesn't like me. Besides, he has a family of his own."

"Then why not apprentice yourself to some other wizard?"

"I don't know any other wizards."

"Why can't you take care of yourself? You're a wizard, aren't you, even if you're just an apprentice?"

"I couldn't do that!"

"Why not?"

"I just couldn't!" She once again looked surprised and hurt, as if Slant was being purposely cruel in asking her such a thing.

He was silent for a moment, considering what to ask next.

"Why come after me, though? What have I to do with you?"

"You killed my uncle."

"Are you after revenge, then?"

"Oh, no, nothing like that! But he was my master, and you killed him."

Slant was afraid he was beginning to understand. "What has that to do with it?"

She looked at the ground, abashed. "You're—you're responsible for leaving me unprotected, you see."

"Am I to be your new protector, then? Did I win you by killing him, as the spoils of victory?"

"I don't know; something like that, I guess."

He stared at her in disbelief. "Are you serious?"

She nodded.

"Do you plan to stay with me, then?"

She nodded again. "If you'll let me."

"What if I don't let you?"

"I don't know." She looked up at him. "Oh, please, though, let me stay with you! I don't have anywhere else to go!"

"You could go back to Awlmei where you belong. Aren't you the heir to Kurao's shop? Couldn't you do something with that?"

"You can have it, if you like."

"I don't want it!"

"Neither do I. I want to go with you."

"You don't know where I'm going."

"That doesn't matter."

Utterly confounded, Slant said nothing more but just stared at her. He did not particularly want her around. If the computer was still active, it would probably order him to kill her, and he would probably obey one way or another; he was glad that he did not have to. He did not like her, but killing was unpleasant and regrettable, and after all the trouble he had gone to on her behalf in killing the dragon, he preferred not to throw his efforts away.

He wondered if she was, as he had first thought, acting on behalf of the wizards of Awlmei. It certainly made more sense than her own bizarre explanation—or non-explanation. Perhaps she had been sent to spy on him, and was much smarter than she appeared.

He had no objection to being spied on; he was doing no one harm. If she was a spy, and he sent her back, that might arouse suspicion and provoke further annoyances. She might be useful to have around; even an apprentice wizard was not something to be taken lightly, he was sure. He was in some degree responsible for her plight—though it was none of his doing that she felt herself incapable of living her life without some sort of protector.

If she were a spy, she had probably been chosen on the theory that her sex would tend to allay suspicion; primitive people often had peculiar ideas about the relationship between men and women. She was attractive, he supposed; with his hormones strictly regulated, he had to judge such matters entirely on a theoretical basis. Had he possessed a normal male sex drive he would almost certainly have gone quietly insane or gotten himself killed long ago; fourteen years of celibacy were not a healthy thing.

She probably expected her appearance to influence his decision, then, and if she had been sent, the wizards would expect the same. He would also be expected to consider her harmless, since in a pretechnological culture such as this women were not physically suited to be warriors and were therefore considered unfit for any sort of fighting at all.

If she were a spy, it would be in his best interests to allow her to accompany him. If she were not a spy, though, she would be a nuisance, and he did not really believe her to be anything other than what she said she was.

What would happen if he sent her back? He didn't

know. It was possible she would pretend to go, then continue following him, at a distance. That would not do; he preferred to have her in sight. She might actually go back to Awlmei, but what would become of her after that he had no idea. It was possible she really was incapable of surviving on her own and would either die or find herself another protector, perhaps one less benevolent than Kurao or himself.

What would become of her if she accompanied him?

Well, he would probably be able to protect her as well as anyone could, though he couldn't continue her training in wizardry. She would tag along, eating his food and drinking his water. She might try to seduce him, but that would be nothing more than a minor nuisance. She might prove useful, since she was able to fly, however badly—he was fairly certain that it was she he had seen fall from the sky earlier. If he got the starship repaired and left the planet, he could take her with him for company. However foolish she might seem, she was a source of human companionship and professed to be willing to accompany him wherever he went.

His growing loneliness decided him, finally. The computer was gone, Thurrel was gone, and he did not want to be alone. He could always get rid of her later, one way or another.

"All right. Come help me with the horses."

"Oh, thank you!" She smiled gleefully and looked ready to jump with delight.

It took several minutes to round up all three horses; they had not fled far but were still nervous, and Slant undoubtedly smelled of dragon. He realized he had blood on his boots, and determined to clean it off at the first opportunity. Ahnao was completely unfamiliar to the horses, so they were wary of her. She professed to know nothing about animals, and her behavior bore out her statement, so Slant had her do nothing more than hold the tethers while he caught the horses one by one by himself.

When all three were collected, Slant fulfilled his promise to clean his boots, wiping off every trace of dragon's blood. He debated retrieving his knife; at first he had almost decided to leave it, when he recalled that his laser was also still back by the dragon, caught in the tree. He did not want to leave the laser; aside from the inconvenience of lighting fires without it, it might be found by a native, and that could be dangerous.

Since he had to go back for that in any case, he found and cleaned his knife as well. He made a quick search for anything else he might have lost but found nothing. With the laser, snark, machine-pistol, and several clips of ammunition back in his pockets and the knife back in the sheath on his belt he felt much more secure.

Ordinarily, if he killed an animal, he took meat from it to augment his supplies; this time, however, he decided against it. The dragon did not look like good eating; the splotchy hide and lack of hair gave it a distinctly unhealthy appearance. Besides, he thought that cat meat was not exactly a delicacy.

When this had been taken care of, he returned to where Ahnao waited with the horses. He had retained the saddles on all three, simply because the easiest way to transport the saddles was to keep them strapped in place and he had not wanted to abandon anything of value; therefore, he went directly to his own mount, the largest of the three, swung himself into the saddle, and motioned for Ahnao to do the same.

She hesitated, unsure of what to do.

"Take the black," he suggested. The black mare had been Thurrel's mount, and was the more placid of the remaining two.

She cast him a worried glance, then walked around to the mare's side.

"Untie the reins from the lead-rope first," he suggested.

"Oh," she replied. She did as she was told, and then returned to the horse's side. The animal stood quietly waiting. Ahnao stood for a moment, holding the reins, and then asked, "How do I get on it?"

"Don't you know how to ride?"

"No."

"You've never ridden a horse?"

"No, never. I grew up in the city; I never had to."

"Would you prefer to fly, then?"

"You can't fly!"

"No, I'm going to ride."

"Couldn't we just walk?"

"I'm going to ride. You can ride, or walk, or fly, as you please. I doubt you'll be able to keep up on foot."

"I wouldn't be able to keep up flying, either. It's hard! I fell six times trying to catch up with you!"

"You'll have to ride, then."

She wailed, "But I don't know how!"

"You'll learn. First, get on the horse."

"How?"

"Grab the saddlehorn with your left hand—that's right, that thing sticking up at the front. Put your right hand across the saddle to steady you. Now jump up and put your left foot into the stirrup, and then throw your right leg across the back."

Ahnao kicked futilely at air.

"No, jump, damn it!"

She tried again and managed to set the stirrup swinging wildly. The horse snorted but did not pull away.

"Steady the stirrup and try again."

Ahnao did as she was told, and managed to hook her left foot in place; her right leg, unfortunately, bumped against the horse's flank and did not go over. She caught herself as she started to fall backward, keeping her foot in the stirrup, and with considerable effort managed to work her leg over the saddle where it belonged. Finally, with what Slant thought to be absurd difficulty, she got herself astride and upright.

Slant said nothing, but watched her to make sure she was securely in place. She shifted about, trying to get comfortable, then noticed his gaze and burst out, "It's not easy!"

"Certainly it is! I haven't done much riding either, and I'm not having any trouble."

"You're bigger than I am!"

This was true; Slant was almost 190 centimeters tall, while Ahnao was scarcely 150. He pointed out, "My horse is bigger. Besides, you should know how to ride."

"Why? I'm a city girl, not a trader or a farmer!"

Slant saw no point in explaining that everyone should

know the basic skills of his or her culture; instead, he dropped the subject and asked, "How did you find me?"

"By magic, of course."

"You flew the entire distance here from Awlmei?"

"Almost; I rested sometimes and walked a little way. I'm not very good at flying; I fell a lot."

"You fell right in front of the dragon, then?"

"My concentration slipped when you started to ride off like that."

"I did that because your idiot shouting woke the dragon."

"I'm sorry; I didn't see it."

"How could you miss something that size?"

"I wasn't looking; I was following you."

The conversation didn't seem to be getting anywhere, so Slant turned forward again and urged his horse onward. After a moment Ahnao managed to get her own mount moving and followed him. The third horse's lead-rope was once again secured to the saddle of Slant's mount, so that it, too, came along.

Slant glanced back every so often and called instructions to Ahnao on handling her horse. She was not a particularly apt pupil but did gradually pick it up. By midafternoon she was doing well enough to come up beside Slant and talk to him.

"Aren't you glad to have me here?" she asked.

"No, not really." He saw no point in flattering her, and so far his impression of her was not favorable; her main character trait seemed to be incompetence. He wondered how she had survived as long as she did, and managed to locate and pursue him.

"Aren't you lonely, though, traveling alone?"

"I was carefully chosen and trained to not be bothered by loneliness. I spent fourteen years with no company except a computer."

"You must want company."

"You're right, I do like to have company. I'm not sure that I'll like yours, though."

"What's wrong with me?" She sounded both hurt and outraged.

Slant did not think it would be a good idea to answer that and said nothing.

Ahnao was insistent. "What's the matter with me?" she demanded.

Silence was not going to serve, it was clear, and Slant had never liked lying. It almost always complicated matters. Furthermore, he was already beginning to wish he had sent Ahnao back to Awlmei after all; she was not proving to be a pleasant companion. Therefore, he told her the truth.

"You're stupid."

"I'm not stupid!"

"Do you call falling out of the sky onto a dragon intelligent?"

"It was an accident!"

"It was a stupid accident."

Ahnao fumed silently for a few seconds, then said, "You're not so smart either; you're the one who had all your machines turned off and wound up exiled."

Slant looked at her in surprise. "You're right," he admitted, "I was stupid, too."

"Hmph!" She snorted, and they rode on in silence.

They made poor time, as Ahnao objected to any pace other than a slow walk, so that when they made camp at sunset they had covered approximately half the distance Slant would have expected. He hoped that this would not cause sufficient delay to make Thurrel's estimate of a three-day ride to Praunce incorrect, but he suspected that it would.

Ahnao was not pleased when she discovered that they would be sleeping on bare ground, unsheltered; she had expected to stay at an inn somewhere, or at the very worst in a tent. She had had enough of bare ground while traveling alone, before she caught up with the cyborg. She complained that she hurt from riding and needed a soft bed, and for the first time Slant sympathized with one of her opinions. He had become more or less accustomed to riding all day long, so that he was no longer actually in pain, but his thighs and lower body were tired and sore, and the thought of a warm soft bed was enticing.

Unfortunately, they had not happened across a village for the last hour or so, so that even had Slant been willing to spend the money, there was nowhere they could go. He explained as much to Ahnao, who remained unconvinced. She did, however, keep further complaints to herself as they ate a meager dinner from his dwindling supplies.

After both had eaten all Slant would allow, he gathered his customary pile of leaves and settled himself down, then told Ahnao, "Make yourself comfortable."

She looked at him oddly, a quizzical look that he could not quite interpret, then lay down beside him, less than a meter away, near enough that Slant could smell her—which was not surprising, since both had been riding all day and had not bathed. She smelled distinctly female. Before he had been cyborged, he thought, he would have found the odor interesting at the very least; now he ignored it.

From somewhere in the depths of his thoroughly trained and conditioned mind arose a warning thought, that he should never sleep that close to another human being who might conceivably be hostile.

He looked at the girl's face and found she was watching him; seeing him look at her, she smiled. He smiled in return.

Moving away would be good tactics ordinarily, he had to admit, but he did not think it would be a good idea in this case. She would be insulted, and there would be arguments and bad feeling. If he was stuck with the girl, he might as well try to get along as well as could be managed.

On the other hand, she hadn't liked being called stupid, but it had not driven her away. She might not be as thin-skinned as she appeared.

He doubted that she was an assassin, however, and if he was to serve as her protector, as she wanted, then the closer he stayed to her the better. This would not have been true in a civilization that used firearms, since it made the two of them a single target, but here, where the most advanced weapon was the sword or perhaps the longbow, it seemed to make sense.

The actual deciding factor was that he was comfortable where he was and didn't want to move. He turned off his smile, closed his eyes, and went to sleep.

Ahnao watched him for a moment; when his breathing told her that he was asleep her own smile vanished, replaced by a slight frown. Vaguely annoyed, she rolled over and closed her eyes.

Slant awoke promptly at sunrise, as he had intended; Ahnao was still sound asleep. He did not bother to disturb her until he had changed clothes and washed himself at the nearby brook; when there was nothing left to do but eat breakfast and be gone, he shook her gently.

She came groggily awake, but said nothing beyond a few vague monosyllables until she had eaten. Then she insisted on bathing, while Slant waited at the camp.

He accepted the delay philosophically; after all, it really made no difference to him how long it took to reach Praunce. A few days either way meant little. It had taken years to go from star to star; why should he suddenly be impatient?

He was usually less irritable in the mornings, anyway.

When the girl came back up the slope from the stream she was wearing the same gray robe, the only garment he had seen her wear, and it occurred to him for the first time that she had not brought any supplies whatsoever, not so much as a pocketknife. She was still thoroughly wet, so that her robe had large dark patches growing wherever it touched her body directly; it clung damply to her hips and breasts.

He had used yesterday's shirt as a towel, then rinsed it out in the stream, wrung it out, and draped it across the top of his pack so that it would be clean enough to wear the next day. His other clothing he had brushed off as best he could, since fur and leather suffered if washed.

Ahnao apparently hadn't thought to wash her robe at all. He considered pointing out the oversight but decided not to. It was her own business, not his. He did not know what the local taboos were regarding discussions of hygiene, and furthermore it would probably start an argument about her intelligence.

They mounted the horses and started off; Ahnao man-

aged to climb into the saddle with slightly less difficulty
this time, though she was still far from quick or graceful
about it. She was still very damp; Slant hoped it wouldn't
bother the horse.

As before, she rode close beside him and kept to a
slow walk. She also made small talk, discussing the
weather, which was sunny and cool, and the trees at
either side of the road. She asked Slant questions about
his past but received only brief and unsatisfactory answers. He asked about her own background, and found
her to be incapable of describing most of what she considered to be a relentlessly ordinary life. He did learn that
she had been apprenticed to Kurao for less than three
months; that surprised him. Though he thought her in-
competent, she had, after all, found and followed him,
and to do that with so little training in magic was fairly
impressive. He also found himself forgiving her some of
her lack of common sense, as she had plainly, until recently, led an extremely sheltered life. Her parents had
been wealthy and overly protective until her father's
business as a grain dealer went bankrupt after some catas-
trophe—probably a fire. While he had tried to recover
financially her mother rapidly drank herself to death; her
father then hanged himself, leaving Ahnao in the care of
her eccentric uncle, the wizard Kurao.

The last few months had not been ordinary, obviously,
but she did not care to speak of them much, and prior
to her father's financial ruin she claimed to have done
nothing of any interest whatsoever. She could not cook,
she could not hunt; when they stopped at noon for lunch
Slant discovered she could not tie a knot well enough
to hold his three exceedingly tame horses.

She could, however, talk endlessly and cheerfully, and
smile at him for hours on end. He found himself smiling
back without meaning to.

He wondered whether some of the regulatory mechanisms in his body were breaking down. He had never
been an emotionless zombie; that was not good for survival. He had, however, been more or less immune to the
automatic social responses of normal humanity. Besides
the obvious sexual reactions, he had also lost the usual

positive emotional response to friendly smiles, slight pupil dilation, pheromones, and other stimuli that help people to like one another—yet here he was enjoying Ahnao's company even though he considered her a useless idiot. Either his initial estimation of her had been unfairly negative as a result of the manner of their meeting, so that he was now reacting appropriately, or his carefully contrived aloofness was coming apart and he was beginning to like her not for what she actually was but because her body was equipped with the right signals.

He wasn't sure whether it made any difference which was true.

By the end of the afternoon Ahnao's riding and self-confidence had improved to the point that the pace had picked up to a normal walk, and Slant had noticed that she had a way of tossing her hair when she was enjoying herself.

As they ate dinner that evening he noticed her watching him steadily, and observed how very big and green her eyes were. He reminded himself that the appearance of large eyes was mostly due to pupil dilation in the poor light in the shade of the trees, and that it was attractive because of an automatic response in the human nervous system. Pupils enlarge slightly when their owner likes or wants what he or she is looking at, and people like to be wanted; that was why dim light had been considered romantic for centuries.

Still, he smiled at her.

When they bedded down for the night she again lay close to him; he was more aware of her than he liked, and found himself wanting to reach out and run a hand along her side. He no longer doubted that the mechanisms that regulated his hormone levels were shot; probably they had shut down at the same time the computer did. He had never known whether they were controlled by the computer or independently; the former now seemed far more likely.

He resisted temptation, refusing to let his glands dominate him. He was rather annoyed to discover they still worked so well after fourteen years. It took him longer than usual to get to sleep.

Chapter Seventeen

THE FOLLOWING DAY HE DECIDED THAT HE WAS PLEASED that his body was returning to normal. After all, he was no longer needed as a military cyborg; the war was long over. There was no reason for him not to lead an ordinary human life, and for that it helped to have ordinary human responses. Sex seemed like an appealing concept.

He still regretted, however, that it was Ahnao he found himself taking an interest in. It was to be expected, since she was the only female he had had any contact with since the computer shut down, but it was still, he thought, unfortunate. He resolved that he would resist any temptation she might offer.

Late that morning, as they topped a rise relatively clear of trees, Slant thought he glimpsed a tower on the horizon. He stopped his mount and peered into the distance.

There was definitely something sticking up to the southeast. He hoped it was Praunce. He was unable to discern details, however, and reluctantly moved on.

When they stopped for their noon meal Slant found that even if Ahnao couldn't cook, hunt, or tie a knot, she could sit gracefully, smile enticingly, and otherwise charm him. She watched his every move with those alluring green eyes; when she moved, he found himself watching the sway of her hips. He had resolved to resist temptation, however, and did the best he could to ignore such attractions.

After they had eaten she managed to get astride her horse with only slight awkwardness; she was learning. Perhaps, Slant thought as they rode on, she wasn't completely hopeless. He asked, abruptly, "Are you proud of yourself?"

"What?" The girl was startled; she had noticed that Slant had grown reluctant to speak to her, and the question was undeniably a strange one to start a conversation with.

"Do you respect yourself?"

Ahnao was still confused. "I think so," she said.

"How can you have any self-respect when you can't do anything useful, can't even take care of yourself?"

"I can take care of myself!"

"Then why are you here with me, instead of back in Awlmei? You weren't taking very good care of yourself running off into the wilderness with no food, no supplies, and no money, and then plopping in front of a dragon."

"I didn't mean that. I know I'm not very good at those sorts of things. I take care of myself, though; I keep myself clean and healthy. I look all right."

"That's just your appearance, though."

"Isn't that what matters for a woman?"

"No."

Ahnao did not reply to that, and Slant lapsed into a sullen silence while the girl turned her attention to the road, the trees, and the horses, rather than trying to figure out this incomprehensible man.

Slant decided that his optimism had been premature; she really was hopeless. He began planning in a halfhearted way to get rid of her. He knew that if he stayed near her he would not be able to keep his hands off her forever, particularly since she gave every appearance of welcoming his advances. His self-respect would not allow him to make love to a woman he thought so little of, he told himself.

He wondered whether it might have been easier if she were to make overt advances; he could refuse them and put a quick end to the matter, at least temporarily. Unfortunately, she did not seem to have any intention of making direct advances; her culture apparently insisted on the male taking the aggressive role.

He should, he thought, be able to get rid of her somehow in Praunce; he would find some man willing to take care of her, perhaps a wizard who would take her as an apprentice. Then he wouldn't have to worry about her any more. His best estimate was that they would reach

Praunce the following day. One more day of celibacy could scarcely be too much to ask of himself.

He found himself wondering, though, whether perhaps the regulatory mechanisms had not merely shut down but reversed. Was the urge he felt really just an ordinary sex drive? He knew, intellectually, that it probably was, and after fourteen years and through the haze of conditioning he could not remember what he had felt before he became a cyborg—but it seemed he could think of nothing else, and if that was the normal state of mankind, how did anyone ever get any work done or think about anything important? He began theorizing that his body was overcompensating for fourteen years of restraint.

Around midafternoon, however, something occurred to distract him—they reached the end of the forest.

There was little warning; the trees did not gradually thin out, but stopped short. They could see from the last bend in the road a hundred meters back that there was much more light ahead, implying that the trees no longer shaded the highway, but it was not until they were almost to the line that they were able to see the actual state of affairs.

The forest ended abruptly in a low stone wall and a simple gate across the road; beyond lay open fields extending over the horizon, broken only by sparse rows of young poplars that had apparently been planted as windbreaks. Every meter of cleared land was lush with crops; Slant could make out corn, wheat, and some sort of bean, as well as others he did not recognize. He reined in his horse a dozen meters from the gate and studied the view.

At first, he had noticed only the farms; now he saw two other important features. First, the gate was guarded; men were peering out at him from behind the last of the forest's trees, and at least two had arrows nocked and aimed. Second, the tower he had spotted earlier was now plainly visible on the horizon, not directly ahead but slightly to the left, which was why he had not noticed it immediately. It was not alone; although the one structure stood higher than the others, half a dozen were visible, forming an impressive skyline. He tried to estimate their height but did not arrive at a reasonable guess; he decided that the nearness of the horizon on this planet smaller than Old Earth was responsible for distorting his judgment. Even allowing for that, however, the tallest tower had to be at least seventy or eighty meters high.

He was quite sure that those towers were part of Praunce, and he wondered why he could not see the city proper. The towers, he decided, must be built on a hill, and the city walls and other buildings lower down, so that they remained just below the horizon. The land was not level; there were several valleys and rises between the forest and the city.

That was all matter for later consideration, however; first he had to deal with the guards.

"Hello!" he called out.

A short, stocky man stepped out from behind a tree. "Hello, stranger," he said. "What brings you here?"

"We're just passing through, on our way to Toyzha." That seemed a better explanation than the truth. If he didn't find wizards here who could remove the thermite and the override, it would be the truth.

The guard looked Slant and Ahnao over carefully; Slant noticed that he looked Ahnao over very carefully indeed, and found himself resenting it slightly.

Finally, the guard stepped back and called, "They look all right to me."

Other men stepped out of concealment; one of the archers did not. There were five altogether.

"Do you want to call out a wizard to check?" one asked.

"Why bother? There are only the two of them."

"They could be spies."

"What if they are? That's not our concern. We're not paid to stop spies, just bandits and raiders."

"I wish they would just station a wizard out here; then we wouldn't have to worry." The voice belonged to a new speaker, a youth scarcely out of his teens.

"The wizards have better things to do," answered the short man.

"Oh, let them go," said the only man other than the archer who had not yet spoken. "What harm can one man and his woman do?"

"We should call a wizard out to check," insisted he who had been second to speak.

The debate continued for a moment longer, but was finally settled by a vote of three to one in favor of letting them pass. The archer never spoke a word.

The short spokesman stepped to the roadside and gestured to Slant that he could pass. "Go on, then."

"Thank you," Slant replied. "That is Praunce I see in the distance, then?"

"Yes, of course."

"You are guarding the border?"

"The border? Hligosh, no! You must have crossed the border days ago; it's too long to guard, though there are patrols. We are the inner guard, and this gate marks the city limits. It's been a hundred years since this was the border."

"Oh." Slant did not entirely understand the term "city limits" in this application but saw no reason to bother asking for further explanation. "Thank you." He urged his mount forward; Ahnao and the riderless horse followed.

A few moments later he looked back and saw that four of the five guards were lounging idly by the gate, talking among themselves. The archer had finally lowered his bow and returned the arrow to his quiver but was still standing alertly by the tree, watching Slant and Ahnao ride on.

For most of the next hour they rode on silently between unbroken expanses of green and gold; occasionally Slant noticed small houses in the distance, scattered among the fields, but he saw no other human beings.

In front of them the city of Praunce grew on the horizon; the towers continued to enlarge as they neared, and Slant realized that his original estimate, dismissed as ludicrous, must have been short of the reality. The towers were huge. He now guessed the tallest to be more than a hundred and fifty meters high.

They had still not come in sight of the city wall but the half-dozen towers had been joined by a forest of other buildings, stretching across a good-sized chunk of the horizon. Also, to the south, Slant now noticed a very odd formation. It was too irregular to be man-made, but it seemed unnatural and out of place among the gently rolling hills; it was a great jutting crag that reared up from the earth, its south face a steep slope, its north face an incredible overhang. He was unable to guess its size, but it was obviously huge, as he could see its shadow on the most southerly of Praunce's buildings while the sun was still well up the sky. Its surface appeared smooth, save for an edge that looked knife-sharp between its two faces.

Looking further, he spotted other, smaller outcroppings; the big one was due south of Praunce, as nearly as he could tell, well to the east of his own position, and the others, three at least, were strung out on an arc extending to the southwest from the city. The last was due south of him. Each was roughly triangular, leaning at an apparently impossible angle, but the direction of the lean varied; the one directly to the south had its overhang to the west, and the two in between leaned northwest at differing angles. Studying them, Slant decided that they all lay along a quarter circle, leaning outward. He wondered what freak of seismology could have produced such a thing.

About an hour from the forest and the gate they topped a good-sized rise and found themselves looking down on a small village and presented with an excellent view of a broad, shallow valley. Like the countryside they had been traveling, it was lined thickly with intensively cultivated farmland, dotted with occasional small houses. Unlike the more westerly land, however, it was also dotted with barren patches.

Slant looked at them in puzzlement; some appeared to be bare rock, which seemed odd when surrounded by obviously fertile topsoil, but the majority were even more perplexing in that they shone and glittered in the sun. They were not water, as they did not move at all in the gentle breeze that was blowing from the north; furthermore, the colors were not right for water. Some were shining silver, others glossy black, and at least one was tinted with red.

There was no pattern to them, nor consistency of size; they were scattered about completely at random and ranged from specks of a meter or so to large dead areas dozens of meters across. They appeared to be more common to the south than to the north.

Beyond the far side of the valley, the city of Praunce was finally visible. It began in straggling suburbs that trailed off vaguely into scattered houses; proceeding eastward the streets straightened and widened and the houses grew more numerous, interspersed with other structures. There was an abrupt end to this stage in the form of a high wall of black stone; beyond that, Slant could see only the towers and high buildings that he had been watching for half the day.

He was surprised by two things; first, it was the only community he had seen on this planet that had suburbs outside the walls, and second, the sheer expanse was overpowering. He had been trained in estimating populations, as that was a simple and obvious requirement in a scout, and he placed Praunce in the half-million-to-a-million range—much larger than he had expected to find on a barbaric planet.

It was still a long way off, as the valley was indeed broad; he did not think he had any chance of reaching the city before dark. That being the case, he turned his attention to the village on the slope before him. It would not do to sleep by the roadside here. There were no concealing trees, no dead leaves. The local inhabitants might take it amiss. Therefore, he decided, he would try to find an inn in this village. That should please Ahnao.

The village consisted of a wide stretch in the highway and a smaller road leading off to the northeast somewhere, each lined with a dozen houses and shops. Like the suburbs of Praunce, it had no walls. At the intersection where the two streets met stood a three-story structure with several large many-paned glass windows; Slant guessed this to be either the seat of the local government, an inn, or both.

It proved, upon investigation, to be an inn. It even had an adequate stable at one side where the horses could be sheltered, fed, and watered for a small fee. Although it was still well before dusk, Slant decided to stay the night. He and Ahnao could easily reach the city by noon of the following day if they left the inn around dawn, and that, he was sure, would be early enough.

To his surprise, the innkeeper insisted that there were no rooms available on the first two floors. Slant had seen no other travelers on the road, and it was still early in the day to be seeking lodging. The stable was not crowded. He made a comment to that effect, and was told that the regular westbound caravan was due any minute. This caravan was a monthly event, and filled the entire second floor to overflowing; it lodged at this inn, close as it was to Praunce, because the entire morning of its departure date was invariably wasted in organizing, so that the caravan never got outside the walls before midday.

Slant agreed that it would not do to antagonize such important customers, and accepted the key to a room in the southeast corner of the third floor.

The gold piece he paid for the room and stabling with was sufficient to cover the house's regular dinner and breakfast; with the caravan expected, the innkeeper was eager to feed Slant and Ahnao and get them out of the way. Ahnao was hungry, and Slant did not see fit to argue, so once they had tended to the horses and dropped their supplies off in their chamber they found a table in the common room and allowed a servant to bring them ale, bread, cheese, fruit, and a thick, gluey stew.

They sat facing each other, chewing idly; Slant spent most of his attention on the nearest window, watching the people of the village drift by, going about their business. Ahnao watched Slant. When she had eaten enough to take the edge off her hunger, she asked suddenly, "How old are you?"

Slant started. "I don't know," he replied.

"How can that be? You must know when you were born."

"Yes, of course, but it's not that simple. I was born about three hundred and twenty years ago. I don't know exactly, because I was born on Old Earth, and years are different here. I was eighteen when I left Old Earth, nineteen when I left Mars."

"I don't understand. That doesn't make sense. I thought you were from Teyzha."

"That's what I've been saying because it's easier and safer than telling the truth. I'm from Old Earth." He was not sure why he had decided to tell Ahnao this; he had avoided her questions previously. But then, he wasn't sure why he had lied before. It had, he decided, probably been nothing more than habit; since he left Mars he had always lied to maintain his cover. If he had told the truth, the computer would probably have killed him—or at least insisted that he kill his listener.

His willingness to speak now, he theorized, was a reaction to the long suppression. He was finally free to do and say what he pleased, like any ordinary man, and he would use that freedom.

"Old Earth is one of the stars, the little lights in the night sky, isn't it?"

He saw no point in explaining the difference between a star and a planet, nor mentioning that Sol was usually not visible. "More or less," he said.

"The stories say that everybody came from Old Earth originally, long ago. Is that what you mean? Your ancestors came from there?"

"No, I mean I was born on Old Earth. I came here in the ship you saw near Awlmei."

"Are the years much shorter there?"

"No; I think they're a little bit longer."

"Then how can you be three hundred years old?"

Confronted with the necessity of explaining something he didn't understand himself, Slant said, "You're right, I'm not. I'm thirty-three."

"So you left Old Earth fifteen years ago?"

Slant hesitated. "No," he said at last, "I left Old Earth during the Bad Times, more than three hundred years ago, as I said."

"I don't understand."

"Neither do I." He gulped down the last of his ale.

There was a moment of relative silence, broken by a commotion in the street; several riders on horseback were stopping in front of the inn. The innkeeper hurried out to greet them, and Slant surmised that the caravan had arrived.

"You really came from the past?"

Slant was distracted by the caravan; the riders had been joined by at least one large wagon. He was unsure if he saw others off to one side. Without thinking about it, he answered, "Yes."

"Did the demon you said possessed you bring you?"

"You could say so."

"How did it come to possess you?"

Answering that required some thought; Slant turned away from the window and looked at Ahnao. "Why do you want to know?" he asked.

She made a vague shrugging gesture. "I don't know."

"How much do you know about the Bad Times?"

"Oh, not very much; the same as anyone, I suppose."

"Did you know that they were a war?"

"Well . . . sort of. Ships from the stars came and destroyed all the cities, I know that."

"Yes, that's right. The ships came from Old Earth. The other worlds had not wanted to be ruled by Old Earth any more, so the ships were sent to smash everything until the other worlds obeyed again." That was the simplest summary of the war he could manage; he hoped it would serve.

"That's not what the stories say!"

"That's the truth, though. I know, I was on Old Earth. The war began two years before I was born, when the colonies stopped sending the food we needed."

"Oh," said Ahnao, in a very small voice.

"Old Earth sent out ships to destroy all the worlds that opposed it, and this world was one of those. However, there were other worlds that they were unsure about. It took years and years to travel between the worlds and carry messages, and there were many places that continued to obey Old Earth and many others that no one was sure about. To find out which side these worlds were on, and whether they might be dangerous, Old Earth sent out a lot of small one-person ships, which visited the worlds and reported back.

"However, the government of Old Earth was worried that, after years of traveling all alone, through space, the people flying these little ships might not obey them any more, that they might join the enemy. In order to make sure that didn't happen, they built a computer into each ship and also put part of it in each pilot, set so that it would kill the pilot if he disobeyed.

"I was one of those pilots, and the computer is what you wizards call a demon."

"Oh. If you had disobeyed it, it would have killed you?"

"Yes, exactly. There is a thing in my head that would explode and burn if the computer told it to."

"The demon is dead, now, so you're safe, aren't you?"

"Yes, but I'd still like to have the thing in my head removed. Then I could bring the computer back to life, but it wouldn't be able to harm me. I would control the demon, instead of the other way around."

"Isn't that dangerous?"

"No, I don't think so," Slant answered promptly, but even as he said it, he was unsure he was right. Was he actually certain he could control the computer?

Yes, he told himself, of course he could. He had the release code.

"Did the demon do anything else to you, besides make you obey?"

Slant shrugged "Sometimes it did." It struck him as an odd question. "Why do you ask?"

"Oh, I don't know; you acted differently before Furinar killed the demon."

"Of course I did; I had to do what I was told or it would have blown my head off." The people of the caravan were drifting into the common room two or three at a time, and the inn servants were rushing to and fro carrying mugs and plates.

Neither spoke for a moment; Slant was watching the caravan crew, and Ahnao was picking at her food and thinking.

"Why," she asked after an interval, "did you come to Dest?"

"The computer told me to."

"Why did it do that? Our cities had already been smashed, hadn't they?"

"Yes, of course they had. The computer wanted to be sure that the survivors weren't doing anything that might harm Old Earth."

"Oh. Why did it make you kill Kurao?"

"It wanted a wizard's head. It thought that wizards might be dangerous; we never found any on other planets . . . I mean worlds."

"Oh." Ahnao lapsed into thought again.

Slant was suddenly uncomfortably aware that one of the men from the caravan was staring at him—specifically, at the back of his neck. He had forgotten that the socket was still there, even with the computer shut down, marking him as something other than an ordinary human being.

He did not want to attract attention or start any trouble; he pushed his chair back and rose. "It's getting crowded in here," he said. "Let's go up to our room."

Ahnao looked up at him in surprise, then looked down at the table. "All right," she said.

Slant realized with annoyance that his words must have sounded like a sexual invitation, which was not at all what he'd had in mind. He was still trying his best to resist his attraction to the girl. Nonetheless, he wanted to get out of the common room; he could straighten out her misapprehension later. They left the table and made their way upstairs.

Chapter Eighteen

THE INSTANT THE HEAVY WOODEN DOOR OF THEIR ROOM swung shut behind them, Ahnao flung her arms around his neck. Reacting automatically, his right hand swept up and then down in a killing stroke; by a ferocious effort of will, he managed to slow the attack before it reached the back of the girl's unprotected neck, but he was unable to stop it completely. As she reached her face up to kiss him, the blow landed.

"Ow!" She jumped back as suddenly as she had approached. "You hit me!"

"I'm sorry; you caught me off-guard and I reacted without thinking."

She rubbed the back of her neck; Slant hoped that he had not done her any real harm. He wondered how she would react to learning that the blow had been intended to kill by snapping the spine, but was not curious enough to tell her and find out. He was committed to spending the night in her company, at the very least, and there was no point in stirring up hostility.

She looked at him resentfully. "I thought you wanted me to do that."

"No, I'm sorry, but I didn't, and I don't."

"Then why did you want me to come up here?"

"Have you ever looked at the back of my neck?"

"No." Her frown vanished into a crooked little smile. "Is it as bruised as mine feels?"

"No. Look." He reached up and pulled his hair to the side, then turned so that she could see.

It seemed he could feel her staring, though he knew that was nonsense. After a long silence, she asked, "What is that? It looks like part of you."

"It is." He let his hair fall back in place and turned to face her. "That's where I was joined to the computer."

"You mean that was where the demon got into you?"

"That's right."

The smile was completely gone again. "That's horrible. How could your people do that to you?"

"I volunteered."

"But how could you volunteer?"

Slant shrugged. "I didn't really know what I was doing."

"Oh. What has that got to do with asking me up here, though?"

"I just wanted to get out of the main room down there. Someone was staring at me from behind. I prefer not to attract attention."

"Do you think he saw that thing?"

"I don't know. That's why I wanted to leave, though. I'm afraid that it had nothing to do with you."

"Oh." Ahnao stood, quietly considering that, while Slant seated himself on the edge of the lone bed and pulled off his boots. When he had done that, he placed them on one side and stared critically at the narrow mattress. He had not specified how many beds he wanted, and the innkeeper had naturally assumed that one would serve, but he was not at all sure it would. He did not care to put himself in unnecessarily close proximity to Ahnao for the night; his resolution was not strong enough relative to his sexual interest for him to be willing to put it to such a test. He would, he decided, let Ahnao have the bed, while he found something for padding and slept on the floor.

As he reached this decision, Ahnao let out a soft little wail. "Why don't you like me?"

He looked up in surprise. "What?"

"Why don't you like me? Why don't you want me? What kind of a man are you, hitting me like that?"

He stared at her for a moment, his mouth slightly open, completely at a loss. The girl was about to start crying, he could tell, and he had no idea how to deal with it. Something stirred in the back of his mind; he stood and was suddenly no longer in control of his body, but merely watching.

One of his construct personalities had come to the fore, one he did not recognize; it was not the warrior or the pilot or any of the cover identities he had used in the past.

He felt the expression on his face softening into a sympathetic smile; his arms reached out, and he heard himself say something soft and soothing.

Ahnao ran to him and fell into his embrace. He bent down and kissed her forehead; a hand brushed away a lock of hair that had fallen into her eyes. She hugged him tightly, and they sank onto the bed.

Somewhere within himself, Slant watched in powerless annoyance as this newly discovered personality systematically made perfect love to the girl. He was little more than a detached observer, going through programmed actions in carefully calculated response to Ahnao's words and motions.

It made sense, he realized. Spies had always had a reputation for romance, and there really were times when seduction was the best possible approach to the gaining of information, the easing of suspicions, or other goals that an IRU might pursue. From the point of view of the Command, it mattered very little what the cyborg happened to think about it, and even less what the target of the seduction thought or felt. What mattered was getting what they were after.

They had never told him how many different personalities they had programmed in, or what they were; most had been built up during long sessions under hypnosis, none of which he remembered at all. He wondered how they had conducted the training of this particular one.

It annoyed him that, when it came down to the point of decision, he had had no choice whether to resist or not. He wondered whether the regulatory mechanisms really had shut down, or whether perhaps his hormones had been triggered somehow to prepare his body for this lover persona's use. Even with the computer gone, he was still a puppet, controlled by his programming and the machines built into him.

As matters progressed he began to marvel at what he was doing, and to wish that he was able to feel it normally and control his own actions. His previous sexual experience had been limited to a few brief liaisons in his last year as a civilian and a few single nights on leave; he had been, like most teenagers, eager and clumsy. Now he was moving with smooth assurance, and Ahnao was responding with enthusiasm in ways none of those long-ago women had responded.

He hoped he would be able to remember some of this later on.

When his primary personality returned to control of his body he was lying on the edge of the bed, relaxed and calm; Ahnao lay beside him, sound asleep, a smile on her face and the sheet beneath her stained with sweat. It was full night outside; he could see stars through one of the room's two windows.

He sat up, careful not to disturb the girl, and looked about, trying to decide if there was anything that should be done before he went to sleep himself. There no longer seemed any point in sleeping on the floor, and though crowded, there was room in the bed.

His supplies were piled in one corner. The horses had been taken care of earlier. He found a chamber pot under the bed. The only thing left to do was to close the shutters and go to sleep.

He rose and crossed to the south window, then paused and looked out at the night.

There was something wrong. It took him a few seconds to identify exactly what it was, but at last he realized that there was a blue glow visible behind the building across the street.

He was on the top floor of the highest building in the village, but his view still consisted mostly of the roof across the street, so that he could not see where the glow was coming from. It had not immediately registered as something out of the ordinary because it resembled the light of a distant city, albeit bluer than most such lights.

On this planet, however, there were no cities that were lit with anything more than torches, to the best of his knowledge. Even if there were enough torches to produce a glow of that magnitude, the color was wrong; torchlight was yellow, not blue.

Did Praunce, he asked himself, have gaslights? He did not recall that any such light had been detected during the orbital inspection of the planet, but it was entirely possible a single such city had been missed. It might have been on the day side during most of the scanning.

He was not content with this explanation, and he realized why. Praunce lay to the east, and he was looking south. There was nothing to the south but farmland and occasional barren spots, and those great upthrusts of bare stone.

He remembered the dragon suddenly and Thurrel's description of Praunce as a city built on ruins, where there were many abnormal births, and realized what caused the blue glow, and what the strange outcroppings were, and why there were barren patches scattered in the fields.

The bomb that had done all that must have been really hellish, he thought. The outcroppings, he guessed, were displaced chunks of surface that had been rammed up against the crater wall and welded in place by the heat and pressure, so that they stayed where they had been flung; the barren patches were caused by chunks of semi-molten stone and metal that had spattered outward from the explosion. The gleaming spots must be resolidified metal, or soil fused into glass.

He wondered how people could live so close to the crater. The environment, he was certain, must be extremely unhealthy. If there was enough radiation to produce that glow, it was surprising there were any live births at all. How could a major city have grown up at the very edge of such a place?

He suddenly found himself wondering whether he wanted to visit Praunce after all. Perhaps the locals were all more or less radiation immune; from a population of two billion there were bound to have been a few people with abnormally high tolerance, and those people would have been far more likely to survive the initial holocaust and to have been the ancestors of the current population.

The local inhabitants might be almost as far removed from the common run of humanity as he was himself. Three hundred years were a mere instant in evolutionary terms, but with the added push of extreme radioactivity a significant selection process might have occurred.

There could even be a connection with wizardry.

His mind was running ahead of itself, he realized. He was guessing. He thought back and recalled that the planet had an abnormally high level of background radiation, but nothing approaching the unlivable.

The inhabitants of Praunce might simply not know any better.

That was a depressing thought. He closed the shutters on both windows, lay back on the bed beside Ahnao, and willed himself to sleep.

His last waking thought was to wish that he had brought dosimeters from the ship.

Chapter Nineteen

SLANT AWOKE THE FOLLOWING MORNING WITH A VAGUE impression that he had had very unpleasant dreams, though he could not remember any of them. He did not let it bother him for more than a few seconds.

Not wanting any unnecessary delay on the day when he expected to finally reach Praunce and perhaps be freed of the bomb in his brain, he woke Ahnao almost immediately. She came awake with a happy smile on her face, and reached up to embrace him.

There was little point in resisting, he decided; it would only confuse the poor girl and perhaps bring his newly discovered personality back into control. He allowed her to hug him but then pulled away.

"We have to get moving," he told her.

The smile faded slightly. "All right," she replied.

Half an hour later they were mounted and on their way. The eerie blue glow that Slant had seen the night before was invisible in the daylight, but he was uncomfortably aware that it was still there.

Ahead of them the towers of Praunce reared up black against the rising sun, the city and its suburbs spread out below. They grew gradually closer throughout the morning, and Slant studied them.

He realized by midmorning that all his previous estimate had been off; the tallest tower was easily two hundred meters high, and they would not reach the city wall—which was also higher than he had thought—by noon.

For the first time, he realized what the towers were. He had been amazed before that such a primitive culture could have built anything so tall; he was amazed no longer. The towers were prewar skyscrapers. Their original glass or concrete walls had probably been replaced; he doubted that the glass could have survived for three hundred years even if it was not shattered—as it almost certainly had been—by the shockwave from whatever had created the crater to the south. The steel frames, however, could easily have stood for a few centuries.

He guessed that the crater had been the planet's main spaceport. That might even be one reason for Praunce's predominance and large population; it had probably been the world capital, or at least the center of trade, and traditions tended to linger.

Shortly thereafter they began to pass scattered houses, growing steadily closer together, until they found themselves riding down streets lined with buildings. Ahead of them the city wall reared up, black and solid; half an hour after noon they reached a point where it blocked the looming towers from their sight.

The wall, Slant was sure, must have been postwar in origin, and it was as impressive as he had first thought the towers to be, a solid, unbroken barrier that at points reached a height of thirty meters above the ground.

Perhaps, if the skyscrapers had survived, some construction equipment had as well; he could not imagine such a structure having been built by hand by the survivors of a nuclear attack.

The street they rode on widened, and traffic increased; where they had passed an occasional pedestrian at the outskirts they were now surrounded by wagons, horses, oxen, and a perpetually moving crowd on foot. There was something subtly wrong with the appearance of the crowd, Slant thought; he looked more closely and realized what it was.

There was too much variation.

In an ordinary crowd there would be a mix of all kinds of people, but the majority would always fall into certain categories. Most would be more than a meter and a half in height, but less than two meters, for example.

That was not quite true here. There were dozens of people of both sexes who stood no taller than children, and others who towered over their companions. Some hands had too many fingers, or too few, or none at all. Some faces were distorted or damaged, eyes shaped strangely, noses enlarged or shrunken or missing. There were a great many bald or balding heads, and far more white hair than was normal.

Perhaps most peculiar of all, none of the people in the crowd paid any attention to the deformities of their neighbors. Obviously, they were completely accustomed to them. Slant wished again that he had brought radiation badges, or that the computer were still active to report radiation levels for him.

The street emptied into a large market square at the foot of the great wall; on the far side of the square was a huge opening in the barrier, a gate into the city proper.

The market was jammed with people; where the crowd on the street leading in had been sparse enough to allow travel at Slant's accustomed pace, here the horses had to advance one step at a time, practically pushing aside the pedestrians who blocked their paths. Their progress was further slowed by the fact that there was a steep slope to the ground; the wall stood along the top of a ridge here, and the market lay on a slant of at least ten degrees leading up to it.

Here, in addition to the freaks and sports that mingled with the more ordinary citizens in going about their business, there were several who were so badly deformed as to be crippled. These, Slant realized, were beggars; bowls in hand—or foot, or their teeth—they accosted their more fortunate fellows. There were more of them the closer one got to the gate itself.

He glanced back at Ahnao; she, too, had noticed the nature of the crowd, and her expression was compounded of dismay and revulsion. Residual radiation was apparently not a problem in Awlmei, Slant thought, or perhaps they practiced infanticide to keep its products under control; in any case, it appeared she had never before encountered creatures like these.

They made their way most of the way across the square without undue difficulty. As they approached the gate, one of the more grotesque freaks, a woman—or at any rate a female—with incredibly long, oddly jointed arms and too many fingers leaped from her place and clutched at Slant's vest. Her breath stank of liquor and rotting teeth. She gabbled something incomprehensible at him.

He thrust her aside, knocking her to the ground, and rode on.

She scrambled to her feet behind him and flung herself upon Ahnao, pleading incoherently.

Ahnao screamed, and Slant turned to see the beggar clinging to his companion's leg. He reined in his horse and snapped, "Let go of her!" His voice was clear and sharp, and there was no doubt that the creature heard him. She glanced at him but did not loose her hold.

They were at the top of the marketplace, directly in front of the gate, in view of hundreds of people, merchants and customers buying and selling and trading, beggars accosting all within reach, friends conversing with one another. Slant paid no attention to any of them.

"I said let her go." His voice was now cold and threatening, and Ahnao looked from the beggar to her protector, suddenly as frightened of him as of the freak.

Again his command was ignored; the wretched creature reached a hand upward to cling to Ahnao's arm.

Slant was totally unaware of his own movement, and it was far too fast for human eyes to follow, but the snark was in his hand and the freak was falling away, to land screaming in the dirt, her many-fingered hand severed at the wrist.

The fingers slowly loosened, and the hand fell from its grip several seconds later.

Ahnao did not scream again but made a curious smothered squeak and turned her gaze away as blood spattered her mount's flank and the hand tumbled a short way down the slope.

The incident had not gone unnoticed; passersby had been watching the little everyday annoyance befalling the strangers on horseback when it had so abruptly ceased to be little and everyday. The beggar's continuing screams were joined by others, and the crowd surged away from the three horses. None touched the bleeding victim until Slant, in a strange state midway between the warrior who had cut off the hand and his ordinary, calmer self, pointed to a bystander and ordered, "Tend to her. There's no reason for her to bleed to death."

The man he had chosen nodded, near panic, and rushed forward; he had no desire to offend such a wizard—if wizard he was. Someone handed him a strip of cloth, and he struggled to bandage the stump of the wrist as the beggar thrashed about in the dust.

Slant paid them no further attention; he wanted only to get away. He urged his horse forward.

The crowd parted instantly, allowing him through the gate into the city of Praunce. Ahnao and the riderless horse followed. In moments they were well into the city, out of sight of anyone who had seen the incident and away from the crowds of the marketplace, surrounded instead by the sparser crowds of the city streets.

Slant found an empty side street and turned into it, then stopped his horse and sat silently thinking. Ahnao came up beside him and said, in a quavering voice, "Slant?"

"Don't bother me," he replied. She lapsed into silence.

It was a beautiful day, sunny and warm; the air was fresh and invigorating, albeit a trifle dusty. White, fluffy clouds drifted overhead, and somewhere on the rooftops birds were cooing at one another. Slant had been feeling pleased with life. He had overcome most of his worries about radiation and his relationship with Ahnao, and was glad to have finally reached the city he had set himself as a goal—and then his good mood had been completely ruined by his combat programming. He had just maimed and perhaps killed a fellow human; however deformed, the woman was still human. He had not been acting in self-defense, nor had he been forced to his action by the computer. He had done it very nearly of his own free will.

It was no comfort to tell himself that it had been another personality in his body; that personality was a part of him, after all, not some mysterious independent entity.

He wished he had never landed on this troublesome planet.

Although Slant never saw her again, the beggar did not die; she recovered nicely and became a minor celebrity among the city's poor. This attention so inflated her vanity that she took to bathing and keeping herself tidy as best she could with her remaining seven-fingered, double-thumbed, double-jointed hand. The pitifully decrepit appearance that had been her main source of sympathy was ruined by this, but the stump of her wrist and her natural deformities were enough to bring her a satisfactory income, and her improved cleanliness and odor made her acceptable in human society for the first time in her life. She was permitted in taverns and shops, as she had not been previously, and her life improved considerably, so that in the end she became almost grateful to the mysterious mounted stranger who had dressed like a warrior but wielded a weapon that was obviously magical.

Slant knew nothing of that, and after a few moments of guilty anger he pushed the whole matter out of his mind as best he could and considered other, more important matters.

He was in Praunce, the city he hoped would have wizards capable of removing the thermite and override from his skull. The next thing he had to do was to locate a suitable wizard.

He looked around. He and Ahnao and their spare horse were in a narrow byway two blocks east of the gate, running approximately parallel to the wall. It was lined with tall, narrow houses, mostly three stories in height and built of stone or half-timbered plaster. It did not look like a particularly interesting neighborhood, neither poor nor affluent. He did not think it likely that there were wizards on such a street. If he were a wizard, he would want to live somewhere out of the ordinary, someplace that would impress people.

The most impressive things he had seen in Praunce were the wall and the great towers. The wall was not exactly a residence, but the towers seemed perfect.

The more he thought about it, the more certain he became that wizards must live in the towers. After all, this culture could scarcely have kept the elevators running in any ordinary fashion; only wizardry could propel anything to the top of a two-hundred-meter building. Nobody, in any culture, would want to walk up sixty flights as a regular thing.

Therefore, he wanted to get to the towers.

That was not necessarily going to be as easy as it might at first appear. He knew the towers were near the center of the city, somewhere to the east of his present position, but visibility was severely limited by the buildings three or four stories high lining the narrow and twisting streets. Although the towers had dominated the view for a full day's ride, dozens of kilometers, now that he was close to them they were invisible.

Still, he knew they were near the center of the city. Accordingly, he headed east, following whichever street seemed to run most nearly in that direction.

Ahnao followed, asking once, "Where are we going?"

"To the towers," he replied. That was enough of an answer to satisfy her, and she rode along silently, not questioning the turns and twists he led her through, even when forced to double back out of a blind alley.

At last, after half an hour of winding through the city, they arrived at a wide intersection from which one of the towers could be seen, looming up to their right, glittering in the sun. Slant was able for the first time to see in detail the side of the structure.

He was now absolutely certain that the towers were pre-war skyscrapers, for there were several places where the walls had not been maintained and chunks had sloughed off, leaving gaping holes in the facade. Through these, Slant could see steel girders. The facade itself was curious indeed, a patchwork of stone and brick and glass, not built up neatly in patterned rows but seemingly slapped together at random.

Now that he had the tower in sight, it was a relatively simple matter to steer toward it, and twenty minutes later he and Ahnao were at its foot. It was not the tallest, but it would do.

There was no question about where to enter; a huge arch, two stories high, occupied the center of each side of the base. Slant, however, did not choose to rush on blindly. He still did not know where in the tower he might find wizards, and did not care to go wandering about fifty or sixty floors, each fifty meters square, looking for them. Furthermore, he was fascinated by the building itself. He had, in his fourteen years of travel, seen other pretechnological cultures, some built on the ruins of bombed-out cities much as this one was. None, however, had ever made use of ruined skyscrapers; he had never seen anything resembling this rebuilt monstrosity.

Where steel girders showed they were slightly askew, rusted and twisted, but still sturdy. The entire building had a slight lean to the north, away from the crater, presumably a result of the shockwave. When the rebuilding began, Slant guessed that the tower had consisted of little more than bare steel and rubble, and the builders had used their own primitive techniques to fill that in. No particular pattern was visible; it appeared that several different people had each filled in sections according to their own whims.

Much of the bottom few meters was clad in concrete, first a clean, straight level that appeared to be surviving prewar work, then a bizarre, patched-together section where chunks of rubble had been assembled with mortar and gravel. Beyond that, Slant saw sections that were half-timbered, or built of cut and polished stone, or walled with fieldstone. There were several ordinary windows of wood frames and small panes, but also large, irregular areas of rough glass, each a single sheet. These chunks of glass were not all transparent; Slant could see blue, green, and red glass, rippled, bubbled, or smooth, all gleaming in the afternoon sun. Obviously, the builders had used what they found in the rubble as it was; perhaps much of that glass had been part of the original walls of the tower.

Slant hoped that little or none of it came from the radioactive crater to the south.

The overall effect of the tower was that of a village built vertically instead of horizontally, and it occurred to Slant that it might have been just that originally, and that the city might have grown up around the towers, in a reversal of the usual pattern where towers grew out of a city for lack of space.

It was odd, though, that the steel frames had survived well enough to make it possible to build these things this close to the crater, and therefore to the blast.

He turned and saw Ahnao staring upward at the tower. She noticed his gaze, and said, "It's so tall!"

"Sixty stories, I'd guess, perhaps slightly less."

"Ftha and Hligosh!"

If he were a wizard, Slant thought, he'd want to live at the top, for the view and the privacy. He remarked, "We may have to find a way up all sixty floors."

Ahnao looked at him in surprise. "Why?" she asked.

"I'm looking for a wizard who can take some of the machinery out of my head; I think one may live up there."

"Oh. Do you want me to check?"

"What?" Slant was startled; he had forgotten that Ahnao herself was almost a wizard. "Yes, if you can."

He had thought that she meant to fly up and report back, but instead she closed her eyes, then opened them again in an unfocused stare, much as she had in Awlmei when contacting Furinar.

Slant waited for the prickle of magic at work but felt only a very faint hint of the tingling he remembered.

Ahnao's eyes closed again, then opened, normal once more. "There is somebody up there, but he's on the next floor down, not at the very top."

"A wizard?"

"Of course!"

"Good. Come on, then, and we'll find a way up." He urged his horse forward and led the way through the great arch into the building's interior.

The arch led into a broad corridor that, had it not been inside a building, would have been more properly called a street. It was seven or eight meters high, and ten meters wide, and extended the full length of the building, to emerge from the other side through an arch very much like the one by which Slant and Ahnao entered. At its midpoint another, similar corridor-street crossed it at right angles, so that the first two floors were neatly divided into fourths.

Both sides of the passageway were lined with shops in two tiers; a balcony ran along either side about three meters off the stone-paved floor, easily reached by half a dozen staircases scattered along its length, providing access to the upper tier's businesses. Since the bright sunlight could not penetrate into the heart of so large a building, the innermost shopfronts were lit by torches made of bunched cornstalks dipped in some black, gummy substance. The

interiors of the shops that had no windows to the outside—
the great majority—were illuminated with what appeared
to be oil lamps.

The shops, being sheltered from the elements as they
were, were not closed in by glass or solid walls but instead
fronted with various sorts of shutters. These varied almost
as greatly as the wall segments of the tower's exterior;
there were sliding metal panels, folding screens of carved
wood, rolled-up bundles of slats that could be lowered like
windowshades, and other ingenious devices. Appetizing
smells of fresh fruit and baking pastry filled the passage,
reminding Slant that he and Ahnao had not stopped for
lunch that day.

Wizards could wait; he was hungry. He reined in his
horse and dismounted in front of a bakery shop. The girl
followed suit.

The proprietor of the shop became very friendly and
attentive the moment silver struck the countertop of polished wood, and as the travelers ate he gladly answered
Slant's question regarding the contents of the tower.

"As you can see, there are our various business estab-
lishments on these first two levels; my fellow businessmen
and myself have our homes on the next four levels—with
our families, of course. Above that there are three more
floors of residence." The baker stopped, with a pleasant
smile.

"What of the rest? That covers less than a fifth of the
tower's height."

"Of course, but that's as far as the stairs go. There's
only storage for most of the rest."

"Storage?"

"Yes, of course. The rest is full of grain and other foods,
in case of siege. The city has enough stored away to feed
the entire population for three years. It is because of that
and the great wall that no enemy has ever successfully
attacked Praunce, and it has helped us to become the
center of the trade in grains."

"Ah, I see. What of the top of the tower, though?"

"As in all the towers, that's where the wizards live."

"Wizards?"

"Yes, wizards. You must know what wizards are."

"Certainly I do. Are there many in Praunce?"

The baker shrugged. "Enough, I suppose. They do their part in defending the city and safeguarding trade, but I never cared for them much. They make me nervous."

Slant nodded. "I might like to talk to one, though. Is there any way up to the top?"

The shopkeeper shrugged again. "There are no stairs. The wizards fly up."

Disappointed, Slant thanked the man, and he and Ahnao left the shop.

"What now?" Ahnao asked.

"We can at least go up as far as we can." He led the way toward the center of the building and up a convenient staircase to the balcony, leaving the horses tied in front of the bakery shop. When Ahnao pointed them out, Slant replied, "They can take care of themselves for now. Nobody is likely to harm them, and we may not need them any more. I can always steal some more."

The balcony was fairly narrow, floored with wooden planks. At the corner where the two passageways crossed another staircase led upward through the ceiling. Slant noticed that the ceiling, too, was wooden; he had rather expected it to be vaulted stone.

They proceeded up this new staircase and found themselves in a large, dim, windowless chamber, lit by oil lamps in brackets on the walls. A dozen doors, each with a name painted neatly upon it, lined the sides of the room, and another staircase led through another wooden ceiling to the next floor.

They continued upward through floor after floor until, eight flights above street level, there were no more stairs but only a closed trap door in a corner of the ceiling that took them a moment to locate. It was a dozen centimeters out of Slant's reach.

He stared at it resentfully, then remembered who his companion was. He turned to her, standing close behind him and very tired from the long climb. "Would you open that for me?"

"Me? How?"

"Fly up to it."

"Oh! Let me catch my breath first."

"All right." She sank to the plank floor and sat; Slant settled beside her, though he was not particularly in need of rest.

When she felt herself to be more or less recovered Ahnao rose to her feet, took a deep breath, and then picked her feet up from the floor, curling herself into a ball in midair, a meter above the planks.

Slant watched in fascination; he had never seen a wizard take off before. He had expected her to leap upward, or to drift, but not to pull herself up as she actually did. He felt his skin crawling and itching from the nearness of magic.

Once she was off the ground, Ahnao slowly and carefully stood up, still unsupported in midair; her hair brushed the ceiling. She reached up and pushed aside the trap door.

Sunlight poured through, and the two of them blinked in the unexpected brilliance; they had long since adjusted to the feeble oil lamps. Ahnao's concentration was disrupted by her surprise, and she fell awkwardly backward. Slant caught her and lowered her to the floor. He looked up through the opening but could not see anything useful; the trap door seemed to open into a vast empty space. That did not accord well with the baker's description of a grain storage area.

"Could you lift me up there somehow?"

"I don't think so," she replied.

He needed a ladder, or at least a rope, but saw nothing in the room that might be useful; except for the flickering lamps, the chamber was completely empty. It was also, he reminded himself, a public hallway, and if he stayed where he was long enough somebody was sure to notice him. If several people noticed him, they might begin to wonder what he was doing there, and he had no good explanation ready.

He could at least send Ahnao up through the opening, though, and perhaps she would find her way up to the wizard and send him down. He was about to ask her if she would cooperate in such an endeavor when she spoke first, saying "The wizard wants to know what you're doing here."

"What?"

"He noticed us banging around and contacted me. His name is Arzadel. He wants to know what we're doing here."

Slant had forgotten that wizards had limited telepathic abilities. Or, rather, he had forgotten that Ahnao did. He was almost pleased to have her along. "Tell him that it's important I speak to him as soon as possible."

He watched as the girl stared off with that peculiar unfocused gaze. When she refocused a moment later, it was to say, "He's on his way."

Slant stood, waiting patiently; a minute or so later a shadow blocked out the sunlight that poured through the trap and a pleasant tenor voice said, "You wished to speak with me?"

Chapter Twenty

"YES," SLANT SAID, "I NEED THE SERVICES OF A WIZARD. I can pay well."

A tinge of annoyance was perceptible in the shadowy figure's reply. "I have no need of money."

"I can pay in other ways, if you would prefer. I really think you should hear me out."

The annoyance was still present, now mixed with resignation. "Very well. As a courtesy to this apprentice, I will listen."

"It is a rather complex matter." Slant did not particularly like speaking to someone he could not see standing above him, and hoped the wizard would invite him to a more comfortable spot.

The wizard did not. "Then stop wasting my time and start explaining it."

"It is not an easy story to believe; therefore, I ask that you test for yourself that I speak only the truth."

"Get on with it." Slant felt a faint tingling.

"I am a cyborg, a creature from the Bad Times, half man and half machine. I was sent out by Old Earth as a spy more than three hundred years ago and just recently arrived on this world. Until even more recently, I was under the direction of another machine, a computer, which controlled devices in my brain. Your compatriots, the wizards of Awlmei, put the computer out of operation by draining its power source; they did this because the computer still believed itself to be fighting a war against your world, and had forced me to kill a wizard named Kurao. I do not fault them for their action. However, I would find the computer very useful if I could start it up without permitting it to control me again. I believe that if I have certain things removed from the devices in my skull I can control the computer, and I know that it will no longer be able to control me. Only a neurosurgeon or a wizard can remove these things without killing me, and there are no neurosurgeons on this world, so far as I know. A wizard in Teyzha told me that he and his fellows could remove them safely; he referred to it as 'exorcising' a demon. If you could perform this service for me, and save me a trip to Teyzha—where that wizard may well be dead by now—I would be glad to pay any reasonable price within my power. Besides money, I have tools and weapons such as your ancestors had before the Bad Times."

Having finished his speech, Slant stopped speaking, and there was a moment of silence. As it stretched into awkwardness, Slant asked, "Do you believe me?"

"I see that you speak the truth as you know it," the wizard replied slowly. "But I am sure you will understand that I find the whole thing incredible. You claim to be more than three hundred years old, and as much machine as man?"

"I was born more than three hundred years ago, on Old Earth, and at the age of eighteen I was sent to Mars as a volunteer, where my skeleton was reinforced with metal and the rest of my body was rebuilt for greater efficiency."

After a moment of further consideration, the wizard said, "Even if you are somehow deceiving me, this is a matter worthy of further consideration. If you will, I will take you up to my home, where we can speak further in greater comfort."

"Thank you. I would like that."

"Then hold still."

Slant obeyed and felt a strange tugging; his skin suddenly tingled so much that it stung. The trap door was closer, then he was through it and moving rapidly upward. The wizard, a handsome young man in a red robe, was rising alongside him; Ahnao was not immediately in sight.

He had a good view, in passing, of the interior of the skyscraper, and saw that it was, indeed, used for storage; although the central area, where he and his companion were, was open and empty as a single shaft twenty meters square and well over a hundred meters high, the sides were divided into floors, some empty, others piled high with sacks and crates. The sunlight that had shone through the trap had angled down from a window several floors up; at other times of day the opening would have been shaded by the partial floors or the stored goods.

Still, the body of the skyscraper was light and airy, far brighter than the gloomy wooden chambers below.

A moment later Slant found himself hanging in midair a pace or so from a metal platform. A stairway led upward from the platform, through the top of the great shaft. This ceiling, unlike those of the lower floors, really was vaulted stone.

Cautiously, he stepped forward, uncertain if the motion would work in these circumstances.

It worked well enough; and he found himself standing on the platform, the wizard beside him. Slant looked at the Prauncer, but he was in turn looking back down the shaft. "Your companion is having difficulty," he said. "She doesn't fly very well yet."

A few seconds later Ahnao rose close enough to reach out and grab the edge of the platform with one hand, whereupon she seemed to lose all her buoyancy. Slant and the wizard both reached out to help her; Slant's hand grasped her right arm well before the wizard's hand was anywhere near her. By the time the wizard managed to take hold of her left arm she was almost onto the platform.

The wizard looked at Slant in surprise. "Hligosh, you move fast!"

"I told you, I was rebuilt for greater efficiency."

"So you did." He smiled. "I may believe you after all. Come, now, into my home." He led the way up the stairs, through a door of wood inlaid with ornamental designs in various metals, into a large and luxurious chamber.

The room was vast, apparently occupying half the entire floor; it was thickly carpeted with fur, and other furs hung on the one long wall that had no windows. Velvet cushions of various hues were scattered about. There were no chairs, but several low tables were visible, of a height convenient to people sitting on cushions. The ceiling was of wood, once again, but rather than bare planks it was elaborately coffered and decorated with gold, red, and white enamel. The three walls not covered by furs were almost completely glass, broad windows separated by stone piers, each window dozens of panes leaded together. Most of the glass was clear, but mingled in each window were panes of yellow and green and red, no two pieces alike. The windows and the pillars between them were all curving, organic forms, reminiscent more of sculpture than of architecture. Sunlight poured through the southern and western walls, the colored panes projecting streaks of monochrome on the furs.

Slant was amazed at the opulence of the place, and spent a long moment simply taking it in, while the wizard and Ahnao seated themselves on cushions at the nearest table. The Prauncer watched with some amusement but finally beckoned to the cyborg, saying "Come join us!"

Slant remembered himself and did as he was bid, seating himself across the table from the wizard, at right angles to Ahnao.

"My name is Arzadel," the wizard said, "and I believe this apprentice called herself Ahnao, but you have not told me who you are."

"I am called Slant."

"You have already told us what you are, if you can be believed. Would you care to explain yourself further?"

"I will be glad to answer any questions you may have."

"You claim to have come from Old Earth, which is a world somewhere beyond the sky, whence our ancestors first came to Dest."

"Yes."

"There are many other worlds beyond the sky, one for every star that we see in the night sky, according to legend. Is this true?"

"Approximately true. There are many other worlds, each circling a star, but I do not believe that there is exactly one for each star in your skies."

"The legends also speak of a world called Sendry, so close that it could be reached by a starship in days instead of years. Do you know anything about that?"

"There is another planet circling your sun that was once inhabited; it was wiped out completely in the Bad Times, apparently, for the computer detected no life there whatsoever."

"Now, you claim to have come from Old Earth, and to have seen all these things that lie beyond our skies. How is this possible? All the starships that our ancestors used were destroyed in the Bad Times."

"I have my own starship. All the ships on your world were destroyed, but not those on other worlds."

"You said that you were sent out as a spy more than three hundred years ago, during the Bad Times."

"Yes."

"Did it take you three hundred years to get here? That is not what the legends say; they speak of a flight lasting five years."

"I did not come here directly, but visited other worlds as well. My flight took fourteen years, but three centuries passed on your world during that time. Don't ask me to explain that; I can't. I don't really understand it myself. All I know is that when a ship goes fast enough to travel between stars, time on board is different from that elsewhere."

"There are stories that speak of time being different on other worlds, the days longer but the years shorter, so I will not call what you say nonsense, though I do not understand it. However, there is something else I do not understand. The Bad Times ended on Dest three hundred and twenty-seven years ago. When did they end on Old Earth?"

"I don't know exactly, but it was at approximately the same time. I had left six months earlier."

" 'Months'?"

Slant realized his mistake; this planet had no moon. "Half a year. On Old Earth the year is divided into twelve parts, called 'months.' "

"Then it has been more than three hundred and twenty years since the Bad Times ended; why have no other ships come before you?"

"Old Earth was destroyed, much like your world, half a year afer my departure from Mars. That was what ended the Bad Times."

"Old Earth was destroyed?"

"Yes."

"Were there any survivors?"

"I don't know. I was forbidden to return."

There was a pause as the wizard considered this; then he asked, "What of the other worlds? Why have none of them sent ships to Dest?"

Slant shrugged. "I don't know. There are many worlds; perhaps they haven't gotten around to yours yet. Starships are still rare and precious things."

"Yet you say you had one of your own?"

"Yes; Old Earth had thousands of them, before it was destroyed, and could easily afford to use them for individual spies like myself."

"What became of your ship, then?"

"It's lying in a gully near Awlmei. Its power source has been drained and its engine shut off."

Ahnao interjected, "It's there; I saw it."

"You crashed, then?"

"No; it was shut down by the wizards of Awlmei in order to stop the computer, which is part of the ship."

"Tell me more about this computer."

"It's a machine that controls other machines; it does not exactly think, but it has a memory and follows instructions fed into it. The computer helped me to pilot the ship and made certain that I followed the orders given me. It has not allowed me to surrender even though the war has been over for years, because its instructions tell it not to; only my superiors on Mars and Old Earth could change those instructions, and they're all long dead."

"I don't understand these references you've made to a war; what war?"

"The Bad Times were a war."

"Oh, is that what you mean! I know, mysterious ships from somewhere beyond the sky came and destroyed all the cities and machinery. That is scarcely what I call a war!"

"It was a war, all right. The ships were not mysterious to me. They came from Old Earth to destroy colonies that had rebelled against the government of Old Earth."

"What? That's insane!"

"It's true, though."

"Why? What had the people of Dest done to deserve such destruction?"

"Your ancestors joined the rebellion against Old Earth."

"I don't understand; why were they rebelling?"

"I'm not certain; I believe it was a protest against the heavy taxation needed to supply Old Earth with food. Old Earth was overpopulated, and only the tribute from the colonies kept the people from starvation."

"But to smash an entire civilization!"

"What would the government of Praunce do if one of its subject villages rose in rebellion?"

"We would send soldiers to burn the village. Yes, I see the parallel; it's the scale that appalls me." He was silent for a moment, then asked, "But if Dest was destroyed by Old Earth, then who destroyed Old Earth?"

"The other rebel worlds. That ended the war. If it's any comfort, your side won."

Arzadel considered this for a moment before asking "Then you were a soldier in this war?"

"A scout, of sorts. I was sent to find out which worlds posed a threat to Old Earth and which could be ignored. When the war ended, the computer forced me to continue, even there was no longer any point in it."

"I see. And in the fullness of time you arrived here on Dest. Why did you kill that wizard you mentioned?"

"The computer was convinced that magic, as you have

here on Dest, was a new weapon that might be a danger
to Old Earth. Therefore, it sent me to find out the nature
of this new weapon. It eventually decided that the best
way to figure it out was to take apart a wizard's brain
and see what made it different from an ordinary person's,
and it made me kill Kurao and bring his head back to
the ship for study."

"You did this?"

"Not willingly, but I did. I had to."

"You have not explained that. How did this machine
control you?"

"This is why I came to you. I don't know how well I
can explain this. Do you know what explosives are?"

"Yes, of course."

"Good. I had not seen any evidence of them on your
world, so I was unsure. There is an explosive charge in
my brain; the computer possessed the means of detonating
it should I disobey its orders. Also, it controlled a device
that could detach my brain from the rest of my body and
control my body itself. I came to you in the hope that
you could remove these two things from me."

"I see. And if I do this, what will you do then?"

"I will return to my ship and try to restore it to working order. I am not certain how I'll do that, but I'm sure
it can be done."

"And what then?"

"I'm not sure of that, either. I think I'll probably leave
your world; I am accustomed to traveling now. I will be
glad to take along a passenger or two, and to try and
reestablish trade and communication between this world
and others—or, if you think it better, I will tell no one
of your existence."

"If you restore your ship, need you restore this machine
that controlled you?"

"Yes; I can't fly the ship without it."

"The machine killed a man, though."

"The machine has killed a great many people, on several worlds. It is not evil, though, it's just doing what it
was told. It cannot think for itself, really; it must follow
its orders. I think I can control it, and change its orders,
so that it will not harm anyone in the future."

"Are you certain you can do this?"

Slant hesitated but knew he could not hope to deceive a wizard. "No, I'm not completely certain. I know a way that should control it, or at the very least let it know that the war is over and its orders no longer good, so that it need not kill any more, but I cannot be absolutely sure it will work." He paused, then continued, "You shouldn't worry, though; even if it doesn't work, you wizards can shut it down again as you did before. If it does work, you have the opportunity to reach the wealth of all the other inhabited worlds."

Arzadel considered this silently for a long moment, then asked, "What if we were to remove the explosive and this other device from your body, but to require in payment that you never restore this dangerous machine to operation?"

It was Slant's turn to consider. Reluctantly, he said, "I'm not sure. I think I would travel further, looking for another wizard who would not impose such restrictions. If I couldn't find one, I would accept your terms. I do not want to be stranded on your world, but I don't want to let the computer control me again, either, nor to go through life with a bomb in my head."

Arzadel sat silently for a moment, then said, "This is too important a matter for me alone. Stay here, as my guests, while I consult with my colleagues. May I offer you something to eat or drink?"

The pastries they had eaten had not been very filling, and the long climb to the ninth floor, followed by their flight up and lengthy conversation, had left both Slant and Ahnao hungry again, so that they accepted gratefully. Arzadel opened a door in the fur-covered wall and vanished through it, to emerge a moment later with a tray holding an assortment of food, two mugs, and a pitcher of some yellowish beverage. He placed the tray on the table, bid them eat, then bowed and departed through another door.

The liquid was something much like lemonade, or at any rate a sweetened citrus concoction; Slant enjoyed it immensely. The food included yellow cakes that proved to be cornbread, a variety of fruits both fresh and dried, and salty meat of a sort Slant could not quite identify. They both ate ravenously.

When they had eaten their fill they sat for a few moments in silence, expecting their host to return momentarily. When he did not, Slant rose, stretched, and crossed to the south wall; he wanted to see the view.

To his far right and far left green, forested hills rolled off into the hazy distance. Nearer at hand were the city's other towers; two were taller, one rising considerably higher into the sky than the other, while two were shorter and nearly even with one another, each ending perhaps twenty meters below the level Slant was on. He was fairly certain that there were at least six towers in all; he could see four, and was inside the fifth, so the remaining one or two he guessed to be around the other side, to the north, where he could not see them.

Below, the city was spread out before him, and except for the massive towers thrusting up from it, it was unremarkable. He had seen hundreds of cities from the air, and this one was nothing out of the ordinary.

Directly ahead, however, visible between the other towers, the view was extraordinary. The southern end of the city was still partly in ruins; twisted steel frames rose in tangled clumps from a thick layer of rubble, occasional bits of concrete still clinging here and there. Beyond the ruins the city ended abruptly in the great stone outcropping he had seen before from the northwest; it reared up over the ruins at a frightening angle, as if it were a falling wall frozen in middescent. It was larger than he had realized before, and he suddenly guessed how the skyscraper skeletons had survived: That upthrust stone had served as a shield against the firestorm and shockwave. He looked to either side of it and found confirmation for his guess; the ruins ended in clearcut lines at the edges of the rock's "shadow." The city walls joined into the crater wall just beyond, so that there was only a narrow strip of desolate level ground on either side between the walls and the ruins.

Slant noticed then that the crater wall merged into the jutting triangle of stone seamlessly, and looked beyond at the crater itself.

Beyond the stony rim the crater was as dead and life-less as if the destruction had occurred three weeks before instead of three centuries; the entire interior was an un-broken plain of incredibly smooth stone that glistened black in the afternoon sun.

The crater rim was jagged and uneven but flowed smoothly up from the crater floor, with no division visible, to end in the middle of its upward curve. Everywhere, the outside of the crater wall was either a sheer drop or an overhang. The jutting crag that protected Praunce was an integral part of the wall, not, as he had previously guessed, a loose chunk that had become attached. All the crags he had spotted previously were parts of the crater wall, as were many other similar formations as well, forming a complete circle that reached almost to the southern horizon. Some of these formations sheltered villages; others guarded ruins that had not yet been reclaimed.

The crater wall was not the usual curving ridge but a sharp, spiky coronet, marking a clear division between the barren plain within and the fertile hills without. Looking at it, Slant guessed something of the nature of the ex-plosion that had created it.

Whatever the weapon had been, it must have melted the bedrock to a liquid as fluid as water; the shockwave had then splashed the molten stone into this eerie ring, where it had frozen again. Since a shockwave travels faster through rock than through air, the promontories that protected the ruins must have risen microseconds be-fore the airborne heat and concussion reached them, which explained why there were still ruins instead of empty plain.

Slant had once seen a photograph of a raindrop striking the ground, its motion frozen by the camera at the instant that it splashed; that raindrop had looked very much like this crater. The raindrop had been water meas-uring a few millimeters across, while the crater was a few kilometers of stone, but they were otherwise identical.

He had spent a year in the wastelands of equatorial Mars, but the interior of the crater seemed far more dead than those expanses of rusty sand.

This had been done by his own government, obliterating millions of people. In retaliation, his homeland had been subjected to even worse—he had heard, at any rate, that the D-series used new and more powerful weapons, but it was hard to imagine anything worse.

He was suddenly depressed and bitter; he turned away from the window and nearly collided with Ahnao as she approached the glass. He let out a wordless noise of surprise and annoyance.

"I wanted to see the view, too," she said timidly.

"Go ahead," he answered, stepping aside.

She was a problem that he needed to consider, he told himself. If Arzadel and his colleagues were to remove the thermite bomb and override, what would he do with Ahnao? Perhaps he could convince someone here in Praunce to take charge of her. It would probably be more difficult to convince her to stay here than to convince someone to accept her. She was an attractive young woman, and friendly, even if she was an idiot.

Actually, he admitted to himself, she wasn't really an idiot. Ignorant and careless she might be, but she was no more stupid than average; her bizarre idea that she needed to be protected and therefore had no use for the basic skills of survival was simply a product of her upbringing—just as his insistence that a person ought to know those basic skills was a result of his.

He seated himself at the table and chewed idly on a section of orange; Ahnao stayed by the window for a long time, staring out at the city, the countryside beyond, and the crater. Neither spoke as they waited for Arzadel to return.

Chapter Twenty-One

THE SUN HAD SET AND THE ROOM WAS DIM IN THE GATH-
ering dusk when the door Arzadel had departed
through opened again. Slant had been leaning against
one of the stone pillars between windows, idly considering
the best means of recharging the ship's drained batteries,
and Ahnao had curled up on the fur-covered floor and
fallen asleep.

When he heard the door's latch, Slant was immediately
alert; he stood upright and began to speak a greeting to
the returning wizard. Ahnao awoke, more or less, and
rolled over to face the newcomer, blinking in the confusion of one half asleep.

The figure that entered was not Arzadel, however, but
a tall, awkward youth in a gray robe; Slant cut off what he
had been about to say and let the stranger speak first.

"Hello, Slant, and Ahnao. I am Haiger, apprentice to
Pleido, and I come to deliver a message from Arzadel."

There was a moment of silence; then the newcomer
continued hesitantly, "You *are* Slant and Ahnao, aren't
you? It's so dark in here!"

"Yes, I am Slant, and this is Ahnao. And it is getting
dark; is there a lamp somewhere?"

"Oh, of course; just a moment." The apprentice reached
up behind one of the fur hangings and brought forth an
oil lamp; a moment later it was lit and set in the center
of the nearest table, casting a circle of cheerful yellow
light.

"Is that better?"

"Yes, much better. Thank you."

"You're welcome."

There was a moment of silence; Slant asked, "You had a message from Arzadel?"

"Oh, yes, I'm sorry! The matter you have brought for consideration is not to be decided lightly; therefore, the full Council of the Wizards of Praunce will meet tomorrow morning, and Arzadel will be occupied for the remainder of the night in preparations for that meeting. He respectfully begs your pardon, and bids you make free use of his home and its facilities, asking only that you remain on this level. He apologizes for the lack of proper bedding and hopes that the furs and cushions will serve. I am to point out to you anything you may ask for; for example, the door to the kitchen is there, and the privy is over there." He pointed to these two locations.

Slant had begun to wonder if all wizard's apprentices were slightly scatterbrained when the lad had been so slow in delivering his message, but he certainly seemed to have covered all the important points neatly, and therefore presumably had remembered everything he had been told to say. "Thank you," Slant said in reply. "Will you then be staying the night here?"

"Not in this room; I will be on the floor above, so that you may have your privacy. Should you need me, you may call up the stairwell. If you don't mind, though, I will stay for a while."

"I don't mind at all. What's on the next floor, then, that you're free to see and we are not?" The question might be impolitic, but Slant was genuinely curious.

"Oh, there's a study, and a library, and the private chambers of Arzadel and Shopaur."

"Is that the top floor?"

"No, there is one more."

"And what is on that level?"

"More living quarters."

"I see." He fell silent.

Ahnao spoke for the first time since awakening. "Are we to have any supper? I'm hungry."

"Yes, of course! What would you like?"

"Oh, anything."

The youth looked pitifully uncertain, and Slant relieved

him by saying "Don't worry about it; just show me where everything is in the kitchen and I'll take care of it."

The youth assented eagerly, and Slant put together a meal of meat, bread, cheese, and fruit for the three of them. The apprentice joined them at the table, and joined as well in light conversation regarding the weather, the differences between Praunce and Awlmei and Teyzha, the difficulties of learning wizardry, and the color of Ahnao's eyes. This last subject was introduced by Haiger but appeared to surprise him as much as it did the others. It also served to put an embarrassed end to the conversation, and a moment later Haiger politely took his leave and departed through the door he had entered by.

Slant studied Ahnao; she did not seem particularly displeased by the lad's remarks, and he suspected that it might be easier than he had thought to talk her into staying in Praunce. As the two of them prepared to settle down for the night, he noticed that for the first time since he had rescued her from the dragon, she chose to sleep in a spot more than arm's length away from his own.

It was still two or three hours until dawn when he suddenly came wide awake, sweating and on the verge of screaming. Unintentionally, from long habit, he mentally phrased a question to the computer, asking "What is it?"

"Request cyborg unit response to reestablish communication."

For a moment he thought that he had answered himself, that some fragment of his splintered psyche had decided to play the role of the computer; then he realized that had never happened before, and that there was no reason it should happen now.

"Computer?" he asked.

"Affirmative."

"You're dead! You can't be there!" He wondered suddenly whether he was still dreaming; he had no recollection of ever having dreamed anything like this before, but it was almost possible.

"Negative. Computer was shut down due to power loss. Minimum power levels for operation of secondary systems have been restored."

"How? Everything was drained!"

"Negative. Number-two repair mechanism is shielded and programmed for power supply operation in the event of on-ground power systems failure."

"What kind of power supply? The drive was shut down and everything was dead!"

"Ship's equipment includes photoelectric units. Number-two repair mechanism is programmed to set up photoelectric units."

"You mean you're running off solar power?"

"Term 'solar' is incorrect. Term 'solar' refers only to the star Sol."

"All right, all right, stellar power, then."

"Affirmative."

"Have you restarted the drive?"

"Negative. Insufficient power available at present."

"I don't believe any of this; I must be dreaming."

"Negative. Cyborg unit is conscious."

"I didn't know there was any photoelectric equipment aboard; where was it stored?"

"Photoelectric units were stored in locker C thirty-one."

That, Slant knew, was a storage compartment he had never had any call to look at, near the ship's nose, below the level of his own compartments. He had no recollection of what was supposed to be in those forward compartments; there might well have been solar cells—or photoelectric units, as the computer called them. He began to realize that he was indeed awake, and that the computer really was, too.

He was right back where he had started, apparently.

No, he corrected himself, he wasn't; his ship was grounded, at least for the moment. "Will you be able to restart the drive? Is it damaged?" he asked.

"There is no evidence to indicate damage to main drive. Sufficient power reserve should permit reignition."

"Sufficient power reserve? Have you got any way to provide that much power?"

"Continued operation of photoelectric units should permit reignition within two hundred hours."

"That's ten days, local time."

"Affirmative."

"Where have you got the photoelectric units set up?"

"Photoelectric units are located on plain approximately twenty meters northwest of ship."

"What if the wizards spot them?"

"Information insufficient."

Slant was able to make a guess; if the wizards of Awlmei found those solar cells and realized that the ship was repairing itself, they would shut it down again and make certain that it was permanent this time.

He wasn't sure if that would be a bad thing. He had intended to revive the computer, true, but he had also intended to bring it under control and ensure it stopped killing people. He couldn't tinker with it while the override and thermite were still in his skull without first using the computer's release code, and he couldn't very well have them removed while the computer was awake.

He did know the release code, though. It was simply his own civilian name repeated three times. He couldn't think of it offhand; he was still not fully awake. That would put him in command when he did remember it.

"I know our release code," he told his computer.

"Release code is not valid over this channel."

That was an unpleasant surprise. "Why not?" he asked.

"Release code can only be accepted over onboard audio or on Command frequency."

"Damn." It had not occurred to him that there might be restrictions of that sort; he had thought that he would be able to use the code to erase the computer's military programming without having to actually speak it aloud and thereby return himself to civilian status, but that was apparently not the case. He had assumed, without giving it much consideration, that when the Command's recording told him that it had to be spoken aloud that it applied only to himself and not to the computer.

He had no way of using the Command frequency, which meant that he would have to return to the ship in order to use the code.

He was not entirely certain he wanted to; he had no idea exactly what the code would do. He knew that it would erase all his synthetic personalities, but he did not know whether he would retain any of his special abilities. He knew that it would turn the computer over to his control, but he did not know how much of the machine's programming might be erased and how many of the shipboard systems might be shut off or destroyed. He did not think that the Command was about to leave a civilian, even a veteran, in control of a nuclear arsenal, so something would have to be done with the missiles aboard. He wasn't even sure he was supposed to be able to fly the starship, though he thought that he would at least be permitted to fly it back to Mars.

He didn't even know whether the computer would still be able to use the override and termination device. It would no longer be able to order him about, and would no longer be pursuing its mission, but it might still play watchdog on his loyalty. That could be as good as a death sentence on a world like this that it considered to be enemy territory.

Of course, he didn't plan to stay on this world. He wasn't sure he wanted to go home, since he had no idea what he could expect to find there, but he had no great fondness for this backwater, even if it was strange and interesting with its wizards and rebuilt skyscrapers.

He had wanted to be freed of the bomb and then to have taken his time in restarting the computer, trying to eliminate some of its more obnoxious programming, or at least to disarm it. That appeared a vain hope now. He was an IRU cyborg again. He had lived with it for fourteen years; he could live with it longer. If it became unbearable, he had the release code. That was something worthy of careful consideration: whether or not to use the code.

"Query: Location and current status of cyborg unit." The computer interrupted his chain of thought.

There was something peculiar about the computer's words; perhaps that was why he had been so willing to consider it all a dream.

"I'm in a city the locals call Praunce, on an upper floor of a tall building that's half warehouse and half residential. I'm uninjured and otherwise normal, so far as I know. I have with me a snark, partially discharged—I don't know the exact level—a machine-pistol, a hand laser, and a few supplies, food, tools, and so forth."

"Locating equipment not fully operational. Describe location more exactly."

He understood now; the "voice" in his head was abnormally soft, with a thin, ghostly quality. The computer must either be operating at extreme range or at low power or both. "Praunce is east by southeast of your present position; I don't know the distance, but your transmission is weak."

"Acknowledged. Describe current status more exactly."

"I have . . ." He paused to phrase his message. "I have successfully infiltrated the stronghold of a wizard resident here, and am his guest. I have with me a captive whom the wizard believes to be my willing companion. In the morning the wizard will be meeting with others in order to decide whether they wish to aid me in repairing the ship; I was not aware that you would be able to restore yourself to operation as you have, and was therefore seeking assistance through subterfuge." He was grateful that the computer could not discern truth as wizards could; it would probably blow his head off if it learned the truth. He was glad that his internal recorders were useless for periods exceeding an hour without computer contact.

A brief pause followed; then the computer replied, "Continue action for present."

That struck him as slightly odd; why would the computer allow him to continue with something that had been rendered completely pointless by the flow of events? Did it perhaps think he could convince the wizards to somehow speed up the recharging process? Had it some ulterior motive that it had not bothered to explain to him?

He decided against asking it, and returned to sleep.

Chapter Twenty-Two

THROWN OFF SCHEDULE BY THE INTERRUPTION OF HIS rest, Slant overslept that morning, and awoke only when Haiger let the kitchen door slam behind him. His hands were both busy holding a tray of breakfast for Ahnao and himself, and the door, which was not hung perfectly, got away from him.

He almost dropped the tray in surprise as Slant came awake in response to the noise; the cyborg rolled over and to his feet in a single incredibly fast motion, the snark ready in his hand, though it had been wrapped in his vest half a meter from where he lay. Once upright, he quickly scanned the room, obviously poised either to fight or flee; when no enemy presented himself, there was a moment of confusion.

Finally, Slant's face relaxed into an expression of sleepy bewilderment, and he lowered the snark. "What was that noise?"

"I slammed the door. I'm sorry."

"Oh." Slant looked about and noticed the snark in his hand for the first time. He crossed to his vest and placed the weapon gently atop it, then turned back to Haiger. "What time is it? How long have you been here?"

"I've been here since just after sunrise; that was a little more than an hour ago." Haiger was standing in the middle of the floor, still clutching the tray; he had not moved since Slant's startling performance. He remembered the tray's existence and asked, "Would you like something to eat? Ahnao and I were about to have breakfast, as we did not know how much longer you would sleep. You're welcome to join us."

"Thank you, I think I will." He postponed considering anything important until he had eaten his fill.

When his stomach felt right, he leaned back on a pile of cushions and asked, "Are you there?" The memory of his conversation with the computer was vague and distorted by sleep, so that he was not completely certain it had not been an unusually vivid dream. That the computer had said nothing since he was awakened by the slamming door served to enhance his doubts.

"Affirmative."

It had not been a dream. "Just checking," he replied.

His situation suddenly seemed precarious. If the computer found out why he had actually come to Praunce, it would almost certainly kill him. If the wizards found out that the computer was operational again, they might well kill him. Worst of all, he could not predict his own actions; he might do something tantamount to killing himself at the computer's insistence. Yesterday he had looked forward to a long life of relative peace; now he was unsure he could live out the day.

"Is there any word from Arzadel today?" he asked Haiger.

"No, not yet; the Council has probably just now met."

"How long do you suppose they'll take?"

Haiger shrugged. "There's no knowing. It might be five minutes or five days."

That added yet another uncertainty, and Slant felt trapped. He wanted to just walk away from this whole mess.

Was there, he asked himself, any reason not to simply walk away, to go back to his ship immediately and stop worrying about wizards? He could not think of any. There was no need to tell anyone of his intentions, except of course for the computer. It might turn nasty if he acted too independently.

"Computer," he said, "I think I've made a mistake in coming here. I want to come back aboard to reconsider the situation."

"Query: Advisability of proposed course of action."

"I don't see any reason to do otherwise. I came here to try and restore the ship's power, but you've done that without my help. My continued presence here serves no useful purpose anymore and puts me at risk."

"Affirmative."

"Then I should return?"

"Affirmative."

A wave of relief swept over him; he would be able to get out without having his brain burned. The only difficulty now was in getting down out of the tower. "Haiger," he said, "has anything been done about our horses? I should go tend to them."

"Horses?"

"Yes; we had three horses. We left them down at the base of the tower."

"I'm afraid I don't know anything about them."

"There's no problem; the Council probably won't need us for a while anyway, so if you could just lower me back down the tower, I'll tend to them myself." An unpleasant possibility occurred to him. "Can you take me back down? I know you're only an apprentice, but it's not that far, and all straight down."

"I think I can manage."

"Good! Then would you, please?"

Haiger still appeared uncertain, and Slant guessed that he had been instructed to keep the two foreigners in the tower. He pretended to think the youth's hesitation had another cause, however, and said, "I'm sure Ahnao will be all right without us."

Haiger looked at the girl, sitting against a wall chewing on a pear and watching the two men. "Oh. Of course she'll be all right. Very well, I'll carry you down."

Slant did not repress his smile; now the only problem would be escaping from this slightly inept young wizard.

The descent from the platform was not as smooth and steady as the ascent had been; instead it was a series of short plunges and sudden slowings, ending in an awkward landing on the wood floor beside the trap door. The tingle of magic was uneven and uncomfortable. Haiger arrived on his hands and knees; Slant came down rolling, as he had been trained.

"Thank you," he said, "I can manage from here. There's no need for you to walk down all these stairs."

"Oh, that's all right. I can use the exercise, and you may need a hand with the horses."

"No, really, don't put yourself out."

"It's no trouble."

Slant gave up; if he protested further it would make the lad suspicious. He decided that it would be best to check in with the computer, however, and asked, "Have you any suggestions?"

There was no answer.

Startled, he asked, "Are you there?"

There was still no response; puzzled, he lowered himself down through the trap under Haiger's watchful eyes and dropped to the floor below.

Haiger followed, floating down gently rather than dropping, as Slant asked again, "Are you there?"

No reply came, then or on any of the eight floors below. The horses were still where he had left them, and with Haiger's assistance he found a stable where they could remain while he dealt with the wizards above.

Walking down eight flights of stairs he had considerable time in which to think, and he decided that he would indeed be dealing with the wizards after all. He had no idea what had actually happened to the computer, but he was able to make a few guesses.

The guess that he thought most likely was that the wizards of Awlmei had found the photoelectric panels and shut down the ship again. He would have expected the computer to have had time to give him some sort of warning, but he didn't really know what the wizards were capable of; they might have blocked the warning, or worked in some manner the computer couldn't detect, so that it was unaware of its own destruction until it was too late.

It was possible that the wizards had simply detonated one of the nuclear warheads aboard the ship; that would be quick, practically instantaneous. He wondered whether the flash might have been visible, or the explosion audible, even at this distance. If one had occurred it had probably been while he was dropping down the shaft a few meters at a time, and he could easily have missed it.

It appeared then that he was free once more, but that this time his ship might be gone beyond repair, leaving him stranded forever on this little planet. He wasn't sure how he felt about that; he considered it as he paid the stablemaster and made sure that the horses were given adequate food and water. He had not wanted to remain on the planet, but it was in many ways preferable to being the computer's slave again, however briefly. At least he had not had to use the release code on himself and still had his extraordinary abilities intact.

The thermite was still in his skull, though, and even with the computer gone that was an unpleasant thought. Furthermore, he could not be certain that the computer actually was gone for good; it had managed one seemingly miraculous resurrection, and he could not lightly dismiss the possibility of another.

He should have time, though, for the wizards to remove the bomb and the override. He would have to ask them to hurry, just in case.

When the horses were taken care of, and Haiger was becoming slightly nervous and impatient, he had decided to carry on as before, as if the computer had never returned to operation. His cheerfulness was only slightly exaggerated as he accompanied the apprentice back to the tower.

The walk up to the ninth floor was wearing, and his cheerfulness faded. He could not be certain what had happened to the computer; what if it had shut itself down, due to some minor systems failure? It might be back in action at any moment.

He could deal with that, however, simply by leaving again. He could explain to the computer that he had thought it had been deactivated again and had returned to obtain help after all.

Haiger helped him up through the trap door by hand rather than by magic; conserving his strength, Slant guessed. A moment later the two of them were rising unsteadily toward the distant platform.

It was at approximately the halfway point, seventy meters from either the trap door or the platform, that he thought he heard a rustling. It grew into a hiss, and he realized it was not in his ears but in his communication circuit. A hundred meters above the floor it had a rhythm and was almost separable into words.

Ten meters short of the platform he could tell it was the computer screaming "Mayday! Mayday! Mayday!"

"What the hell is the matter?" he demanded.

The computer's reply was faint, but it strengthened with every meter he rose. "Cyborg unit has passed extreme limit of communication range without permission or prior warning."

"What?" That was not the response he had expected; he had guessed that the computer was in the process of reviving itself again.

"Cyborg unit has passed extreme limit of communication range without permission or prior warning."

"I did?"

"Affirmative."

"All I did was to go down to the base of the tower and a couple of blocks up the street." The platform was within reach; he caught it and hauled himself upward.

The computer did not reply until he and Haiger were on the stairs, when it announced, "Evidence indicates that city designated 'Praunce' by cyborg unit lies below broadcast horizon. Communication is possible only while cyborg unit maintains sufficient altitude to remain above broadcast horizon."

That, unfortunately, made sense. The ship's transmitter had enough power to communicate at great distances—it would have had no problem reaching from Old Earth to its moon—but it could hardly be expected to reach through a planet, or even just a slice of one. That possibility had not occurred to him when he was considering what might have happened to the computer.

Although it appeared at first that his situation was exactly what he had thought it to be at breakfast, he realized as he entered the main room again that that was not the case. The solution to all his problems was at hand. All he had to do was to return to ground level, with Arzadel, and have the override and thermite removed there; the computer would be able to do nothing to prevent it, would not even be aware of it. Then he could return to the ship and do as he pleased with it.

He would even be able to bring someone else aboard to speak the release code, while he stayed out of earshot and thereby retained his own special abilities. He would be free to pilot the ship anywhere he wanted then—at least, he would if the computer did not have some sort of injunction against it in its civilian programming. Even if it did, he should be able to alter the programming and get around it.

Everything, he told himself, was working out beautifully!

"I came back up here because I thought you'd been shut down again," he told the computer. "I was planning to ask the wizards for help after all, but now I don't need to, so I guess I should start back to the ship."

"Negative."

"Why not?"

"Interruption of communication between ship and cyborg unit for extended periods of time is not acceptable."

"Then how the hell am I supposed to get back to the ship?"

"Cyborg unit will remain in present location until main drive is fully operational. Ship will then be relocated within communication range. Cyborg unit will then return to ship."

"But I could be stuck here for ten days!"

"Affirmative."

"The wizards may not let me stay that long."

"Cyborg unit will terminate any personnel who interfere with acceptable course of action."

"I may have to kill every wizard in Praunce!"

"Affirmative."

"I can't do that!"

"Failure to comply with acceptable course of action will allow termination of cyborg unit."

"You damn idiot machine!" Nothing was working out after all. He was stranded in the tower; if he tried to descend that would be an unacceptable course of action, and the computer would kill him.

He was worse off than before—at least until the ship could fly again. Then he would be able to leave and use the release code to put everything to rights, sacrificing his supernormal abilities.

He would be able to do that only if he survived the next ten days. He was not optimistic.

It struck him as incredibly bad luck that he had been in the tower when the computer first restored communication. Coming to Praunce had been a mistake; if he had gone on to Teyzha, he would have remained below the broadcast horizon until the bomb was safely out of his head.

Was that necessarily true? What if it had taken him another ten days to reach Teyzha? Then he might have been in an even worse situation than he was in at present, as the ship would have come looking for him. At least now he had several days to try and figure out a way to improve the situation. He might find some way to convince the computer that he should be allowed to descend, assuming he didn't get killed first.

He was back in the main room; he had nodded politely to Ahnao but refused to say anything more than a vague mumble to either her or Haiger, as he was too concerned with his own thoughts and the computer's actions.

Seeing that Slant was not paying any attention, Haiger made light conversation with Ahnao; the two gradually drifted off to the far end of the room, leaving Slant alone to glower out one of the great irregular windows at the world below.

Chapter Twenty-Three

IT WAS MIDAFTERNOON WHEN ARZADEL APPEARED, AND Slant had not devised any way to improve his situation.

The wizard was not alone; several other men and women accompanied him, clad in flowing robes of red, black, or gold. When Slant rose politely to greet them, Arzadel introduced the wizards, Pleido, Shopaur, Marse, Arrelis, and Dekert.

The six seated themselves, and Arzadel started to speak; before he could say anything, Slant interrupted him.

"Forgive me, but before you tell me of your decision, I want to thank you for even considering my request that you aid in the repair of my ship."

He hoped the wizards would take the hint; he did not want the computer to know what he had actually requested.

There was a moment of confused silence; Arzadel studied Slant's face and then said, "Of course, of course. I think, however, that the matter may require further consideration, after all; this committee will have to discuss it, and we may want to reconvene the whole Council. Is there anything that we can do for you immediately, here and now?"

"I do have a favor to ask."

"Ask it."

"I am weary from traveling; would it be possible for me to remain here as your guest for nine or ten days?"

"Ten days?"

"Yes. I would also ask that someone see to our horses, as I do not feel that I can manage the trip down to ground level again for a while."

"I think that can be arranged."

"Thank you. I am grateful for your hospitality."

"I think we had best depart now, and consider your request further." Arzadel arose, followed by his five compatriots, and the group trailed out through the door.

Haiger remained behind, obviously confused. "I thought they had reached a decision," he said.

"So did I," Ahnao agreed.

"Apparently they hadn't," replied Slant.

There was a faint crawling of his skin; the cyborg informed him, "Minor gravitational anomaly occurring in vicinity of cyborg unit."

Haiger's eyes were unfocused, staring at something beyond the ceiling. He rose, and his eyes returned to normal. "I have to go," he said. "They're calling for me."

"Go, then. We can manage for ourselves," Slant said.

"Must you go, Haiger?"

"I'll be back when I can, Ahnao." He smiled at her,

then followed his superiors, closing the door carefully behind him.

Slant decided that he would have no further trouble with Ahnao; she would probably be eager to stay in Praunce. He was not entirely sure he liked the idea after all; she might have been good company once he taught her a few things.

The remainder of the day passed in quiet boredom; Slant and Ahnao were both tired of admiring the view, discussing the weather and the furnishings, and sitting around doing nothing. Ahnao took to pacing the length of the room impatiently and poking about in the kitchen; Slant, with years of practice in boredom, sat back and lost himself in thought, running through familiar old games, working mathematical problems, considering his situation. He came up with nothing new. He was trying to remember his name when Haiger returned, shortly after sunset.

"Arzadel has sent me," he announced, "to ask your help in a small matter."

"What is it?"

"Someone was sent to tend to your horses but encountered some difficulty. If you could come down for just a moment, I'm sure the whole matter can be straightened out quickly.

"Well, computer? It will look suspicious if I don't co-operate, and it will just be a few minutes."

"Negative. Cyborg unit will remain in present location until main drive is fully operational."

"I'm afraid I can't, Haiger."

"I really think you should."

"I'm sorry, I can't. You people will just have to deal with the horses as best you can without me."

"I'll tell them what you've said." He turned and left again, with only a brief glance at Ahnao.

Haiger did not return that night; Slant and Ahnao made themselves an adequate dinner from the stores in the kitchen and, after another hour of sitting around doing nothing, went to sleep. Again, Ahnao remained a few meters away from Slant; she was obviously over her attachment to him.

Haiger had still not returned when they awoke in the morning. They prepared and ate breakfast, and waited.

By midmorning Ahnao could no longer stand the boredom and announced, "I'm leaving."

Slant replied, "Take care of yourself."

"I'm going to find Haiger and find out what's going on."

"Good luck, then."

She looked at him angrily and marched out through the door the wizards had used. Slant simply sat where he was and watched her go. He was pleased that she was removing herself from the danger of his presence.

Shortly after noon, as Slant was gathering himself his midday meal, he heard a door open and close; he put down the orange he had been peeling and returned to the main room.

Haiger had returned. "Oh, there you are," he said as Slant emerged from the kitchen. "We have to leave; the tower isn't safe. Something's gone wrong with the frame; one of the beams has rusted through, and the whole thing could collapse. We're getting everybody out as fast as we can."

"Computer? I think I better go with him. I'll go straight to the top of one of the other towers and contact you from there."

"Negative. Cyborg unit will remain in present location."

"I can't; didn't you hear? The building's about to collapse!" He did not for a moment believe that to be true, but it was an admirable lie.

"Cyborg unit will remain in present location."

"Do you want me to get killed? You're not being rational!"

"Computer dysfunction remains within acceptable parameters. Cyborg unit will remain in present location."

"What computer dysfunction?" Slant was much more seriously worried by the computer's words than by anything Haiger had said.

"Computer is marginally dysfunctional as a result of general wear and damage suffered during recent power loss."

"Slant?"

"Just a moment; I'm thinking."

"We have to hurry."

"Listen, computer, I have got to leave!"

"Negative. Recommend enemy personnel be terminated."

"Why?"

"Cyborg unit will remain in present location."

"You're not making any sense; are you sure you're not seriously damaged?"

"Slant, we have to go." Haiger reached out to take the cyborg's arm.

Slant reacted automatically; he picked Haiger up and threw him across the room. The apprentice landed hard, the wind knocked out of him, but the furs and cushions kept him from serious injury; he lay dazed where he had fallen.

"Recommend enemy personnel be terminated."

"No, damn it, I won't kill him. I won't kill anybody." Six words spoken aloud aboard his ship would put an end to this idiotic behavior—but the computer wouldn't let him reach the ship to speak them yet. He refused to kill anyone else when he was this close to freeing himself from the computer's control.

"Please take proper action."

That phrase meant the computer would use the override if he continued to disobey; Slant didn't care. He headed for the door to the stairs leading down.

The override came on, and his legs stopped obeying him. He fell forward and lay face down on the rug, twitching as he fought the computer for control of his body.

"I won't kill him!"

The distance was extreme, and the computer had no power reserves; for the first time in his life Slant was able to resist the override, though with only limited success. His right hand jerked, swinging in an arc from his elbow, as the computer tried to force him to draw a weapon; while it concentrated its attention on his arm, he was able to roll onto his back, so that his vest was flung open to one side, the weapons out of reach again.

The arm jerked back, and the machine-pistol was

knocked free. It fell to the floor beside him. He fought for control of his arm, and his hand flapped wildly back and forth.

Behind him a door opened, and the six wizards he had met with the previous morning entered the room.

"Enemy action occurring. Failure to cooperate in termination of enemy personnel will permit termination of cyborg unit."

"Damn it, I won't kill them!" He waited for the explosion as he continued to struggle. He was lying on his side, his right arm reaching out toward the gun; the computer was winning. Perhaps, he thought, that was why it was taking so long in carrying out its threat.

His hand touched the gun; he was concentrating now on keeping his fingers from closing on it. He remembered that the computer was weak on fine control at long range. He could no longer make any motion of his own; the computer had stopped that somehow, strengthening its hold. All he could do was slow down and throw off the moves the computer tried to make.

In a flash of intuition, he wondered if the computer's termination threat was a bluff; if so, he had called it, and so far nothing had happened.

His fingers closed loosely on the pistol grip, and the electric tingle of magic touched him. His index finger groped toward the trigger, and abruptly the crawling sensation became a vicious shock; his limbs jerked spastically, his hand slamming itself against the fur-covered floor but retaining its hold on the gun.

He was no longer able to control his movements at all as he flopped about, but apparently the computer was also incapacitated by the magic; he was flung onto his belly, and the back of his neck burned with an electrical fire that was beyond anything he had ever experienced before. He was no longer completely conscious, and wondered vaguely whether the incredible pain was due to thermite igniting or some new sort of wizardry.

"Cyborg unit has been captured. Immediate termination essential." There was a sudden dull hissing thump, horribly loud, behind him; his body was pressed down viciously, his face rammed into the fur, as if the building had indeed collapsed upon him. The back of his head was abruptly laced with lines of burning agony, and he smelled singed hair and scorching flesh. He lost consciousness.

Chapter Twenty-Four

H E WOKE UP IN A BLAZE OF PAIN, UNABLE TO MOVE HIS head or neck. It took several seconds to focus when he opened his eyes.

He was lying on his back on something cool and soft, looking up at a coffered ceiling painted white and gray. There was no sound he could identify, though the world around him was not completely silent; he heard a faint something that might have been wind or rain, and a rippling sound that could have been distant voices or running water.

It might have been pleasant had he not hurt so much.

Sunlight fell from somewhere, but he could not turn his head enough to see anything but ceiling and could not tell where it came from.

The pain was mostly in his neck and the back of his head, with other spots down his back and a dull grinding headache in his temples. Most of the damage felt like burns, but by no means all; he thought he could detect cuts, abrasions, bruises, and other injuries as well. Cautiously, he lifted his arm; that appeared normal and moved as he wanted it to. He reached up and felt the side of his head.

His hair was gone, and part of his beard; his hand touched dried blood and raw flesh, and he gasped, his vision blurring again, as the faint pressure increased the agony beyond what he had thought possible.

He was alive, but he had no idea where; he was obviously injured, though he was not sure what had happened to him. Somebody was apparently caring for him, since he appeared to be in a bed; the coffered ceiling suggested Praunce. He wondered what had happened to the computer, why it wasn't screaming at him.

"Are you there?" he asked tentatively.

"Affirmative. Please state identity."

He winced; the mental voice seemed unbearably loud. Its question was odd; the computer had never asked him that before. He wondered how badly damaged it was.

"I'm Slant, of course."

"Cyborg unit designated Slant has been terminated."

"Oh." That explained the question, and a great deal more as well. He wondered how he had survived; had the wizards had something to do with it? He thought they must have, as he could vaguely recall his struggle with the override and that magic had been in use.

If he had been terminated, then the thermite was gone and he was free. The only serious question now was whether he could take control of the computer and use the starship for himself.

"I am Slant," he told the computer. "Is there anything in your programming that says I can't communicate with you after being terminated?"

"Negative."

"Then we can just go on as before, right?"

"Negative."

"Why not?"

"Termination of cyborg unit initiates self-destruct procedure."

"It does?" He didn't really have to ask; he knew it did. That was why the computer had wanted him dead. "Then why are you still operational?"

"Programming requires that self-destruct operation be preceded by infliction of maximum possible damage to enemy installations."

He had known that, too. "Then why haven't you done your damage and shut yourself down, or blown yourself up?"

"Maximum possible damage requires use of main drive. Main drive is not presently in operation."

Slant did not have to ask any further questions. He did not want to ask any further questions.

If the ship were to blow itself up where it lay, in the gully, it would be a big, messy explosion, assuming all the various warheads went off, but would probably not hurt anyone except a few farmers who happened to be in the area. He would be stranded on the planet permanently, but relatively little harm would be done. Even the fallout wouldn't be significant when compared to the radiation level already present.

However, if the ship were to get airborne again and distribute its firepower effectively against the various cities, it could reduce the planet to a state fully as bad as it had been in three hundred years earlier. It could probably wipe out the entire civilization.

Slant had to stop that.

He felt a moment of panic as he wondered whether he *could* stop it, but that passed. Of course he could stop it. All he had to do was get back aboard the ship before it took off and use the release code. Even if it refused to recognize him he could get aboard; he knew all the emergency boarding procedures. Once aboard, anybody could use the release code. All he had to do was speak his name three times.

First, though, he had to get to his ship before it took off.

"How long before you can restart the drive?"

"Continued operation of photoelectric units should permit reignition within one hundred and twenty hours."

Before Slant had not worried too much about details, but he knew they could be crucially important now. "Is that a maximum time?"

"Affirmative."

"Allowing for bad weather and so forth?"

"Affirmative."

"Then what's the minimum?"

"Twenty-one hours."

Time was suddenly rushing by; every second increased the urgency. He realized for the first time that if he was still in Praunce when the ship began its attack he would be killed along with the hundreds of thousands of innocent natives. He had traveled for seven days to reach Praunce from the ship, and though he had been moving at a leisurely pace, he doubted he could get back to the vessel in less than three days. If the weather was bright, he had only a single day.

If the weather was cloudy, though, he might have as much as six days. An average of the two figures was three and a half days, or seventy hours. He could probably manage that if he got moving immediately. He had at least a decent chance of success, then.

There was no time to waste, however. He had to get out of bed and start moving. He would need help in getting under way; he guessed that he was probably still atop a tower, and would need a wizard to lower him to the ground. He tried to sit up, ignoring the surge of pain in his head, and shouted as he did so, calling as loudly as he could "Help! Help me!"

The near-silence vanished in a rush of footsteps and voices; a door slammed open somewhere nearby.

He managed to push himself into a sitting position on the edge of what was, as he had thought, a bed, and with some effort he brought his eyes back into focus, ignoring the drifting colored shadows that he knew were tricks of the mind and eye. He was in a room with soft gray walls and a deep golden carpet; the far end, a dozen meters away, was a single expanse of glass and lead, the panes clear or yellow or green, and smooth or rippled or bubbled. Nothing but open sky was visible beyond.

He was still in Praunce, and still atop one of the towers. He had time to see that much before his bed was surrounded by people. Arzadel was the first, followed by Haiger and Ahnao and others; they gathered at his bedside.

"You shouldn't be sitting up," Arzadel told him.

"I have to. I have to get to my ship as soon as possible."

"Why? What can be so urgent? You're badly injured; we got the explosive out of your head before it went off, but you were still much too close to the blast. You're severely burned from the top of your head halfway down your back, and I'm not sure we got all the fragments out.

We had to work on you for hours; it was a very delicate procedure, with all that metal and strange wiring in your head. We had to make a few changes so we could manage it, do something so you could live and heal—we don't ordinarily make changes without the subject's cooperation, but we had to."

"I know I was injured, I can feel it. The computer thinks I'm dead, though, and it has orders to take revenge for my death by destroying everything it can reach."

"The demon machine is still operating, though it believes you dead? We feared it might be."

"Oh, yes; it isn't stopped as easily as that. It plans to destroy as many of your cities as it can before it kills itself."

"How can it destroy cities? It's only a single machine, isn't it?"

"It controls a starship, armed with the same kind of weapons that made that crater to the south." He saw no point in subverting his own argument by mentioning that his ship's warheads were only a tiny fraction of the size.

Arzadel sucked in his breath, then asked, "What can be done to stop it? Can you fight it?"

"If I can get aboard the ship before it has enough power to take off, I can change its orders. I think I can make it obey me."

"How long do we have before it has enough power?"

"That depends on the weather, because it's taking energy from your sun's light, but it's between one day and six. If I leave immediately and ride hard, I might get there in time."

"You can't ride in your condition. It isn't possible. We'll fly you there."

That eased his worry somewhat. He had not thought of it. "Good," he said. "But I still have to hurry."

"Where is your ship?"

"In a gully a few kilometers south of Awlmei."

"Where is Awlmei?"

Slant was startled that the wizard didn't know, but answered, "It's on the plain to the west of here; I traveled for seven days, two by foot and five by horse, to get here from there."

"Due west?"

"No, slightly to the north."

"We'll find it."

Slant was not as confident as Arzadel, but he nodded. The motion hurt his neck. He was beginning to feel very unsteady, and lay back on the bed. "We have to leave as soon as possible," he said.

"We will. You rest here; I'll make the preparations and wake you when we're ready."

Slant nodded again, carefully; Arzadel turned and left.

When he had gone, taking most of the others with him, Slant said to Haiger, "I'm sorry I threw you around like that."

"That's all right."

"That was a good idea, claiming the tower was going to collapse. I don't know why it didn't work."

"It was Shopaur's idea, not mine."

"Thank him for me, for trying."

"I will. I was wondering . . . how do you know that your machine wants to do these terrible things?"

"It talks to me. It told me what it was planning?"

"It talks to you even when it thinks you're dead?"

"I guess it thinks I'm a ghost."

"A what?"

"Never mind." Either Slant had used the wrong word, or these people did not have ghost stories; in any case, it wasn't worth explaining. "It was told to answer my questions; nobody ever told it I had to be alive at the time."

Haiger said something else, but Slant did not hear it; he had fallen asleep.

When he awoke again the room was full of wizards. Arzadel was nearest him, and spoke.

"We're ready to go. We plan to take turns carrying you; that will be best. Have you any suggestions? We know nothing of this demon you must battle."

An idea had come to him while he slept. "Wizards can control the weather, can't they?"

"Sometimes."

"Could you contact the wizards in Awlmei, and ask them to to make it cloudy? That would give us more time."

In his fuddled state it didn't occur to him that the wizards of Awlmei would probably take much more direct steps if they became aware of the computer's reawakening.

"The mind-talk doesn't work that well, I'm afraid; we're limited to a few kilometers at most, and Awlmei is much too far away."

"Then I have no other ideas. Let's get started."

"Right." Two wizards reached down and picked him up, trying to be gentle, but his head fell back against the pillow as one's hold slipped slightly, and he was suddenly blinded by pain.

When he could see again he was unsure how much time had passed, and whether he had remained conscious or not; the wizards were gathered around him still, but he was no longer in bed or in the gray room but on a rooftop. A strong wind blew out of the north—at least, he thought it was the north, assuming that the sun was in the southwest. He was unsure why he thought it to be afternoon rather than morning; it was the feel of the air as much as anything else.

A moment later he was in midair, supported by the two wizards; the others followed, trailing slightly behind. These were not the wizards who had accompanied Arzadel to bring him the decision of the Council, but others he had not met before, for the most part. He saw Arzadel among them, and one other was familiar. There was nothing he could do to help; his life and the lives of the computer's potential victims were in the hands of the wizards. He glanced at the ground far below; the city wall was passing beneath them, and the fields lay spread out ahead, the forests beyond them.

There was nothing he could do; he gave in to the pain and fell asleep again.

When he next awoke the sky was dark. He was gratified to see clouds dimly visible overhead, though there were not very many of them; the drive might take longer to restart than he feared, if those clouds lingered. He looked about and noticed that the wizards were flying at a much lower altitude. They were probably tiring, he told himself. He wished he were able to help.

Although it was hard to be certain by starlight—and his

vision seemed to have blurred again, as well; he hoped that he had not suffered any permanent damage to the optic centers—he thought that the two who were carrying him were not the two who had picked him up from his bed. He looked around and could see only six wizards, where there had been eight originally. The missing two, he was fairly sure, were the pair who had first carried him; they must have tired, passed him on, and returned or landed to rest.

He blinked, trying to clear his vision, and for a moment seemed to see everything through strange polychrome distortion; the wizards were ringed in golden red, the ground below was suffused with indigo, the sky was a seething pale-blue mass. The effect faded but a curious rippling remained, as if the air were heated, though the night was cool.

The wizards holding him dipped abruptly, and he forgot about his eyesight as he grabbed instinctively for a better hold.

"You just keep still," one of the pair muttered. "Don't try and do anything; it'll only interfere. We'll get you there."

Slant nodded weakly. "How long before you restart the drive?" he asked the computer.

"Continued operation of photoelectric units should permit reignition within ninety hours."

"What's the minimum time?"

"Twelve hours."

He looked down, ignoring the distortion in his vision, and saw nothing but dark forest in every direction. "How far do we have to go?" he asked.

"I don't know," replied one of the wizards.

That was little help; he gazed down at the forest rushing by underneath. The pain in the back of his head and neck had lessened; he could bend his neck slightly. His headache was no better, though.

A new worry occurred to him; he reached up and felt for the socket in the back of his neck.

It was still there, but bent completely out of shape; his fingers came away with soot on them. The metal was partially oxidized.

He would be unable to pilot the ship without the direct-control cable; he was stranded on this planet forever unless he could control the computer and force it to fly the ship for him.

He wouldn't be able to fly the ship at all if it destroyed itself. He had to reach it before it took off. The forest rolled away beneath; he watched it for a time, his vision finally clearing, and then dozed off again.

"Slant?"

The voice awakened him; he was still in midair, slung between two wizards, but the forest was gone; instead the ground below was open plain. It was daylight, cloudless and bright, and they were hovering, not moving forward. There was a faint hint of a heat shimmer to the landscape below, and he could not be certain if it was in the air or his vision. Remembering the trouble he had had before, including the momentary flash of weird colors, he hoped that it was not a sign of brain damage. He would have to ask the wizards to check the optic centers of his brain out very carefully, if he ever got back to Praunce.

That could wait, though; someone had awoken him. There must be a reason.

"What is it?"

"We've reached the plain, but we don't see a city or your ship anywhere. Can you direct us?" It was Arzadel who spoke.

Slant looked down and saw nothing but open prairie; behind, a few kilometers away, was the edge of the forest and the start of the hills. There were no landmarks he recognized.

"Where am I?" he asked the computer.

"Information insufficient."

"What do you mean, 'information insufficient'? I thought you always knew my location!"

"Cyborg unit has been terminated. All information received from cyborg unit must be considered invalid."

"That's ridiculous."

The computer did not reply.

"Look, tell me where I appear to be, then. I don't care if the information is invalid. Am I north or south of you?"

"Apparent location of cyborg unit is south by southwest of ship; distance unknown. Locating equipment not fully operational."

"Turn north," Slant told Arzadel. "And look for something flat and shiny black." The photoelectric cells would be far more visible than the camouflaged ship.

The wizards obeyed, turning to parallel the edge of the forest, and when they were moving again Slant asked, "How long before you start the drive?"

"Continued operation of photoelectric units should permit reignition within twenty-five hours."

"What's the minimum?"

"Three hours."

"What?" For the first time, Slant noticed that the sun was in the west; he had slept away the entire morning. Furthermore, the sun was bright and warm; not a single cloud was in sight anywhere. Only four wizards were left in the party.

He did not go to sleep again, but watched as best he could the ground ahead.

Slightly over two hours later he thought the terrain was beginning to look familiar. Before he could say anything, though, one of the wizards called, "Look ahead!"

He tried; he turned his head, and the pain in his head and neck blurred his vision momentarily. When it cleared he saw a dull glint amid the grass below.

"I think that's it," he said. Relief trickled through him; he had begun to worry that he would not make it in time. The weather had been bright, clear, and sunny all day. He had wondered how the wizards could possibly have come out so far off course, and whether the computer had told him the correct direction.

Now he was no longer particularly worried. He only had to get aboard and speak his name three times. All he had to say was his name.

He couldn't remember it, but he still had time.

"How long before you can start the drive?" he asked.

"Continued operation of photoelectric units should permit reignition within a maximum of fourteen hours. Given current weather conditions, reignition will occur in approximately forty-five minutes."

Slant had suspected for some time that the minimum time would prove sufficient because the weather on this continent had been consistently clear and sunny since he landed.

A few moments later the wizards landed; at Slant's suggestion they stayed well away from the ship, in case the computer had devised a way to defend itself. He would approach alone, on foot. This was to be entirely his own battle.

"Be careful, Slant," Arzadel said as he staggered to his feet.

"I will," he answered. He was unsteady for a moment; he had not stood upright on his own for more than a day, and his body's reserves had undoubtedly been depleted by healing the wounds on his head and neck, whatever the wizards might have done to help. He realized he hadn't eaten since before the thermite bomb went off; he had not had the time. His body had suppressed his hunger automatically, as it was trained to do. Perhaps that was why his vision had been so faulty, and not improved since first he awoke after the blast. Even now, he seemed to see a bluish shimmer to the ground before him. He blinked, and it was gone.

As he walked slowly toward his vessel it occurred to him that he might be able to stop the ship from taking off by smashing the photoelectric panels, but he decided against trying it. The computer probably had some way of defending them, and if he was unable to get at them, for whatever reason, he might waste too much time in the attempt. The release code was a sure thing. Even if he could not remember his name, he knew it was written on a slip of paper stuck in a book in the case in the control cabin.

He would do better to get aboard the ship quickly than to waste time with the photoelectric equipment. Besides, if he wrecked the panels, he might never get the ship off the ground once he had taken control.

He arrived at the lip of the gully, on the far side from the ship. Carefully, he began climbing down the slope.

His feet went out from under him on the loose sand, and he slid feet-first down the side of the depression; the spray of dust raised by his body stung painfully on his burns. He lay still for a moment at the bottom, then slowly sat up. He hand, when he raised it to shield his eyes from the slanting sunlight, shook from fatigue and hunger.

He was twenty meters from the ship; it loomed up before him, an irregular mass of green plastic camouflage covering most of the opposite slope of the gully for meters in either direction. The airlock, he knew, was around the far side, above the wing. There were other entrances, but that was the one that was most easily breached.

It was possible he wouldn't have to breach anything. "Open the aft emergency hatch," he told the computer.

"Cyborg unit has been terminated. Commands given on this channel are therefore invalid."

He had expected that. "How long until reignition?"

"Approximately thirty-two minutes."

That was not bad, though he was cutting it closer than he liked. He made his way across the gully and up the far side in eight minutes, staying well clear of the camouflage cover in case the computer decided he was dangerous. The stream at the bottom helped cool him and wash the dust away, and he paused while wading across to drink a few handfuls of water.

Once he was above the camouflage he approached slowly and cautiously, taking his time in finding his way through the plastic and along the wing in the cool green darkness.

The computer did nothing to stop him and said nothing; he judged he had slightly under twenty minutes remaining.

The airlock door did not cooperate; the manual control was being overridden by the computer, and the computer ignored his commands to open.

"Can you hear me?" he asked aloud.

"Negative," the computer replied through his communication circuit. "Exterior audio inoperative for reasons of power conservation."

There was still a way in; the manual control that the computer had overridden operated the same hydraulic mechanism the computer itself used, but he could use an emergency panel just aft of the hatch to uncouple the mechanism, allowing the door to be cranked open by hand, just as he had cranked it shut when he left the ship. He found the panel and pried it open, breaking a fingernail on the metal.

The coupling lever inside was stiff from long disuse; it took all his strength to throw it. When it finally came free he was unable to stop his forward momentum, and sprawled awkwardly on the ship's wing.

He lay there for a few seconds, then got to his feet, his ears ringing. Ghost images danced before him, and the metal sides of the ship had a golden sheen. The airlock was still closed. The computer told him, when he asked, that he had fourteen minutes.

It took one of the fourteen minutes to work the hatch open far enough for him to slip inside. He left it as it was; he had no time to waste in recoupling the hydraulics or cranking it shut.

The inner door was also shut; he cursed his own caution. There was no need to find an uncoupler for this door; the regular manual mechanism could not be overridden. He had it open in thirty seconds.

There was an unspeakably foul odor filling the interior of the ship; he gagged when it first reached him, and stopped where he was. It was nothing familiar, no simple failure of the ship's ventilation as had sometimes occurred over the years. It was the smell of something dead and rotting.

The air within was stagnant; the ship's ventilators had not been running. The computer had been conserving power. "Turn on the fans," he ordered aloud. "Clear that smell out of here."

There was a soft whirr as the computer obeyed. It was programmed to obey certain orders from anyone inside its hull, so that time would not be wasted on authorization during emergencies; any request for essential life-support systems, such as air circulation, would be fulfiled.

The stink subsided gradually, and Slant realized what it was. He had left Kurao's head on the acceleration couch in the control cabin.

That was a minor consideration, however. He was aboard ship, with perhaps ten minutes remaining before the drive could be restarted. All he had to do was speak the release code.

He couldn't remember his name. It began with something that sounded a little like his code name—Slan? Slam? Sant?

None of those sounded right.

"Computer, what's your cyborg unit's civilian name?"

"That information is restricted."

He had spoken aloud to avoid argument about his termination, so the computer had replied over the ship's speakers; its voice was strange and unfamiliar, very unlike the "voice" that he heard over the communication device in his skull. It had a pleasant contralto, though it spoke in a monotone. He had not expected it to have a feminine voice.

It might be willing to answer its cyborg; he tried subvocalizing. "What's my civilian name?"

"That information is restricted, available only to personnel authorized by the Command. Cyborg unit does not have authorization."

He was not worried yet; he still had time. The drive would not be started for a few more minutes, and it would take time to heat up the engines. Once aloft, it could take time to choose and approach a target.

His name began with an S sound, he was sure. It was a two-part name.

He couldn't think of it.

"How long until ignition?"

"Approximately seven minutes."

He would have to find that slip of paper in the bookcase. He could not remember the name. He stepped through the inner door of the airlock and moved cautiously down the corridor to the control cabin. The lights were on, dimly, as if during Slant's sleep period.

The smell of rotting flesh was not completely gone here; it made him want to turn back, to find somewhere to vomit. He forced himself to keep moving forward.

The storage lockers were still open, as he had left them;

he was surprised that the computer had not closed them. It was apparently serious about using the minimum power required by its programming. He was glad that it was required to keep open the communication channel he used, or else he might not have know what it was doing in time to stop it.

The chameleon fur was a neutral gray color; apparently the computer was not able to keep power from revitalizing it. He had no time to play with it; even though the gray was ugly, he ignored it.

Kurao's head was a mass of decay, lying on the canvas sack he had carried it in; the idea of having it in the room while he searched through the books was more than he could stand, and he carried it to one of the disposal chutes.

If he had had more time he might have done something slightly more respectful, but he had six minutes.

He returned to the control cabin and crossed directly to the bookcase. The smell was already fading. He opened the glass doors and pulled out a handful of old paperbacks.

The acceleration couch had an unpleasant stain where Kurao's head had rested; it had seeped around the edge of the plastic dropcloth. He did not want to touch it. Instead, he seated himself on the floor beneath the bookcase and began thumbing through books.

Almost immediately, he found a slip of paper; he unfolded it and read, "#7 locker has broken latch, open with screwdriver."

He threw the paper and book aside, and picked up the next volume.

The note with his name on it was not in any of the first dozen books; he paused and looked up at the shelves. They were jammed full. Those dozen books had not made a visible dent.

It would take half an hour, at least, to go through the entire bookcase, even if he gave each volume only a quick riffle—and the note might be wedged in where a quick riffle would not find it.

"How long until you start the drive?"

"Approximately four minutes, thirty seconds."

He had to remember, and quickly. If he could not remember his name, he had to remember where he had put the note.

"Computer, do you know which book has my name in it?"

"Negative."

He had expected that; the computer's memory was not unlimited, and it couldn't keep records of everything he did. There was nothing to do but keep looking; he pulled down a fat book on late–nineteenth-century art.

When the warning chime sounded, he sat amid a pile of books he had thumbed through; he had found half a dozen notes, mostly reminding himself of particularly good features in the computer's video library.

"What is it?"

"Main drive has been reignited. Prepare for launch."

There was a sudden series of banging sounds as the computer used its now-plentiful power supply to take care of its postponed maintenance and close the doors to the storage lockers. The lights came up to full brilliance; Slant blinked. Each light appeared haloed in red; he blinked again, and they were normal.

He had to get onto the acceleration couch, he knew, but he didn't want to leave the bookcase, or to touch that dark-brown stain. He tried to think of his name.

The pain in his head distracted him. It was no use trying.

He got to his feet and grabbed another handful of paperbacks from the bookcase, then started toward the couch. He was reaching out toward it when he heard the engines starting. He wasted no more time but threw himself onto the couch, turning as he did to try and get into the proper position. He almost made it.

The ship's takeoff vaporized the green plastic camouflage; the nose shredded the cover into thousands of fluttering shreds that vanished completely when the heat of the exhaust hit them. The side of the gully collapsed as the ship tore free.

The photoelectric panels were shattered and partially melted by the shock and heat, but they remained where they were, glinting dully in the sun.

To the south, four wizards from Praunce watched wordlessly, certain that Slant had failed and that their doom was upon them. To the north, a few Awlmeian farmers saw the launch and wondered what it could be.

Aboard ship, Slant was slammed back against the couch. He was not properly aligned with the depression in the couch designed to fit his body, so although the machinery performed its function, thrusting upward against him to counteract the acceleration, his head and arm were banged against the edge. Red waves of staggering pain poured through him from the blow to his injured head.

His body was equipped to handle pain, he told himself.

There was a pounding and bumping all around him; he managed to pry his eyes open against the pressure of acceleration, and saw through blurred vision that most of the bookcase was empty. He had left it open, and the books had fallen out, tumbling past him to collect at the back of the cabin.

The acceleration suddenly subsided; the couch shifted under him, adjusting to new acceleration, and he realized the ship was turning. It was preparing for its first attack run.

"Stop it! Damn it! I know our release code!"

"Release code can be accepted over onboard audio."

"It's my name!"

The computer said nothing. Slant reached for the direct-control cable but then remembered that he couldn't use it.

"My name, damn it, repeated three times!"

He knew what it was; he twisted his neck, ignoring the pain, and glanced at the pile of books, tumbled haphazardly against the curving wall. He did know what it was; he only had to remember it. Slat . . . Satta . . . San . . .

"Sam!" His name was Sam, he could remember hearing it many times; a girl had whispered it in his ear, his father had called him that. Samuel.

"My name's Samuel Turner!"

That was it!

The computer said nothing.

He remembered that he had to repeat it three times.

"Samuel Turner, Samuel Turner, Samuel Turner!" he shouted. "I'm Samuel Turner!"

The computer clicked and whirred, and answered, "Affirmative. Release code accepted. Awaiting orders."

He barely heard it; his mind felt as if it were tearing itself apart and being rammed back together. He felt himself to be eighteen people, each distinct, all jammed into a single body and being forced to merge with each other.

The pilot was gone, and Slant himself realized he knew astronomy and navigation; cover personalities were fading into nothingness, leaving him their skills and memories. He remembered his seduction of Ahnao—or her seduction of him, whichever it had been—and knew why he had made each move, what each of the proper responses had been. The memories of the warrior persona mingled with his own as it faded, last of all, and he was revolted by the knowledge that he had killed and maimed with his own hands—though he had had the ability to do worse, and would still have it, if he survived; he could mangle other human beings in ways he found hard to believe. He had been aware that he had done these things, or that they had been done with his body, but now he felt them himself, knew what bones breaking under his hands felt like.

He did not want to know everything he had done and thought in all his guises, but as he reabsorbed each schizoid personality that knowledge ran through him and into his own memories, leaving no distinction between himself and the person who had done it.

It had been he, Samuel Turner, who had decapitated an innocent old man and dissected his brain; it had been he who killed Teyzhan guards with his bare hands, he who cut off a beggar's hand, he who seduced a foolish young woman, he who had made sense of a synesthetic mess of data in order to steer the ship, he who had spent fourteen years wandering in space killing any who interfered with him. He knew how he had done all these things, and he remembered committing each act.

Then the memories were blanked out by a wall of pain. The back of his head was a mass of raw flesh and exposed nerves, and the mechanisms that kept him in control of the pain from those wounds had just shut down.

He struggled to reconstruct them, to somehow block out the agony; his vision was bathed in red haze. He was unsure he could remain conscious much longer, and he had to stop the computer from destroying the planet's civilization. "Don't attack!" he called feebly. "Stop!"

"Affirmative. Cessation of all computer activity in five seconds."

"What? He remembered the computer's death wish, and that one of the ways it could die was a shut-down order following its release code; it was misinterpreting his command. It would shut itself off if he didn't countermand himself in the five-second grace period, and without the computer he could not control the ship. It would crash, or drift off into space if it had reached escape velocity, or possibly fall into orbit around the planet. He would die.

No! He would not let himself die! Not after surviving fourteen years of drifting through space, fourteen years in which he had killed dozens, hundreds of innocent people so that he could survive. After living through all that, he would not die now because the computer chose to suicide; he would not let the machine take him with it. He would not give in to it this final time.

He struggled against the pain, trying to phrase a command; his communication circuit was dead, so it would have to be spoken aloud. He sat up, so that the computer would hear him more clearly.

That proved a disastrous mistake; a new wave of pain swept over him as he moved, and he blacked out for an instant.

That was enough. There was a click, and the computer was gone. The ship was dead, running entirely on its simple fail-safe systems, coasting along its set course.

He could not restart the computer; he had absorbed the personality in charge of ship's maintenance, and he knew that it was gone, that it could only be revived by slow, step-by-step reprogramming. If he was to survive he would have to land the ship himself—or else boost it clear of the planet, to drift on until the life-support systems failed. That wouldn't take long, without the computer to regulate them, and he didn't want to die, alone in the void, when food or air or water slowly gave out.

He had to land the ship, any way he could. Any landing he could survive would do; keeping the ship intact was of relatively little importance.

There were no manual controls; the ship had been designed for the use of a cyborg and computer. It had intentionally been made so that it was impossible for an ordinary human to pilot, to prevent capture and use by the enemy. The closest he could come would be to rip out the control leads to the engines and short-circuit them into jury-rigged switches.

He didn't have time for that. He didn't have time for anything at all, without the computer or the direct-control cable. The ship might crash at any time; he had no idea what its trajectory was. He wished he could see where he was.

The cabin seemed to flicker around him in a reddish haze; his eyes were playing tricks again.

Perhaps the socket in his neck was not beyond hope, he thought. He snatched up the direct-control cable and tried to shove it into place.

It wouldn't fit. He felt an eerie whining sensation as a pin contact brushed against the side of the socket, where insulation had burned off and left bare metal; that was not where the contact was intended to go, but a signal of some sort was coming through.

That was something. He pushed the cable in harder, trying to ignore what that did to the raw tissue of his neck; there was a faint scrape of metal on bone as he drove the socket up against his spine.

There seemed to be some sensation, a faint electric tingle. He strained to feel the contact, to tap into the ship's sensors and see the data he needed.

He could sense, vaguely, that something was coming through; he closed his eyes. The cabin did not vanish; an after-image, etched in vivid spectral colors, lingered and seemed to brighten. He did not want that; he wanted contact with the ship's sensors. He concentrated, and the image of the cabin distorted, shrank, and vanished, and he saw where he was.

The ship was traveling a long, shallow curve; it had already passed over Awlmei, its first target, without strafing, and was sailing eastward across the forested hills. It would crash somewhere northwest of Praunce. He took that in in a single quick glimpse, then lost contact again.

Something was wrong, though; the information had not been in the right form. He had *seen* it, rather than having to interpret coded data; it was as if the ship had suddenly turned transparent around him. His skin was tingling strangely, most particularly on his forehead and the backs of his hands.

Could it have something to do with his use of the release code? Did he see things differently now, because Samuel Turner rather than the pilot was seeing them?

He had no time to consider such things. He had to get the ship down in one piece—or at least, in few enough pieces to ensure his survival.

Nothing was wrong with his present course, but the speed was too great; the ship would be splattered over several square kilometers. What the computer had considered a slow strafing speed was still more than a thousand meters a second. If he braked and did nothing else, though, the ship would drop steeply, and again he would have no chance of survival. He had to slow the ship and bring its nose up simultaneously and gradually, and drop it down to a belly landing, using the trees to cushion the impact.

He had to manage somehow. He thought his orders into the cable, or tried to; nothing happened.

He concentrated, eyes tight shut, his right fist clenched around the plug, his left hand clamped on the edge of the acceleration couch. His head ached, and his scalp tingled; he wondered if current were seeping into his skin from a faulty contact.

Suddenly he made a connection again and saw the ground below, coming up at him; he tried to order the ship to brake.

There was a response; the ship veered suddenly as one braking jet fired. He had to correct that, he knew, or he could wind up in a spin; he shoved harder at the plug.

That motion, combined with the sudden sideways acceleration from his uneven braking, bent several contacts and snapped a piece from the edge of the socket, sending his right hand, still holding the plug, scraping across the side of his neck. His skin crawled, pain surged through him, and he almost screamed; he *had* to hold the image of the ground, to keep control of the ship! If he lost it now he was dead.

He did keep it; the other braking jets fired, and he watched as the ship leveled off, then slowed and began to drop smoothly toward the woods beneath.

The plug, though, was nowhere near the socket. His skin felt as if it was rippling across his body, and his hair seemed to be standing on end, as if his body were charged with electricity.

He opened his eyes and brought the plug around to where he could see it. It was ruined, its contacts bent or broken, yet he was in control of the ship through it. He saw it clearly, and at the same time saw an intricate web of red and yellow light woven through it; his image of the approaching ground was also in that light, somehow, and the means of controlling the ship as well. It was wizardry of some kind, he was sure.

He had no time to wonder what was happening; he had to land the ship. He saw the trees coming up, corrected the ship's angle, corrected again, braked—and hit.

It was a bad landing, a very bad landing; Slant could hear and feel the ship coming apart around him in roaring, splintering fragments as it smashed its way through the trees. He knew, though, that he shouldn't have been able to land at all. The only thing that had enabled him to was magic.

That was his last conscious thought before the ship hit the ground.

Chapter Twenty-Five

HE AWOKE TO THE SMELL OF BURNING INSULATION AND the sound of crackling flames and spitting sparks. He opened his eyes and saw nothing but smoke. Acting from conditioned response, he moved immediately trying to escape the smoke; it could be more deadly than fire itself.

Blinking, his eyes watering, he managed to make out his surroundings. He was still in the control cabin, lying on a pile of battered books; the impact had thrown him off the acceleration couch, but the books had broken his fall. He felt no new injuries beyond a few minor bruises. Some mechanism in the couch had apparently overloaded; it was the base, near where the direct-control cable emerged, that was afire. He noticed for the first time that he still held the plug from the cable; he must have ripped it free without intending to when flung aside.

The swirling smoke reached him again, and he coughed. He had to get out immediately, he knew; the ventilation systems had shut down or been destroyed in the crash, he guessed, since their hum could not be heard and the only movement in the air was the convection caused by the fire's heat. He scrambled across the room and found that the corridor outside was tilted at an almost unmanageably steep angle. His lungs ached, and the back of his battered head and neck still roared with agony, but the lingering headache that had plagued him seemed to have faded, and he was able to think with some semblance of clarity.

He struggled his way up the passage on all fours, keeping low where the air would be better, though in fact most of the smoke was still in the control cabin. Storage lockers had been ripped open by the impact, their contents strewn about, and he found himself picking his way over scattered tools and broken machinery.

The inner door of the airlock was also open, and twisted hopelessly out of shape; he squeezed past it.

The airlock itself was a shambles; shorted connections sputtered, warning lights flashed, and a ruptured supply line was spraying hydroponic nutrient solution across the chamber. The outer door was still halfway open; the computer had been unable to reclose it with the hydraulics uncoupled, and had flown with it as it was. That might have contributed to his poor control of the landing, he thought, by interfering with the ship's trim. He clambered across the sloping floor toward it, ducking under a buckled ceiling plate, and began to climb through.

He stopped himself suddenly. His leading foot had not met resistance where he expected. He looked down and discovered that the entire wing had been sheared off and lay in pieces a dozen meters away.

Cautiously, then, he eased himself through, taking a deep gulp of the fresh forest air, and lowered himself down as far as he could before letting himself drop.

Again he landed badly; he had not seen a twisted hull plate, still very hot, beneath him. His knee struck it hard and gave under him, and he rolled forward.

That was nothing, really, he told himself. The pain in his burned and bruised knee and the hands that had unexpectedly had to absorb the shock of the fall was nothing compared to the continuing agony of his neck. He ignored it all as he staggered away from the ship.

The main drive was probably down again, he told himself, and wouldn't blow; if the nuclear warheads hadn't gone already, nothing would set them off now. Therefore, any explosion would be caused by the conventional armaments or the various chemicals stored on board, set off by the electrical fires that were obviously burning all over the ship. Those could make some fairly spectacular little explosions, all right, but nothing that would kill him if he could put a few hundred meters behind him first.

Of course, if the main drive hadn't shut down and was still running unregulated, the plasma might eventually find a way out of its containment vessel and, if there was enough of it, melt down the entire ship. He had no idea what that would do to the warheads, or whether it would happen fast enough to be an explosion in its own right. He hoped the drive was down.

It should be; the impact should have smashed the lasers, or at least thrown them out of alignment, in which case they might burn holes out through the sides of the ship eventually. He would watch for that.

For now, he had limped his way out beyond the last smoldering scraps of metal and splintered fragments of trees, into the undamaged part of the forest. He was at the limit of his endurance and knew it. Once he was safe from explosions, he would settle down and rest, he told himself. Another few meters would do it.

That thought was the last thing he remembered.

When he was aware again, the first thing he was aware of was a voice. Someone was speaking, saying something in a language he knew he should know, but he was still too drowsy to make sense of it.

He rested a moment longer, then tried again. This time he could follow it. He was still on Dest, and the voice was speaking that world's barbaric language. It was commenting on someone's strength of will and potential for the future.

As well as the voice he could hear a breeze making its way through trees, and a set of footsteps somewhere not too far away; he smelled green growing things and rich earth and smoldering plastic, and other odors as well.

He was also aware, in a way he couldn't quite explain, of the presence of four people besides himself, and of the subtle tug of the planet's pull upon him, and of the flowing of the air around him.

Reluctantly, he opened his eyes.

"Hello, Slant," someone said. "It's good to see you awake again."

"Hello," he replied. "Where am I?"

Even as he asked, he knew part of the answer; he was lying comfortably on a patch of grass, in the shade of an oak tree, not far from where his ship had crashed. He did not, however, know where the ship had come down. His final maneuvers had gotten him quite lost.

"Oh, we're in the forest somewhere about two days' ride west of Praunce."

It was one of the wizards he had met in Praunce, one who had carried him, who spoke; he thought that man's name was Dekert. He was young, and wore a golden robe.

Two other wizards sat nearby; he recognized one as another member of the group that had carried him but was unsure of the other. The footsteps he had heard belonged to Arzadel, who was approaching at a casual pace. He had apparently been investigating the wreckage.

"Would you like something to eat?" The wizard he couldn't identify held out a crockery vessel and lifted the lid; a savory smell of meat and vegetables emerged. Slant felt his stomach knot itself in response to the odor; he was ravenous.

"Yes, please," he answered.

The wizard handed him the pot, full of hot stew, and a wooden spoon. While he ate the four gathered about him, waiting politely until he had eased his hunger.

When he felt that he could survive awhile longer without stuffing more food into his belly, Slant put aside the stewpot and spoon and asked, "What are you doing here? How did you get here?"

"We came seeking you," Arzadel answered. "We flew."

He considered that for a moment; then Dekert asked a question of his own. "Is the demon dead?"

Slant looked at the wreckage, visible through the trees. There had apparently been no explosion, but there could be little doubt, nonetheless. "Yes, it's dead."

"That's good."

"How long was I unconscious?"

"Your ship flew here the day before yesterday," Azradel answered. "You might have awoken sooner, had we let you, but we kept you asleep so that you might heal better, with our aid."

He sat for a moment, considering that, and remembering how his ship had come to crash here. "You people helped me control the ship, didn't you?" he asked.

The wizards looked at one another in confusion. Arzadel replied, "We did nothing to aid you while the ship flew. We knew of nothing we could do, once you were aboard the vessel."

"I don't understand," Slant answered. "There was magic helping me; I couldn't have survived the crash without it." He was certain that it had been wizardry that let him control the ship without the socket in his neck, and that had let him see where he was flying.

"Oh, I see!" Arzadel said. "No, Slant, that was not us. That was your own power."

"What?"

"I told you, back in Praunce, that we had worked on your head for hours after the explosion. One of the things we did, so that you might help to heal yourself, was to give you the gift of wizardry. It was very tricky, with all that extra wiring you carry, but we managed it. We had also thought that as well as helping to heal you the change might be of aid in your battle with the demon, should it continue after you recovered; we did not know then what would happen after the bomb was removed. Some of us felt that it might be unwise, but they were overruled; however, it was decided that, as a compromise, we should not tell you what we had done until we could supervise your training. An untrained wizard can be very dangerous, to himself as well as those around him. Then, when you awoke and told us what the demon intended, there was no time for training—or for much of anything."

"You mean I'm a wizard?"

"Yes, and most likely to be a very powerful one, I would judge. You say you used wizardry aboard your ship—to have used the power without knowing you had it is a very good sign indeed that you will be quite adept, with practice. We will have to find you an apprenticeship immediately." He smiled.

This was rather more than Slant could take in at once; he was silent for a few seconds, sorting it out. It fit, though. The distortion of his vision, he realized, must have been the beginnings of the "wizard-sight" Kurao had mentioned. The headaches had been caused, he guessed, by his brain's readjustment. Already he seemed to be over those unpleasant side effects; with training, he was sure, they would not recur.

"You're offering me an apprenticeship in Praunce?" he asked at last.

"When one can be found for you, yes. The sooner the better."

That was all right; Praunce seemed as good a place as any to live, now that his ship was gone. He might someday try to do something with the wreckage, but for the present he could not plan on leaving Dest. It would be good to have a place, to belong somewhere; he had been a wandering outsider for far too long already.

There was something else that bothered him, though.

"How can you take me in, though? I've killed innocent people, caused untold destruction, slain at least one wizard."

Arzadel made a gesture of dismissal. "You did what you had to, while the demon possessed you. We saw you fight the demon for Haiger's life in Praunce, and saw you struggle, despite your wounds, to do final battle and destroy the demon. We saw you succeed and bring the demon-ship falling out of the sky. These were not the acts of an evil man. Your old life is behind you, Slant, and forgiven; you have done what you could to atone, and you will repay us further, I am sure. There is no one else on Dest with your knowledge of the old ways, the old magic from before the Bad Times; you will be a great asset to us. You are one of us now, Slant of Praunce!"

He considered that, and accepted it. He would do the best he could for these people; they had already done well for him. There was one more thing, though, to be done, before he could leave his old self behind.

"Call me Sam," he said.

About the Author

Lawrence Watt-Evans was born and raised in eastern Massachusetts, the fourth of six children. Both parents were long-time science-fiction readers, so from an early age he read and enjoyed a variety of speculative fiction. He also tried writing it, starting at age seven, but with very little succes.

After finishing twelve years of public schooling in Bedford, Massachusetts, he tried to maintain family tradition by attending Princeton University, as had his father and grandfather. He was less successful than his ancestors, and after two attempts left college without a degree.

During the break in his academic career, he lived in Pittsburgh, a city he considers one of the most underrated in the country. At this time he began seriously trying to write for money, as that seemed easier than finding a real job. He sold one page of fiction in a year and a half.

In 1977, after leaving Princeton for the second and final time, he married his long-time girl friend and settled in Lexington, Kentucky, where his wife had a job that would support them both while he again tried to write. He was more successful this time, producing a fantasy novel that sold readily, beginning his full-time career as a writer.

Enchanting fantasies from

DEL REY BOOKS